RETIREMENT SCHEME

Jack Dillon Dublin Tale 16

Second Edition

RETIREMENT SCHEME

Jack Dillon Dublin Tale 16
Second Edition

Mike Faricy

Library of Congress Control Number: 2023920764
paperback ISBN: 978-1-962080-91-0
e-Book ISBN: 978-1-962080-92-7

MJF Publishing books may be purchased for education, Business, or promotional use. For information on bulk purchases, please contact the author directly at mikefaricyauthor@gmail.com

Published by

MJF Publishing
https://www.mikefaricybooks.com

ACKNOWLEDGMENTS

I would like to thank the following people for their help & support: Special thanks to Nick, Roy, Julie, Mittie, and Toui for their hard work, cheerful patience and positive feedback. I would like to thank family and friends for their encouragement and unqualified support. Special thanks to Maggie, Jed, Schatz, Pat, Av, Emily and Pat, for not rolling their eyes, at least when I was there. Most of all, to my wife, Teresa, whose belief, support and inspiration has, from day one, never waned.

To Teresa
"You've driven me demented!"

PROLOGUE

AIB, Allied Irish Banks, is one of the big four commercial banks in Ireland, with over a hundred and seventy branches in the Republic. The Grand Canal Dock Branch is located at 2 Hanover Quay, between the South Dock Steak House and a bar called Boojum, a Mexican Burrito Bar. At 3:54 on Friday afternoon, the bank was due to close in six minutes. Two men approached the bank from opposite directions. Both men wore faded caps, disposable face masks, wigs, and latex gloves beneath their dark brown cotton gloves.

The older of the two held the door for his partner. The partner nodded and whispered, "Four minutes," as he stepped inside and headed toward the bank's teller counter. The older man stepped over to the table in the center of the lobby. A rack filled with blank deposit and withdrawal slips was in the center of the table. He stood with his back to the teller counter, facing the desks of two bank officers.

The older woman in front of the man at the teller's window thanked the teller, arranged her cash in her billfold, set the billfold in a pocket of her purse, zipped the purse closed, thanked the teller again, and stepped to the side.

The man took a deep breath, stepped forward, and said, "I'd like to make a withdrawal." He handed the bank teller his note and a shopping bag. The note read, 'Empty your drawer. I have a gun.' In case the teller had any questions, he pulled back his windbreaker, revealing the pistol in his belt. Her eyes grew wide, and he politely said, "Do it now, please."

She nodded and began to quickly pull the stacks of euro notes from her cash drawer. As she did so, the teller four feet to the left, a woman named Tierney, asked, "Megan, what are you doing? Megan?" She glanced over at Tierney.

"Megan, give her the shopping bag. Fill it up, be quiet, and nothing will happen," the robber said.

"What do you think—" She stopped and stared as he pulled back his windbreaker.

"Better just do it," Megan said. She quickly handed the shopping bag over to Tierney just as an elderly woman stepped up to the counter and slid a deposit slip and two twenty euro notes toward the teller.

"Pardon me, ma'am, I was just finishing a transaction here," the robber said as he stepped over and gently moved her aside.

"Excuse me. I think you might want to consider waiting your turn. Good heavens, where did you learn your manners?" She made a move to step back in place, but he held his ground and gave her a not-so-gentle shove. "Oh, what in the name of—"

The man at the table pulled a pistol out, fired toward the ceiling, and shouted, "Everyone on the floor, now. Come on, move, get down on the floor. Don't even think of pressing a button, you stupid slapper. Move away from your desk and get down on the floor. Everyone follows directions, and no one gets hurt. Let's go, do it now," he shouted and waved his pistol at a wide-eyed woman still seated at her desk staring at him. She suddenly moved from her chair and onto the floor. "Face down on the floor. Move. Now."

The robber reached over the teller counter, took hold of the shopping bag, glanced around for any additional currency, and headed for the door. He nodded as he passed his partner, who quickly followed.

As they stepped out of the bank, the older man took an olive drab canister from his windbreaker, pulled a pin, and tossed it into a distant, empty corner. The canister exploded a few seconds later, immediately filling the bank with a gray-white smoke. The smoke was too thick to allow anyone to make it to the door, so everyone remained on the floor, coughing and crying.

A few minutes later, a couple stepped out of Boojum, the Mexican Burrito Bar. They noticed the smoke in the bank lobby, and the man held the door open, gradually releasing the smoke outside, while his girlfriend called 999, the Irish Emergency Response

number. The first Garda vehicle arrived four minutes
later.

ONE

US Marshal Jack Dillon, assigned to Dublin's An Garda Síochána, Special Branch, got the call as he settled onto the couch next to his dog, Lucifer. He had just turned on the 6:00 news, where the leading story was a bank robbery on Hanover Quay, when his phone rang. He checked the screen on his phone, Emergency Response and answered, "Dillon."

"Sir, Emergency Response calling, requesting your presence at 2 Hanover Quay. An AIB bank has been robbed."

It figures, Dillon thought. "Have you contacted DI Suel?"

"Yes, he is en route, sir."

"Mark me as on my way."

"Thank you, sir," the caller said and disconnected. Dillon repeated the address to himself as he entered it into his cellphone's GPS. He turned off the TV, let Lucifer out into the front garden, and hurried up to his bedroom. He strapped on his shoulder holster, pulled a jacket from his closet, and coaxed Lucifer back inside with a biscuit.

He cautiously approached his car, careful not to step in Lucifer's recent deposit, and headed to Hanover Quay. The squad cars, double-parked in front of the AIB bank, identified the location from two blocks away. The building was a seven-story structure. The upper six stories featured all glass housing units with large balconies that were probably going for a million euros each. As he approached, a taxi was just driving away from the South Dock Steak House. Dillon pulled into the spot, took the An Garda Síochána identification sheet from his glove box, and set it on the dashboard. He climbed out of the car, draped the lanyard with his ID around his neck, and headed toward the bank. The building's ground floor units were dark gray concrete with the name of the various businesses, South Dock Steakhouse, AIB Bank, and Boojum, in steel letters above the windows. The bank had a nondescript entrance except for the fact that, right now, the area was taped off by white tape with blue letters that read '**An Garda Síochána**.'

All the lights were on inside the bank, but there was a substance on the windows that limited the view. As he approached, Dillon ran a finger across the exterior of the window but didn't get any residue. Apparently, whatever was on the windows was on the inside. A uniformed officer was standing at the door. As Dillon stepped beneath the An Garda Síochána tape. He held up his ID. The officer nodded and moved aside so Dillon could enter.

At this hour, it was largely An Garda Síochána on the premises. He nodded at a couple of familiar faces and glanced around. He saw three security cameras mounted in different corners. Hopefully, they had been able to record the incident. He headed over to his partner, DI Paddy Suel, who was talking to two individuals at the teller counter.

"Oh, here he is now, finally," Suel said as Dillon approached.

"I literally just got the call not twenty minutes ago. How long have you been here?"

"Five, maybe ten minutes. That's all it took for me to proclaim that a robbery had taken place."

Everyone chuckled. Dillon wrinkled his nose. "I'm guessing they set off a smoke device on the way out. I can smell it, and it's all over the windows."

"And over everything else in here," Suel said and nodded at all the footprints on the floor in what appeared to be very fine dust. "Fortunately, no one was hurt. Two senior individuals were taken to Mater Hospital just to double-check. They were having difficulty breathing after lying in that cloud for ten or fifteen minutes. There's a security tape, not quite four minutes long. We can check it out in the Operations office. It's already been sent to Special Branch. Come on, it's back this way," Suel said and led the way past the teller counter and through a door. There was a short hallway with four doors. They walked past an open office with two officers Dillon recognized. They were speaking with a white-haired man, maybe fifty years old, seated behind a desk.

The nameplate next to the door read Thomas Mullen, President.

The door further down was labeled Operations. Suel knocked on the door as he opened it. Two men were inside. Dillon recognized one of them, Jim Burke, from the Tech Department in the headquarters building. Burke's specialty was facial recognition. They were seated at a desk with three screens mounted on the wall in front of them.

As they stepped in, Burke turned around and said, "Good evening. This is Dermot Casey."

Casey looked up and nodded at Dillon and Suel.

"Dermot has been kind enough to send files to Special Branch and a number of other units. Derm, you want to run that tape for these gentlemen? They're with Special Branch."

Casey nodded but still didn't say anything. His hands flew across the keyboard, and a moment later, three frozen images came up on the screens. One screen focused on the entrance, one focused on the lobby, and the third screen focused on the teller counter. Each image had a twenty-four-hour time in the upper right-hand corner of the screen. At the moment, all three screens displayed the time as 15:54:21. Dillon and Suel stepped behind the two men, and Burke said, "Okay, Derm, play it at normal speed first, then we'll show them the focused version."

Casey ran his fingers across the keyboard, and things began to move on the screen covering the teller counter and the screen covering the lobby. At 15:54:37, the entrance door opened, and two men stepped in. They had long hair that hung over their ears, and they were wearing faded caps, disposable masks, sunglasses, jeans, and what appeared to be navy-blue windbreakers. There were no identifying characteristics on the caps or the windbreakers. One man headed for the teller counter and stood in line behind an older woman. The other man stepped to the counter in the center of the lobby.

As the woman in front of the man stepped aside, he moved forward and handed a note to the teller along with a brown paper bag. They watched as the teller said something, and the man pulled his windbreaker back, exposing the pistol tucked into his belt. As this was going on, the man standing at the counter in the middle of the lobby appeared to be focused on something or someone out of camera range.

The man at the teller counter suddenly moved in front of the woman in the line next to him and said something to the teller. The woman he moved in front of did not appear to be happy and said something to him. Suddenly, the man at the lobby table drew his pistol, fired a shot over his head, and shouted something.

The shot apparently got the attention of everyone, and they began to stretch out on the floor. The teller quickly filled the shopping bag with cash from her drawer. Both tellers disappeared from the screen as they crouched down below the counter. Three individuals could be seen on the lobby screen. All three were lying face down on the floor. One of them, a gray-haired woman, had her hands placed on either side of her head. Both robbers appeared on the lobby screen for a brief moment and then at the door. The man with the shopping bag stepped out of the bank while the other man paused at the door. He took a canister from his windbreaker, pulled a pin, and tossed it into a corner behind him. A moment later, all three screens fogged up. The time in the upper right corners of the screens read 15:58:43. The entire episode took just a few seconds over four minutes.

"There you have it, lads. A few seconds longer than four minutes, probably due to your wan telling your man to mind his manners. They're in and out and disappear."

"What's with the smoke bomb? They're almost out of the place, and no one's going to stop them."

"I'd guess just a precaution," Burke said. "Delay any emergency phone calls or someone following. Teams are in the process of gathering CCTV tapes from surrounding businesses. Anything stand out to you two?"

"That smoke bomb your man sets off. It looked like there was an ID number on the thing. I think his hand was covering up some of it, but I could see L83 in white letters on the canister."

"It's a British military training device," Burke glanced over at a sheet of paper on the desk in front of him. "The actual number is L83A1. A smoke bomb for training purposes in the British army."

"They didn't appear to be current members in the Army," Suel said. "You think they came down from the north?"

"Bring up the images of them stepping in the door, if you would, please, Derm."

Casey typed again, and the clocks on all three screens reverted back to 15:54:21. Only the screen focused on the front door began to count the seconds off. Casey froze the image once both men were present on the screen.

"A few things. As we review the tape, you'll notice these are the only two people wearing face masks. Also, I can't prove it, but my sense is at this early stage that both men are wearing wigs beneath those caps. The windbreakers are nondescript, as are the hats, and I would suggest that both have probably been discarded if not destroyed."

Dillon and Suel studied the image on the screen. Casey's comments made sense.

"With the masks, the sunglasses, and the caps, what chance do you have at facial recognition?"

Burke shook his head. "Almost none. I might be able to narrow it down to a few hundred individuals, but there's almost no chance of coming up with a specific person."

"Do you think this was their first dance?" Suel asked.

"It's quite possible, but if it is, they've studied up on what to do and not to do. If I had to guess, I would say they're students looking to get an advanced degree."

"Students?" Suel asked.

"Not someone attending a university. I meant they're learning as they go along. This may well be their first dance but be prepared to see them again."

TWO

They watched the tape at least a half-dozen times and didn't come up with anything new. Dillon and Suel went back out to the lobby. Dillon walked over to the lobby counter and gazed up at the ceiling, studying.

"What are you looking for?" Suel asked.

"On the security tape, your man pulled out his pistol and fired into the ceiling to get everyone's attention, and he yelled at them to get on the floor."

"Yeah, shooting the gun is certainly one way to get folks to pay attention."

"Take a look and tell me when you can see a bullet hole. I certainly can't find one. He was standing just about here," Dillon said, moving to his right about half a foot. "This rack of deposit and withdrawal slips was centered on his chest on the tape. He raised his arm over his head, pointed at the ceiling, and fired, but I don't see a bullet hole."

Suel looked up and stared at the ceiling, searching. "You think he fired a blank?"

"Right now, I'd say that's entirely possible. I can't see where it hit, and it should have been almost straight upward if it was a live round."

Suel studied the ceiling. "I'm not finding anything. So if they're loaded with blanks, and they've gone to a lot of trouble to get a reasonably small amount of cash, what does that mean?"

"I think it means they've got a lot to learn."

"Did we learn anything from the witnesses?"

Suel shrugged. "The woman that your man jumped in front of was positive he had a Dublin accent. He told her he wasn't finished with his transaction. She told him he should wait his turn and then asked him where he learned his manners. I don't know. It's just not adding up."

"And they've no one working security?" Dillon asked.

"Only before holidays, the last two days, and the first two days of any month. Those would naturally seem to be their busiest times. Dermot Casey is the only employee still here, and he was locked in the room with his security cameras during the robbery. There's Mullen, the president, but he's currently being interviewed, and I suspect they'd take an awfully dim view if we stepped in. You want to wait around until they're finished?"

Dillon shook his head. "I'm thinking we head out, maybe grab a pint. Casey sent us the four-minute tape. It would be interesting to check it out. See if, indeed, they were wearing wigs, for starters. I don't know, Paddy.

You think they might have gone online and just gotten information on how to pull off a robbery? There are all sorts of sites that would have that information. Tell you to wear a disguise. I'm guessing that with the cotton gloves they had on, they probably were wearing latex gloves beneath the cotton to eliminate any DNA trace. No mention of a vehicle parked out front."

"There's a parking ramp around the corner, Dillon. How about this? They park in the ramp. Pull off the robbery and remove the wigs, sunglasses, and windbreakers. One of them hides in the back seat, and the other one drives them out of the garage to someplace where they change. Maybe the car is stolen, they set it on fire, drive off in their own cars, and pretty much vanish into thin air."

"Not so far-fetched. Hopefully, we can trace them on CCTV tapes tomorrow. It's just…I don't know…it doesn't seem to be adding up."

"Yeah, I'm with you. You want to check out the parking ramp around the corner?"

"It couldn't hurt," Dillon said.

"I was afraid you'd say that. Come on, let's do it, but you're buying the pints when we're finished."

The parking ramp was a four-story concrete structure. Payments were all made with credit cards, no cash was accepted, Which meant that the operator's office set between the entrance and exit was empty, and the lights were off.

Dillon and Suel split up, with Suel taking the even levels and Dillon the odd ones. The ramp was only a third full. Lots of open parking places and nothing like windbreakers or wigs lying around. Dillon lifted the lids on the trash bins next to the elevators and found exactly what he expected to find, cups, wrappers, newspapers, junk mail, and three different empty half-pints. He also found a black bra, which was not what he had expected. He had taken the elevator up to the fourth level and worked his way down. It barely took a half-hour. Suel was waiting for him at the exit gate.

"Find anything?" Dillon asked.

"Absolutely nothing. You?"

"Nothing unusual other than a black bra, but I figured you already had one, so I left it in the trash bin."

"Probably a good idea. Hell, we don't even know if they parked in here," Suel said.

"Yeah, although this would be the closest place to disappear from sight. Change to another quick disguise, and one of you hides in the back or even inside the boot, and off you go. With that smoke bomb, even if the Garda arrived in a minute or two, they'd be involved in getting people out of that mess, and the robbers would have all the time in the world to casually exit and drive out of town."

Suel nodded and said, "You aware of a car set on fire anywhere?"

"You mean destroying the evidence? No, I haven't seen anything come across on my phone. Of course, once they're out of the immediate area, hell, they could drive up to Meath or down to Wicklow County and destroy the vehicle or just leave it on the street with the keys in the ignition for some idiot to make off with the thing thinking he'd made a big score."

"I think the best thing we could do would be to adjourn to the Autobahn pub, where you can buy me a pint, and we can discuss what our next move is going to be."

"I can't believe you're starting to make sense, Paddy. Let's go."

THREE

Dillon glanced around the pub and asked, "What do you think?"

Suel took a deep breath and exhaled. "I still think we're going to see these two again. Unfortunately, I believe Burke was right. They're using this as a learning experience. How much money do you think they got from today's effort? One, maybe two thousand euros? It strikes me as an awfully big risk to take for that small amount. Given the sense of planning they seem to have put into the operation, wouldn't they have realized, at some point, that there was a finite amount of cash?"

A waitress approached, and Dillon raised his hand, signaling for two more Guinness. "If what you say is true, Paddy, and I'm not suggesting you're wrong. But if that is the case, my thought is we'll see them again sooner rather than later. And if that's the deal, where is their next target? A larger bank? A busier bank? It's not rocket science to realize that today's robbery occurred at a small neighborhood bank for a couple thousand euros. Even if they want to move up the ladder, a larger bank isn't going to work because the place will be too big for two individuals to rob. Plus, a larger bank will have security people who would be armed. That's an entirely new problem that they would have to deal with."

Suel nodded. "Yeah, you're right. But I just can't see them continuing at this level, a couple thousand, and if you're caught, you'll be spending six to ten or maybe even twelve years behind bars."

"But these guys, I don't know. Maybe the ultimate target isn't a bank. Maybe it's a business, someone's office, a jeweler, or even some kind of warehouse."

"It will be interesting to see what, if anything, we're able to get on CCTV footage. Maybe if we—"

The waitress suddenly appeared with two pints of Guinness. She set one in front of Suel and the other in front of Dillon. "Fifteen euros," she said.

"My dad told me he'd buy both pints," Suel grinned and nodded at Dillon.

She looked at Dillon, glanced back at Suel for a brief moment, and joked, "No doubt hoping to get his wayward son back on track."

Dillon laughed, pulled out a twenty euro note, and set it on her tray. "Keep the change. Your comment was worth it."

They clinked glasses and both took a hearty sip.

"You're not aware of these two showing up anywhere in the past, are you?" Suel asked.

Dillon shook his head. "No. If I were, I would have mentioned it. I think it will be interesting to see what comes up on CCTV. My guess is we're going to be looking at next to nothing. At no surprise, the note your man passed to the teller was printed off, so there is no handwriting to compare. A total of seven words, short and to the point."

"Looking at the tapes, what do you think they did wrong?" Suel asked and took another sip.

"In all honesty, not much. Were it not for your wan, giving the man a hard time, they may have been able to walk out of there, and no one would have been the wiser. Only firing the pistol, apparently, a blank, is what got everyone's attention and got them on the ground. I find it interesting they didn't collect wallets and purses. It's not unusual to gather all that up."

Suel nodded. "Yeah, but in the instances where it's been done, there's usually a group large enough to have one or two people in charge of that. Just the two of them? It would have put them on the security cameras for another minute, maybe two. The fact that they didn't do that suggests they had at least a rudimentary plan going in. It seems obvious they wanted to get out of there as quickly as possible."

"Yeah, and it seemed to work. I still like the idea of the smoke bomb being used to get the Gardai focused on moving people out of the lobby and not looking for the robbers, or at least giving them time to casually disappear and not attract any attention. Hopefully, we'll get a car and license number on CCTV, and that will be the end of it. I'm still coming back to why in the hell anyone would do this. They've got about a ten percent chance of not getting caught, and for what? Two thousand euros? It's crazy."

"Yeah, that's the bottom line." Suel drained his glass. "Hey, thanks for the pint. I'll catch you in the morning."

They walked out together and headed home. Dillon drove past Tara's house, just across the lane and up a couple of doors from his place. There was a gray Volkswagen Golf parked out front, and the drapes in the sitting room were drawn, meaning she was entertaining someone or being entertained. He pulled into the front garden, let Lucifer out, and made himself a grilled cheese sandwich. Once he finished eating, he let Lucifer back in. He scanned the TV for a movie, but nothing caught his interest. He watched the tail end of the late evening news and headed up to bed.

FOUR

Since it was Saturday morning, Dillon woke up forty-five minutes before his alarm would normally go off. He hadn't set the alarm, so, of course, he didn't sleep in. He crawled out of bed, pulled on a sweat suit, and headed downstairs. He put the coffee on and turned on his laptop. He had eleven emails waiting, not one of any interest. He didn't need a new mattress, he was happy with his car and home insurance, and then there were the three political emails from people he would never vote for. He deleted one after another and cleared his emails in about ten seconds. He logged into YouTube, brought up last night's US evening news, and listened to that while he prepared his breakfast.

Halfway through breakfast, Lucifer appeared, and Dillon let him out into the front garden. He finished breakfast, filled Lucifer's food and water dishes, and let him back inside. He checked the local Dublin news, nothing really of interest and only a brief mention of the AIB robbery yesterday afternoon. He went upstairs, shaved, grabbed a shower, and hopped in the car. As he backed out of his drive, it wasn't lost on him that whoever belonged to the gray Volkswagen Golf at Tara's house across the lane was still there this morning. He drove to his office in the An Garda Síochána Headquarters building located alongside Phoenix Park.

He parked close to the main door and entered the building. Once in the Special Branch section, he settled in at his desk and opened the first of a half-dozen files regarding yesterday's AIB robbery. He examined the images of the two individuals as they entered the bank. He focused on the faces, enlarging the images and examining the little he could see of the hairlines on the two individuals. Burke had suggested that both men were wearing long-haired wigs beneath their caps, and Dillon was inclined to agree.

The two men had on disposable masks, but Dillon noted that the suspect with the blonde hair had what appeared to be maybe a half-day's beard growth in the area of his sideburn and hairs in his ear that appeared brown or possibly auburn. If he'd shaved first thing in the morning, the beard growth Dillon was studying would make sense at almost four in the afternoon.

The sunglasses on both men were reflective, and for a half moment, Dillon recalled snapshots of his father as a young man in a US Army uniform wearing mirrored sunglasses upon his arrival home from Viet Nam.

He studied the wrists on both individuals looking for a hint of latex gloves underneath the brown cotton work gloves. The gloves were tucked into the elastic-reinforced sleeves of the nylon windbreakers, and he was unable to detect any latex. Examining other images, he noted the remnants from labels that had been cut off from the rear of both pairs of blue jeans.

He couldn't be sure, but the pistol that the one suspect held and fired appeared to have a black carbon fiber finish. He enlarged the image, but it blurred what he thought might be the manufacturer's name to the point that he couldn't make it out.

He made a list of questions and suggestions regarding the wigs, actual hair color, and the type of weapon and sent them to Emily down in the Tech Lab. That done, he headed out of the office, made a quick stop at his local Aldi grocery store, and drove home. This time, the Volkswagen Golf was gone from Tara's house.

Lucifer met him at the door and hurried out into the front garden. Dillon put the groceries away, grabbed the leash, and took Lucifer on a walk. They did three laps around Albert Park just outside of DCU, Dublin City University. Each lap was 1.2 miles, and when they'd finished the third lap, both Dillon and Lucifer were ready to head home.

Dillon placed a call to Aiofe McDonald, a woman he'd dated off and on, and ended up leaving a message. "Hi Aiofe, Jack Dillon calling. It's been too long since we went out. Just wondering if you'd like to join me for dinner this evening. Nowhere in particular, but I'm in the mood to eat in a restaurant for a change. Just let me know, and I'll gladly pick you up."

He disconnected, then went upstairs, changed the sheets on his bed, vacuumed the bedroom, and cleaned the bathroom sink and the glass in the shower. He had dozed off on the couch in front of the TV when his phone rang. He cleared his throat and answered in what he hoped was a sexy voice, "Jack Dillon."

"Are you okay, Dillon? You sound like shite," Suel said.

"Oh, you, I was hoping it was a woman I'd called and left a message asking her to dinner."

"Oh, for lord's sake, forget it. If she has any brains, she won't be calling the likes of you back. Hey, listen. I'm going to be watching the rugby match on the telly tonight. We're playing the All Blacks, New Zealand's team. If you're not too busy, why don't you pick up some beer and come over."

"Yeah, I suppose I can do that. If I don't hear from that woman in the next thirty minutes, I'll give you a call and—"

"Dillon, it's almost 5:00. You're not going to hear from her. Come on over. Oh, and don't forget the beer," Suel said and disconnected.

Dillon walked into the kitchen. Suel was right. It was almost 5:00. He'd apparently been asleep for an hour and a half. Aiofe hadn't returned his call, and whether he liked it or not, he knew he probably wouldn't hear from her. He let Lucifer out into the front garden, then went upstairs, showered, and changed. On the way to Suel's, he stopped at a local shop and grabbed a twelve-pack of Smithwick's Blonde Ale. He parked in front of Suel's place ten minutes later.

Given Suel's character, you'd expect a place with overgrown grass, gardens filled with weeds, and maybe two or three newspapers on the front steps. Just the opposite was the case. The lawn was always neatly trimmed, and the gardens, edged with stones painted white, had a number of different flowers, not to mention a half-dozen rose bushes and two rose trees. The two front windows had flower boxes with a lovely array of red and yellow flowers.

Dillon stepped into the front garden. Just as he closed the gate behind him, Suel opened the front door wearing jeans, a long sleeve Irish rugby jersey, dark green with a white collar, and a black apron. "Aww, Paddy, how nice of you to get all dressed up for me."

Suel shook his head, took the twelve-pack of beer from Dillon, and said, "Believe me, I didn't dress up for the likes of you. Come on in. You're the first one here."

Dillon stepped inside and followed Suel into the kitchen. He could see three roast chickens through the window on the oven door. "The first one here? You've got other folks coming?"

"Not to worry, the two of us plus my friend Sean and three others."

"Three others? You should have told me. I would have picked up a case of beer instead of just the twelve-pack."

"We've plenty of beer and wine, and if things get desperate, I have a half-dozen whiskeys. Here make yourself useful and toss this," Suel said as he slid a wooden salad bowl across the counter to Dillon. A salad fork and spoon were already in the bowl.

Dillon began tossing the salad as Suel opened a bag of green beans and dumped them into a frying pan. A moment later, the doorbell rang.

"Oh, that should be Sean. Would you mind letting him in?"

"I'm on it," Dillon said as he hopped off the stool and stepped into the entryway. He opened the door and was about to say, 'Hi, Sean,' until he focused on the red-haired woman holding what looked like a white bakery box.

She was maybe six inches shorter than Dillon. Dressed in tight white shorts, with a black belt and a red and white striped off-the-shoulder top. She smiled and said, "Oh dear. I hope I'm in the right place. Does Paddy Suel live here?"

"He does, and he's cooking in the kitchen at the moment. I work with him. My name is Jack Dillon," he said as he held out his hand.

"Noreen Rooney, nice to meet you," she said as they shook hands.

"Let me take this for you," Dillon said and took hold of the bakery box.

"Dessert," she said. "Thank you. So you work with Paddy? Are you the American he's always talking about?"

"Probably, but don't believe whatever he said. I'm really a very nice guy."

She laughed as Dillon closed the door behind her. "He only says nice things about you."

"Then he's one of the few," Dillon said, and she laughed again as they headed into the kitchen.

"Oh, Noreen, thanks for coming. The other girls should be here shortly. Can I get you a beer or a glass of wine?"

"A glass of wine would be wonderful. White, if you have it."

"Coming right up. You met my partner, Dillon? Hopefully, he didn't say anything too rude or insulting."

"No, he was very polite. Oh, I baked all day and made a dessert, then placed it in that box."

"How very thoughtful," Suel said as he filled a wine glass and handed it across the counter to her.

"Thoughtful? You told me I had to bring it, or you weren't going to let me in."

The doorbell rang, and Suel said, "There's trouble. You mind letting them in, Noreen?"

She took a sip of her wine, set the glass on the counter, and said, "Watch this for me, and don't let Paddy drink any, please." The doorbell rang again as she stepped into the entry.

They heard the door open, and then a male voice said, "Oh, Noreen, here to keep us all in line?"

"Come on. We're all in the kitchen. How you keeping, Sean?"

"Good, thanks for asking. Not a bother."

Everyone chatted, sipped their drinks, and Suel eventually took the chickens out of the oven. "We shouldn't wait any longer for the Mahoney sisters. They'll simply have to catch up," Suel said just as the doorbell rang.

Noreen hurried out of the kitchen, and a moment later, the three men heard shrieks and laughter. "Oh God, prepare yourselves, gentlemen. With the three of them we'll be lucky to get a word in."

FIVE

They were eating in front of the TV, all six of them: Suel, Dillon, Sean Hanahan, Noreen Rooney, and the Mahoney sisters, Ann and Linda. The sisters were twins, identical except for the fact that one was blonde and the other was dark-haired. Dillon couldn't determine which one had dyed her hair. The women were talking nonstop, and occasionally Dillon glanced at the rugby match on the TV, but he found the women's conversations so interesting that the match had taken a backseat. At the moment, the women were discussing the breakup of a couple that apparently everyone but Dillon knew.

"Well, how long had she been having this affair?" Noreen asked.

"Dennis thinks at least two years. He told me he was the last person in Dublin to find out. He's filed for divorce, but they have to be separated for a year before the divorce proceedings can even begin."

Suel glanced over at Dillon, mouthed the 'F' word, then said, "Who's ready for some dessert?"

"I'll help you bring the dishes into the kitchen, Paddy," Dillon said as he rose to his feet. He took the almost empty plate from Noreen, placed Sean's empty plate beneath it, and then took the Mahoney sisters' plates. Suel followed Dillon into the kitchen with his own plate.

"God, the Gillford divorce. It's Saturday night. Let it be, for Christ's sake," Suel said.

"Well, they apparently know the Gillfords and this guy the wife hopped in bed with."

"Yeah, Connor Wright, Dublin's biggest criminal contractor. He owns a bunch of buildings and screws everyone he's ever hired. Constantly in court for not paying bills or wages, the bastard is a complete bollix."

"So why would this woman climb in bed with him?"

"That's the big question, and it's not even the worst part."

"Your wife screws some guy, and he's a real jerk. What could be worse?"

"Gillford's wife's best friend is, or rather was, Connor Wright's wife."

"Oh, man, talk about messy. So they got divorced too?"

"The Wrights? Not that I know of, at least not yet. I think—" Dillon's phone suddenly rang. Suel gave him a look as Dillon pulled it out of his pocket.

"Shit. Emergency Response." He put the phone to his ear and said, "US Marshal Jack Dillon. Yes. Shots fired? Okay. Text me the address, please. Yes, probably no more than thirty minutes. I'll have to go home first.

Thank you," he said and disconnected. "You'll probably get a call in the next few minutes. A robbery and—"

"Don't tell me it's another bank."

"Not exactly. It's a check-cashing service. Are you familiar with J&R Credit?"

"All over town, I've been past them but never been in one. Pretty much like a bank, they cash your checks and charge a hefty fee. I think somewhere between four and six percent."

"Yeah, well, this place is over in Coolock on Main Street," Dillon said.

Suel nodded. "I know where it is, right in between two pubs. The Cock and Bull and Kyles pub. Actually, when you think about it, a check cashing place located between two pubs is a pretty good idea."

"Yeah, a good idea for J&R Credit. Anyway, armed robbery about an hour ago. Without knowing anything, my money is on the two idiots who hit the AIB bank. I'll have to—"

Suel's phone suddenly rang. "Oh shit. Really?" He answered the call. "Detective Inspector Suel. Yes. In Coolock? Yes, I'm familiar with the area. Thirty or forty-five minutes. Good evening," he said and disconnected. "Damn it. I had such high hopes for later tonight. I'm going to tell my guests to stay here and enjoy the wine. With any luck, we can be back in a couple of hours, ten o'clockish. Not too late. What do you think?"

"I think we should drive separately. Just in case we get tied down. At least there wasn't a shot fired, although it would have been interesting to see if it was a blank, like at AIB.”

“Stack all the dishes in the sink. I’ll give them the word. Maybe with the desserts Noreen brought, we can talk them into staying.” Suel picked up the bakery box and headed back into the sitting room. “Did you settle the Gillford divorce?” Suel asked.

“Would you like me to put those cupcakes on a plate, Paddy? It might be a little classier than eating them out of the box.” Noreen laughed.

“Well, unfortunately, Dillon and I have just gotten the word from Emergency Response that they can’t succeed without us. We’ve to run out, solve a case, and then we’ll be back. Please, if you wouldn’t mind, stay here and enjoy the wine and beer. Treat yourselves to one of these cupcakes Noreen brought, and we’ll be back just as soon as we can.”

“Oh, dear, I’m sorry, lads, and on a Saturday night. I think Linda and I should head for home and—“

“Ann, why don’t we at least have a cupcake since Noreen went to all the trouble,” Linda said, and everyone laughed.

“Please, stay as long as you want. We’ll be back just as soon as we can,” Suel urged.

Dillon said his goodbyes and hurried out the door. He was back home ten minutes later. He let Lucifer out and went upstairs to the bedroom. He draped his ID around his neck and attached his pistol to his belt. He

coaxed Lucifer in with a biscuit and headed over to J&R
Credit in Coolock.

SIX

S uel had been correct. J&R Credit was placed right between the Cock and Bull and Kyles Pub. The Cock and Bull looked to be about three times the size of Kyles, with a flashing neon sign across the front of the place and a half-dozen folks just stepping inside. Kyles looked like a cozy little local place where neighborhood folks would go and drink until closing. In between them was a narrow building with a sign in red letters that read J&R Credit. At the moment, it was taped off by the standard white tape with blue letters, '**An Garda Síochána**.' The interior was all lit up, and Dillon counted four officers inside. Two of the officers were taking pictures. Two uniformed officers were standing outside the front door. Four squad cars were parked on the 'No Parking' side of the street. Dillon pulled past Kyles Pub and around the corner. He found a parking place four doors down the street.

As soon as he rounded the corner, he could hear music coming from the Cock and Bull. He lifted the '**An Garda Síochána**' tape and held up his ID. The officers at the door stepped aside as he approached.

"Having a fun Saturday night?" Dillon asked.

One of them shrugged and said, "At least nothing crazy is happening, and the music next door isn't all that bad."

"You know what happened here?"

The officer shook his head. "Only that it was robbed about ten minutes before it was due to close."

"Were there two guys wearing disposable masks, and they told everyone to get down on the floor?" Dillon asked.

"Apparently, two plonkers. Haven't heard anything else except that they were in and out in a minute or two."

"I can't believe they got away with much," his partner said. "Only in there for just a couple of minutes. I think they're still taking statements from the employees in a back office."

"Enjoy the rest of your evening," Dillon said and stepped inside.

The lobby, such as it was, was a small room with a small counter in the middle where you would fill out forms. Three stations made up the teller counter. They were all behind thick panels of glass that Dillon presumed would be bulletproof. The glass had no indication of having been tampered with or fired at.

The four officers inside all turned and stared at Dillon. One of them looked familiar. "Evening, lads, Jack Dillon, Special Branch. Anyone in charge?"

One of the officers raised his hand and waved Dillon over. He looked a little older than the others. Dillon guessed he might be forty, give or take a couple of years. "James Gibbons," he said and held his hand out.

Dillon shook hands. "Jack Dillon, Special Branch. My partner Paddy Suel should be along at any moment. What can you tell me? I just got a call giving me the address and telling me there'd been a robbery. Was anyone hurt?"

Gibbons shook his head. "No, just one teller was here, and she's okay. There were two of them. One stood at that counter over there while the other passed a note to the teller who was at that end spot," Gibbons said and pointed to the far corner of the teller counter. "She opened her cash drawer, and as she did that, she pressed the alert button next to the drawer. It sends a silent alert to the offices in back and flashes an alert inside the teller area above the glass. It can't be seen from out here in the lobby. The other thing it does is immediately lower a metal security shutter. The tellers are trained to drop to the floor and huddle in a protected area beneath the counter, which she did. I don't believe the two dunderheads got any money."

"Any shots fired?" Dillon asked.

Gibbons shook his head. "No, not even sure if they were armed. I haven't seen any video, but I'm presuming they've got images of both knackers. Cameras in both corners," he said and nodded at the two security cameras, one up against the ceiling at either end of the teller counter. "I think they're still interviewing the teller and the manager somewhere in the back office. You're free to go back there if you want. We're sort of twiddling our thumbs out here waiting to get the all-clear so we can leave."

"I'll check it out. I've got a partner who's due to arrive at any minute. If you would send him back there when—"

"Might he be wearing a rugby jersey? The match against the All Blacks was on the telly tonight, and I was hoping to catch it," Gibbons said and nodded toward the door.

Dillon turned just as Suel stepped inside and headed toward them. "Well, Sergeant James Gibbons, trying to set my partner straight. Are you giving him directions so he can find his way home?"

"Paddy, fancy meeting you here. So you two are partners? In Special Branch?"

"Afraid so. No one else would have him," Dillon said, and all three laughed. "Based on what Gibbons said, it sounds like they may have gotten little or nothing. I was just about to head into the back office. They're still interviewing the teller and the manager."

"Let's do it. Maybe we can get out of here at a decent hour."

"Amen to that," Gibbons said, then followed up with, "Nice to meet you, Dillon. Good luck."

Dillon held the door for Suel, and they stepped into a small hallway with two office doors opposite each other. In one office, a uniformed officer was talking to a heavyset blonde woman. There was a desk in the office, but they were seated in the two chairs in front of the desk. The woman held a can of soda on her lap, and the officer held a notebook. A small recording device rested on the desk.

"Dillon, why don't you check on these two, and I'll do the other office. I have a feeling this isn't going to take very long, with the attempted robbery being shut down before any cash was taken."

"Good idea," Dillon said and knocked on the door frame. The woman and the officer looked up as Dillon introduced himself. "Hello, Jack Dillon, Special Branch. Mind if I interrupt?"

"Actually, we've just finished," the officer said. "A botched attempt due to the quick thinking of Miss O'Mara."

"You're the teller, Miss O'Mara?" Dillon asked. She nodded. "Jack Dillon," he said. "I'm sure you're anxious to just get home, but could you tell me what happened?"

"Please, call me Colleen. Like I was telling the officer, it all happened so fast. There were two of them. They were the only ones in the lobby. It was right before close, and it had been a slow day."

"When did your day start?"

"I work the three to seven shift. There hadn't been anyone in for at least fifteen minutes. Then these two men entered. They were both wearing face masks. I thought that was strange, but I didn't think for a moment that they were going to try to rob me. One waited at the middle counter, and the other stepped to my window and handed me a note. I occasionally get people with a speech problem or someone who doesn't speak English, so I didn't think anything of it until I opened it, and he wanted all my money."

"Do you recall what the note said exactly?"

"It said, 'Give me all your money,' and then after that, it said, 'I have a gun.'"

"Was it hand-written?"

She shook her head. "No, it was printed, you know, like from your computer."

"It's filed for evidence, or it will be when we leave," the officer added.

"So, then what happened?"

"I opened up my drawer, and as I did that, I pressed the silent alarm button. There's one at each teller's position. That also makes the rolo come down, and we're taught to go below the counter. There's a space we're trained to crawl into. It's lined with steel, so we're safe in case someone tries to shoot us."

"Did he try to shoot you?"

"No, but the rolo drops so fast that, by the time he would have his gun out, it would be down."

"All the glass is bullet-proof," the officer said. "About the only thing he could do would be to leave, well, unless he wanted to be arrested, in which case he could just wait there for three or four minutes."

"Can you describe what he looked like?"

She nodded and said, "He had long blonde hair and this mask, you know, like we wore during COVID. The mask was black. He was wearing a windbreaker, a navy-blue windbreaker, oh, and he had on a cap and a pair of sunglasses. The strange thing was he had on a pair of gloves. When he handed me the note, I saw the gloves. That gave me the first real warning this bollox might be up to something."

"And then they left? He didn't try to lift the rolo or anything?"

"Not that I'm aware of, but by that time, I was under the counter, and we're supposed to stay there until the manager gives us the all-clear. That's exactly what I did."

"When the rolo comes down during working hours, it immediately sends an alert to the station. You can check, but the initial response was no more than a couple of minutes," the officer said.

"Anything else you can think of, Colleen?"

She shook her head. "No, it was all over so fast. It couldn't have been more than fifteen or twenty seconds."

Dillon handed his card to the officer. "Can you make sure whoever is in charge sends us a copy of your recording with Colleen?" He took Dillon's card and then handed him one of his. "Thanks. Sorry to take up more of your time, Colleen. I'm glad you're okay, and thank you for stopping this robbery before they barely got started."

"I live nearby, and as soon as I'm out of here, I'm heading into Kyles."

"I don't blame you one bit. Enjoy, and thank you both."

SEVEN

Colleen and the officer left about sixty seconds after Dillon stepped out of the office. They nodded goodbye to Dillon and hurried out to the lobby. Dillon twiddled his thumbs for another ten minutes waiting in the hall for Suel. He eventually stepped out of the office, followed by an officer and the manager of J&R Credit, who was wearing a white shirt and a tie. Suel introduced them, but it was obvious both men were anxious to leave. After the introductions and Dillon stating that he was glad no one had been hurt and the robbery had failed, the officer and the manager smiled and wasted little time in heading out to the lobby.

Once they were gone, Suel asked, "Did you learn anything?"

"Only that the event probably took less than thirty seconds from start to finish. They didn't get any money. The teller's description matches the two idiots who robbed AIB, and fortunately, no one was hurt. What'd you learn?"

"Pretty much the same thing. I watched the security tape. It's the same two plonkers. Copies of the security tape have already been sent to Special Branch. I find it interesting that this place has substantially tighter security than the bank. You see the idiot passing his note to the teller, and the next thing you see is him jumping back from the counter as the rolo comes down. He looks at his partner, and the two of them hightail it out of the building. They've got a team working on collecting CCTV footage. Maybe we'll be lucky and get a license plate number."

"Yeah, the teller told me they're trained to activate that rolo. They crawl under the counter into a steel-lined area and remain there until someone tells them it's safe to come out. I gotta say, I was impressed. Oh, and then the teller told me as soon as she gets out of here, she's going over to Kyles."

"Can't say that I blame her. Let's check and see if there's anyone else we need to talk to. Otherwise, I'm for heading back to my place."

"Yeah, I'd say we lucked out. Nothing was taken, and no one was hurt."

Five minutes later, Dillon was following Suel back to his house. The lights were still on when he pulled into the same spot he'd parked in earlier. Three cars were still parked on the street, and Dillon crossed his fingers that no one had left.

"Well, that was fast," one of the women shouted from the sitting room as Suel stepped into the house. Dillon was right behind him.

"Case solved, and we found all the money," Suel said and made his way into the kitchen.

"What? Really?" the sisters asked.

Dillon stepped into the sitting room. "Yeah, well, actually, it turns out the robbery was just an attempt. A quick-thinking woman ended the whole thing before it had barely started," Dillon said and went on to give a brief rundown of the event.

Suel suddenly appeared with two beers and handed one to Dillon. "What's up with the rugby match? Is it half-time?"

"It was boring, and no one was scoring," Linda said. "Besides, there's a new Vera on tonight, and we wanted to watch it."

"Vera? That grandmother series where she's supposed to be a detective? They're kidding, right?" Suel asked, looking over at Sean.

"They said they wanted to watch it, and it was three against one. What was I supposed to do?"

"Please tell me you set my internet up to record the match before you turned the channel."

"How in the hell am I supposed to know how to do that on your telly?"

"Oh, for the love of—Let me check, here," Suel said and pulled out his phone. A moment later, he shouted, "Oh my God. We won. We won. We beat the All Blacks by ten points, 32-22. I can't believe it. We won! We won the bleedin' match. Okay, not to worry. I'll pay to get a recording of the match. Oh, this is great. Who's up to celebrate with a whiskey? I've got a good one."

Linda started to raise her hand, but her sister Ann pushed it down and shook her head. "No, Linda. You're driving. I'll have Linda's whiskey, Paddy."

"I'll have another wine," Noreen said.

"I better have one. Don't want you celebrating alone," Sean said.

"Dillon?"

"Yeah, of course. Why not?"

Suel hurried out to the kitchen. He was back a few minutes later, carefully carrying a large wooden tray with six Waterford glasses and a bottle of Paddy's Irish Whiskey.

Sean exchanged a funny look with Linda and said, "Hold on a minute, Paddy. You said you'd a good whiskey."

"I do. Look at the name. It's Paddy's, the best in the house. In fact, it's the only one in the house. Now, if you don't want—"

"No, no, it will do just fine. Just asking is all."

Suel cracked the seal on the cap. He filled all six glasses with an inch of whiskey and passed five of them out. Then he set the tray on the coffee table just in front of Linda and gave her a wink.

"No, Linda, I told you before, you're driving."

"Oh, come on, Ann, just the one. If you're really worried, yous can spend the night here. I've two empty bedrooms," Suel said.

Ann rolled her eyes and said, "Okay, but just the one. God, here we are sharing a whiskey with two Gardai, Special Branch no less, and we're instructed to misbehave. Honest to God, you can't make it up."

Dillon eventually poured a second glass, but maybe just half as much. He took his time, pulling the glass away just as the whiskey began to touch his lips. The conversation and laughing had grown louder over the next two hours, and suddenly the bottle was empty. No one was staggering or slurring too many words, but five of the six people weren't feeling any pain. Sean said he'd sleep on the couch, but then Ann and Linda flipped a coin to see which one would sleep with Suel so Sean could have a bedroom. It was all carried on as a joke, but there was an element of truth.

Noreen and Dillon said their goodbyes at the same time and left. "Oh, God, I think I had a couple more than I should have. I don't think I should be driving," Noreen said once they were outside.

"I didn't drink that much. Where do you live? I can give you a ride."

"Mmm-mmm. Thanks, but I'm all the way out in Skerries."

"Well, you're right. You shouldn't drive. At least not that far. Tell you what. I've got two guest rooms. Why don't you stay at my place? I'll bring you back early tomorrow, and you can get your car before the others are out of bed. They'll never know."

"Are you sure?"

"Yeah, you don't need to lose your license or worse. It's not a bother. Honest."

"Oh, that's really nice of you. Thank you. Yes, I'd love to stay."

Dillon held the door for her as she climbed into his car, then hurried around to the driver's side. The drive home was uneventful other than some casual conversation. Noreen Rooney taught third class in a primary school. She grew up in County Mayo, came to Dublin city at the age of twenty-two with a teaching certificate, and landed a job in the Dublin school system.

Dillon pulled into his drive and hurried around the car to open the door for Noreen. It had just been a ten-minute drive, but based on a couple of slurred words, he guided her by the arm as he led her to the front door. He opened the door, and there was Lucifer on the other side. He leaped out and assumed the position next to the driver's door of the car.

Noreen seemed oblivious and stepped into the house. "Oh, how lovely," she said as she examined the entryway that looked pretty much like eighty percent of the homes in Dublin.

"Come on into the sitting room. Would you like some water? Or, I've got some cranberry juice or—"

"I'd love another whiskey if you've got it."

"I do, coming right up. Grab a seat in front of the fireplace," Dillon said as he headed into the kitchen. He took two glasses from the cupboard, Waterford but not the same pattern as Suel's. He poured a healthy serving of Bushmills Black Bush whiskey into the glasses and took them into the sitting room.

Noreen was seated on the couch, and she grinned as Dillon handed her the glass.

"Here's to you, Noreen," Dillon said as they clinked glasses and took a sip.

"Mmm-mmm, God bless Paddy for having us over for that crazy night, but this is a much better whiskey. It's nice to be able to get to know more about you without a rugby game or a crime show playing in the background. You mind if I ask how you ended up here, in Dublin?"

"Not at all," he said and quickly gave her the short version, not mentioning the shooting at Terminal 2 at the airport or really anything else he'd been involved in crime-wise. He mentioned some of the things he liked about the country and the people.

When Noreen finished her drink, Dillon took her upstairs and let her choose which guest room she wanted to sleep in.

He went downstairs and let Lucifer back in the house, washed the Waterford glasses, and headed upstairs. He left the hall light on, turned on the night light in the bathroom, and climbed into bed. He was almost asleep when the door to his bedroom opened, and the naked silhouette of red-headed Noreen Rooney appeared. She walked around to the far side of the bed, pulled the covers back, crawled in, and snuggled up next to Dillon.

EIGHT

Dillon was wide awake just after 6:00 in the morning. Noreen was still sound asleep and breathing heavily. After their initial 'get together,' he woke her around 2:00, and she'd done the same to him just before 5:00. He debated waking her again but thought he might be pressing his luck. He slipped out of bed and pulled on his jeans and a t-shirt out in the hall.

He turned on the coffee pot and placed a tea bag in a mug for Noreen. Just before 7:00, he turned on the kettle and took a fresh tea and two aspirin upstairs to her. She was in the bathroom, and he knocked on the door and said, "Good morning, fresh tea and a couple of aspirins on the dresser in the bedroom for you. I'll be downstairs. We can get your car whenever you want, but happy to make breakfast for you."

"Thanks," she replied, not quite groaning but sounding like she was feeling the effects of last night's beverages. She was downstairs looking beautiful fifteen minutes later with an empty tea mug. She set the mug on the counter and said, "Umm, I think as much as I'd like to stay for breakfast, I should probably go get my car."

"You took those aspirins?"

"Yeah, thank you for that too."

"Not a problem. Let's go before anyone is up over at Suel's and the word gets out."

"I hope you don't mind. I just don't want to—"

"Relax, I get it. You could have come over to say the rosary, and by the time the word got around, it would end up we were both photographed in the back seat of the car, and a neighbor had to tell us to keep the noise down."

She laughed at that. "Not far from the truth."

"Come on before they get up. God only knows how late things went."

"Probably not much later than when we left, but only because Paddy ran out of whiskey."

They drove over to Suel's. When they turned the corner, his house was halfway down the street. Sean Hanahan's and the Mahoney sister's car were still parked out front. As they approached, all the shades appeared to still be drawn.

"Thank you for last night, Noreen. Great to meet you, and, well, thank you very much. I'd still like to make you breakfast. You've got a half-hour drive to Skerries, and if you have a hangover, there's no better way to deal with it than to have someone cook you breakfast."

She seemed to think about that and said, "You know, I really appreciate that, but—"

"I'll just cook you breakfast. You don't have to climb back into my bed. God, you wore me out last night. Not a complaint, by the way."

"Yeah, okay, that would be nice. I'd love breakfast. Thank you."

"I'll see you back at my place," he said as he pulled next to her car.

She studied Suel's house for a moment and then said, "Yeah, see you back at your place," and hurried out of the car. Dillon was halfway back to his place when headlights flashed in his rearview mirror, and he noticed Noreen's car behind him. He pulled into his drive, and she drove up over the curb and parked on the sidewalk. He waited until she stepped into the front garden, and they headed into the house together. Lucifer met them at the door, gave Noreen a quick inspection, and hurried outside.

Dillon began to prepare a breakfast of French toast with maple syrup from Minnesota. He set two places on the kitchen counter, placed a side dish of blueberry yogurt at each place, and filled the kettle. Noreen was upstairs in the shower, and once he heard the shower turn off, he waited a couple of minutes, then turned on the burner and made six slices of French toast.

He heard the bedroom door open upstairs and filled her tea mug as she came downstairs.

"Mmm-mmm, it smells delicious," she said, stepping into the kitchen. Her red hair was pulled back, and she appeared even more beautiful without makeup.

"Everything okay with the shower?"

"Just what the doctor ordered." She smiled as he slid the fresh mug of tea across the counter.

"You take milk?"

"Yes, please."

Dillon took the quart of milk from the refrigerator and set it next to her tea mug. Noreen cautiously tipped it and placed no more than two drops into her tea. Dillon had seen the routine before and didn't comment. They chatted about nothing in particular while they ate. Noreen had another tea with two more drops of milk, and then Dillon walked her out to the car. They kissed at the driver's door, not just a peck but a bit of a lingering event, and then Dillon held the door as she climbed in. He got another kiss, this time more of a peck, but it was on the lips. She started the car, blew him a kiss, and drove down the lane. He watched until she disappeared around the far corner.

He went back into the house and cleaned up the kitchen, then went into the sitting room. Lucifer was up on the couch chewing on something Dillon didn't recognize at first until he realized it was, or rather, had been, a thong. A powder blue floral lace G-String thong. He'd never seen it before, and Noreen must have left it in the guest room before she slid into bed with him last night, never realizing Lucifer would grab it in a heartbeat.

"I can't blame you, boy," he said and turned on the TV.

NINE

Monday morning, Dillon was filling his coffee mug in the break room. Suel wandered in, turned on the kettle, and placed a tea bag in his mug.

"Paddy, why don't you bring your own tea bags to work? You know you hate the tea here. You're going to cringe, swear, and then dump your tea down the sink."

"I do it for the same reason you drink that shite from the coffee machine. You made it home okay Saturday night?" Suel asked, clearly fishing for some information.

"Yeah, what about you? Did one of the Mahoney sisters warm up your bed?"

"I only wish, no wait a minute, on second thought, I'm glad they didn't. After yous left, they opened up a bottle of red wine, and after going through that, they opened a second bottle. Sean went up to bed, and I eventually told the girls to turn off the lights when they were finished, and I went upstairs. I left the bedroom door open, hoping one or both of them would join me. Instead, I woke up around 3:00 to the sounds of someone throwing up in the bathroom. That went on for the next hour or so, both of them taking turns groaning and erupting. I think they were trading places. As soon as one of them finished, the other would start up. Then they'd go into the bedroom, and the other one would be throwing up again five minutes later. God, I had to pull a pillow over my head to muffle the sound. They slept until about 10:00, then came downstairs looking like death warmed over, said their goodbyes, and hurried out the door. What about you?"

"Me? I just went home and enjoyed a quiet Sunday. About all I did was take Lucifer for a walk around Albert Park, and we—"

"Dillon, I was talking about Noreen. She was giving you the eye all night. We all picked up on that, well, except for you, apparently."

"Noreen? I just walked her to her car, and she drove home. Told me she lived out in Skerries and had to get home."

"You didn't invite her to your place?"

"No, I just told you. She said she had a long drive and had to get going."

Suel shook his head. "I give up. I'm heading back to my desk and going to see what we've got as far as CCTV footage on these two idiots who robbed AIB and ran out of J&R Credit."

"I'll go over the tape from inside J&R. It's only a half-minute long. Then I'll check on CCTV footage from around the area. I want to check with Emily about these two wearing wigs. They may be idiots, but they've got some basics, wigs, disposable masks, sunglasses, and gloves. They're doing something right."

"I still think they've got their heads up their bum." Suel took his first sip of tea, shuddered, and mumbled, "Oh, why in the hell do I even bother?" He dumped the remainder of the mug into the sink. "Don't say a word, Dillon."

Dillon ran his fingers across his lips, pretending he'd zipped them shut, and they headed out of the break room. Once back at his desk, he phoned Emily in the Tech Lab.

"I don't have anything for you at the moment, Dillon," was how she answered.

"Hi, Emily. I was just checking in to see how your weekend was."

"Yeah, sure you were. I'll be studying the tape you sent me from the AIB robbery, and with any luck, I'll be back to you later this morning."

"Okay, I'm out of your hair," Dillon said and hung up. He phoned Jim Burke in the Tech Department.

"Burke," was how he answered.

"Hi Jim, Jack Dillon calling. Any luck on the facial recognition of those two idiots robbing AIB?"

"I wish. Unfortunately, between the face masks, the sunglasses, and the caps, we're down to just a couple of points. To put it bluntly, no, we don't have anything useful, and unless we get a better image showing eyes, cheekbones, nose, mouth, and chin, we won't be able to obtain a match with the images in our system. We're really working in the dark. I received a copy of the tape from the botched attempt Saturday night at J&R Credit, but that was more of the same. I wish I had better news for you, Dillon, but unfortunately, I don't."

"Look, Jim, I get it. These two clowns have managed, in their ineptness, to prevent us from finding out exactly who the hell they are and hauling their asses to jail. Hopefully, something will change, and we can get them off the street."

"Let me know if you get anything. Based on these two events, I fear we have not heard the last of them."

"Thanks, Jim. I'll keep you posted," Dillon said and hung up. He replayed the thirty-two-second tape from J&R Credit. The two men walked in. One stopped at the lobby counter. The other proceeded to the teller window, passed the note, and the rolo window came down five seconds later. They both hurried back out the door.

One thing seemed obvious to Dillon. They had been there before. They knew exactly what they were doing. In fact, it was as if they had practiced. He brought up the AIB tape and watched it. More of the same, they entered just prior to close. One man goes directly to the teller. The other stands at the counter in the middle of the lobby, theoretically keeping an eye on the surrounding area. It appeared to Dillon that it wasn't their first time in the bank. The man heading to the teller's window moved there without any hesitation.

Did they check both places out, or were they regular customers? Dillon placed a call to Dermot Casey, the person in charge of the security tapes at AIB. He answered just before Dillon expected to be dropped into voicemail.

"Casey."

"Hi, Dermot. This is Jack Dillon with An Garda Síochána, Special Branch. We met last Friday after the robbery. I'm going over the security tape, and I'm curious, how long do you hold onto your recordings?"

"Recordings, you mean of the front lobby and the teller's window?"

"Yes."

"Standard process is six months. That would be the same for the ATM on the front of the building."

Six months? Dillon figured it would take about that long to review the tapes.

"Why? Are you thinking they were here before? That they may be customers?"

"Not that they would be regular customers, although we're not discounting that. But in reviewing the tape, they seem to clearly be familiar with the lobby and the teller's window. I can't detect any hesitation in their movement. It's direct, but they're not racing. They seem to be moving confidently. I might even say very confidently."

"It's interesting you say that. Obviously, we're not a large facility, and yet, if you were planning to rob us, my sense would be that three individuals would be more to the point. You'd theoretically be able to have all the cash drawers emptied in little more than one minute. But that brings up the next question, which is why would you rob the tellers? They represent a limited amount of currency. On a busy day, that might amount to twenty-five hundred euros. A bank officer would periodically check any large cash deposits and place them in the vault. In today's world, virtually anyone needing cash would use their bank card or credit card at the ATM. Most of our in-person deposits are in the form of checks unless it's possibly a retail business. People nowadays use their credit cards for purchases as small as two or three euros without even thinking."

"Would you be able to send your lobby recordings for the previous week, prior to the robbery, to me here at Special Branch?"

"Yes, I'd be happy to do that. Let me give you my email address. Please send me an official request, and I'll send them to you immediately. I believe I have your card. Let me check. Oh yes, your card, along with Officer Suel's. I can get these to you as soon as I receive your request."

"You'll see it in the next thirty minutes," Dillon said and hung up. He actually had the request on the official form ready to go ten minutes later. He double-checked it and then sent it off. Fifteen minutes later, he received Casey's email with the previous week's recordings.

TEN

Dillon began to work backward with the tapes. Starting an hour before the robbery late Friday afternoon and running the tape back toward Monday morning at 9:00 AM. There was a lot of time when either no one was in the lobby, or there were individuals who clearly weren't one of the two men on the actual tape of the robbery—women, youngsters, and elderly. That still didn't mean it wasn't a time-consuming undertaking.

"I'm going out to get some fish and chips. You interested?" Suel asked a little after 1:00.

"Would you mind picking me up an order? I've technically got sixty-five hours of tape left to run through from AIB."

"What in God's name are you looking for?"

"I was thinking those two idiots seemed to be familiar with the place. I'm hoping to spot one or both of them checking the lobby out and not wearing masks or sunglasses."

Suel shook his head and said, "Yeah, I'll grab some fish and chips for you. Sounds like you're gonna need it. Good luck with mission impossible. Just remember, they probably aren't going to be wearing disposable masks or sunglasses."

"Gee, now, why didn't I think of that?" Dillon said. He worked his way through more of the tape. Suel dropped a bag of fish and chips on Dillon's desk twenty minutes later. Dillon continued to review the tape and came up empty-handed. He still had eight hours left to review when Suel suggested a pint at the Autobahn might be a good idea.

They parked on Glasnevin Drive and stepped into the Autobahn. It was a full house, but they were able to grab a table just as a couple left. They placed an order with a waitress for two pints of Guinness.

"You come up with anything reviewing the tapes from AIB?" Suel asked.

"Not a damn thing, and I've still got all of last Monday to go through. I just have to believe the robbery wasn't their first time in the place. They knew exactly what to do and didn't hesitate. Didn't stop at the counter in the middle of the lobby and look around. One went right for the teller's window while the other kept an eye on the two loan officers at their desks."

"You think that was the same situation at J&R Credit?"

"I do, as far as the lobby was concerned. What they didn't know was that there was a button next to the cash drawer that the teller could push in the event of a robbery and the rolo would be coming down five seconds later. But again, they were smart enough to clear out at that point. Your man didn't try to stop the rolo from closing. They simply hurried out of the place. You learn anything today?"

Suel shook his head. "Not really. They left AIB and headed into the parking ramp around the corner. Based on the tapes I watched, they're still somewhere in the parking ramp. Same thing after J&R Credit. They go into an alley. Cameras are at either end of the alley, but they never appear."

"I'm beginning to think these may not be bumblers but rather someone who knows exactly what they're do-ing and—"

The waitress suddenly appeared carrying a tray with two pints of Guinness. As she set the glasses on the table, Dillon handed her a twenty euro note and said, "Keep the change."

She smiled and stepped away. "You Americans, you're always tipping too much and ruining it for the rest of us. Still," Suel raised his glass toward Dillon and took a sip, "You were about to tell me how these two knackers are actually very smart. I guess you're right. What in God's name was I thinking when they were shut down at J&R Credit in less than thirty seconds, and they risked spending six years in prison for the princely sum of no more than a thousand euros apiece after robbing AIB?"

"Yeah, but if they're so stupid, why are they wear-ing the masks and sunglasses, so we can't do any facial recognition? Why do they have latex gloves on under-neath the cloth gloves? If they're so stupid, why haven't you been able to spot them on CCTV tape driving off in a vehicle? Why haven't I spotted them on the previous week of AIB's security tape?"

"If I had the answer to those questions, they'd be locked up by now."

"I don't know, Paddy. They're up to something. I'm just not sure it's robbing these places."

"Then what, Dillon? Clearly, they're beginners. Okay, maybe they've been lucky, I'll give you that. But they haven't planned these bumbling attempts. If they had, they never would have entered either place. You're never going to get lots of cash from a teller's window. It's like something from a half-century ago. Something from out of a movie, a bad movie."

Dillon's cell phone suddenly rang, and he pulled it out of his pocket.

Suel said, "Oh, please. Don't tell me they're at it again and tried to rob a grocery store. We both need a break."

Dillon looked at his screen, Noreen Rooney. Thank God it wasn't Emergency Response. "Relax, just a neighbor calling. Wondering if I'd like to stop by for a glass later tonight."

"Oh, that sexy one across the lane from you. What's her name, Sarah?"

"No, Tara, and yeah, that's who called. I'll swing by on my way home. Better limit myself to one pint tonight."

"Oh, for Christ's sake. I still haven't recovered from my night with the Mahoney sisters. The two of them and one crazier than the next. You can't make it up. It has to be the only time I've ever been thankful neither one crawled into bed with me. Unfortunately, I can still hear them groaning and throwing up in the bathroom."

"I wish I would have stayed. I would have loved to direct them into your bedroom."

"Well, there's the lesson. Plenty of whiskey and two bottles of red wine do not make for a pleasant night's sleep for anyone. You know, Dillon, you should consider giving Noreen Rooney a call. I wasn't kidding. She had her eyes on the likes of you all night long. When the two of you stepped out together, I was sure it was the beginning of some great event. But then that would require you to pay attention and be aware of the women around you, so she's safe."

"Sorry, Paddy, it never occurred to me."

"Don't I know it."

They finished their pints, said goodnight, and headed out to their cars. Suel gave a quick honk as he drove past Dillon, just climbing into his car. Dillon pulled into his drive, opened the front door, and let Lucifer out. He settled onto the couch in the sitting room and called Noreen back.

She answered on the second ring. "Oh, hi. Hope I'm not interrupting whatever you've got going."

"Oh, no, sorry I didn't answer. I was driving home and didn't want to take a phone call. Had I known it was you, I would have answered."

"How sweet. I'm thinking I owe you dinner after the wonderful breakfast you made me. I had a nice quiet Sunday due in no part to your French toast and aspirin. Left to my own devices, I would have been in bed most of the day with a pounding headache."

"Listen, thank you so much for a most wonderful evening. I'm just glad you made it home okay. Your little geniuses were okay in school today?"

"Yes, plenty of energy on any given day. I had called wondering if you might be free for dinner some evening this week."

"I would love it. Would you like to meet somewhere?"

"No place special. I thought it might be fun to actually have a conversation with you that I'd be able to remember the next day."

"Well, if you want to choose a place, I would be happy to meet you there on two conditions."

"Oh?"

"Yes, the first would be I pay for dinner. The second would be that we schedule something with the understanding that, based on my work, I may have to cancel at a moment's notice."

"I'll agree to both those if you'll agree to my condition."

"Which is?"

"You come out here to Skerries."

"I agree."

"Wonderful. Is there any particular evening that would work better?"

"Not really. I'm such a boring guy that any night is open at this stage."

"Oh, well, how about tomorrow night? Do you know where the Stoop Your Head pub is in Skerries?"

"I do, as a matter of fact. It's right on the harbor, if I remember, and that would be perfect. It's a wonderful place."

"Shall we say 7:00?"

"I'll see you at the Stoop Your Head, Noreen, to-morrow night at seven."

"Well then, I'd better rest up. See you tomorrow. Bye, bye, bye," Noreen said and disconnected.

Dillon sat on the couch and stared at the phone for a very long time, replaying Noreen's 'I'd better rest up' statement.

ELEVEN

Dillon was up the following morning before his alarm went off. He showered, shaved, dressed, and then packed an overnight bag with clean underwear, deodorant, and a razor. He let Lucifer out into the front garden, filled his food and water dishes, and then coaxed him back into the house with a biscuit. He placed the overnight bag in the trunk of his car just in case things got crazy at the end of the day.

Over the course of the next nine hours, the clock appeared to be moving backward as he checked the time every ten or fifteen minutes. He reviewed the tail end of the AIB tapes and never saw anyone who remotely resembled either of the two robbers in size or shape. In what only felt like seventy-two hours, the hands on the wall clock in Special Branch finally headed toward 5:00.

"What do you say to a pint?" Suel said as he pushed his chair in and headed over to Dillon's desk.

"Oh, I'd love to, Paddy, but I promised to help a neighbor move some things. She's going to be fixing dinner and—"

"Is it that hot sexy one across the lane from you?"

"That would be Tara, and she has more sense than to ask me over. No, this is an older woman around the corner. To be honest, she told me her name, but it went in one ear and out the other. I just say, 'Hi, how are you,' and no one picks up on the fact I've forgotten their name."

"Or they probably know, but they figure, what's the point? This bollox won't remember if I tell him again."

"Yeah, now that you mention it, that's probably more the case. Anyway, I better head out. I don't want to keep her waiting. Besides, she's an excellent cook."

"Enjoy, and I'll see you in the morning," Suel said.

Dillon tidied his desk and headed out of the office. He drove home, let Lucifer out, then hurried upstairs to change clothes. He chose a freshly ironed, light-blue shirt and a clean pair of jeans. The Stoop Your Head pub was a casual place, but he wanted to look nice for Noreen in the hope it might lead to a more eventful evening.

He checked the US news on his laptop for a few minutes and decided if he listened to much more, he'd end up in a foul mood, so he shut it down. He coaxed Lucifer in with a biscuit, turned a lamp on in the sitting room, and headed out the door. It was a good thirty-minute drive out to Skerries at this time of the day, but he pulled into the harbor parking lot ten minutes early. He sat in his car and looked out into the small harbor.

A pair of seals were swimming along the harbor wall next to a fisherman's boat, probably dining on the dregs of the day's catch. He watched for a few minutes, then got out of his car and headed into the pub. The place was nicely crowded. He caught a wave from Noreen, seated in a back booth, and headed toward her.

"Oh, right on time," she said as Dillon leaned down to give her a peck on the cheek. She turned quickly and kissed him on the lips, squeezing his hand in the process.

"Thank you," Dillon said as he slid into the booth across from her.

"Thanks for coming all the way out here. I really appreciate it."

"Not half as much as I appreciate the offer. Just remember the rule. I'm paying."

"Would you like something to drink?" a waitress asked.

Dillon nodded at Noreen.

"I think I'll have a glass of your Sauvignon Blanc," she said.

"I'll have the same," Dillon said as the waitress placed menus in front of them. "Do you know what you're going to have?" Dillon asked.

"I always get the fresh salmon. I love it."

"Enough said. That sounds perfect. Great choice."

They chatted and had another glass of wine with their salmon dinners. Dillon talked Noreen into ordering a dessert, not that it took much pressure. Once he paid the bill, she asked, "Are you anxious to head back to Dublin?"

"Actually, no, I'm enjoying the evening and your wonderful company."

"Could I talk you into seeing my place?"

"You certainly could. Lead the way."

Dillon followed Noreen's silver-colored Volkswagen Passat through the village and out to a country road. Just outside of the village, she turned onto a lane with a row of attached houses overlooking the water. At the end of the lane and across from the attached units was a very contemporary-looking place with a gated parking area. The Passat stopped, and the gate began to open automatically. She pulled in, and Dillon followed, parking next to her and facing the water.

"Oh, man, this is gorgeous. Have you lived here long?"

"Oh, yes. Actually, most of my life. My father was an architect, and my parents built this in the 1990s with help from my mom's brothers, and lucky me, this is where I live."

"Gorgeous view," Dillon said, gazing out onto the Irish Sea.

"Oh, don't I know, and wonderfully quiet. Come on, let's go inside."

Dillon took a final gaze out across the sea for a few seconds and then followed Noreen into the house through a double door. With a glass of white wine in hand, Noreen gave him a tour of the modern structure. Tile floors were throughout the entire place, with thick Asian rugs in every room but the kitchen. Three bedrooms, each with a fireplace along with fireplaces in the kitchen, the sitting room, and even the pink bathroom, all gas so you'd never have to clean them out or maintain a stack of firewood.

"Oh, that's really cool," Dillon said, examining the bathtub, complete with jacuzzi jets and the fireplace behind a glass panel.

"I'd be lying if I said I never used it. At the end of any given day, I make my way into the tub with a glass of wine and just decompress for a half hour. When I was a teenager, all my girlfriends wanted to come over and try it out. When I turned fifteen, I had three girlfriends spend the night, and they each got twenty minutes in the tub with the fireplace on. My mom was in charge."

"Do you have any pictures of that?" Dillon asked.

"Oh, now, wouldn't that be something? No, I don't have any pictures. I gave them all away to the boys at school," she said, and they both laughed.

They chatted in front of the sitting room fireplace while enjoying another glass of wine, and then Noreen led the way into her bedroom. She had a four-poster queen-sized bed. The headboard had a brass reading light on either side of it and held a dozen books on a shelf. After an exhaustive interlude, they eventually drifted off to sleep with Dillon's arm around Noreen snuggled up against him. He woke about five minutes before her alarm went off, just in time to remember he'd left his overnight bag out in the car. He considered getting dressed and going out to get it, then decided against that idea.

He waited until the alarm went off and Noreen woke up. She crawled out of bed and went into the bathroom. She was out of the bathroom five minutes later, wearing a terrycloth robe cinched tightly around her waist and sending a message.

"Would you like me to put the kettle on? I think I might have some instant coffee."

"Oh, thanks," Dillon said, "but don't worry. I should head back to town. I have to get ready for work and let my dog out."

"Oh yes, what was his name again, Devil?"

"Close. Actually, it's Lucifer," he said, pulling on his jeans and then picking his shirt up off the floor. He buttoned the shirt as he followed Noreen out of the bedroom and toward the front door. They shared a passionate kiss. Each said thank you, and promised to call later on, then Dillon headed out to his car. As he backed up, Noreen apparently activated the gate because it slid open as he approached. He turned onto the road, tooted his horn, and headed back into the village of Skerries. He was home twenty-five minutes later and was making a fresh pot of coffee before Lucifer was even awake.

TWELVE

Dillon was in Special Branch before 9:00. He wasn't aware of it, but he apparently had a smile on his face because, when Suel entered the office, he glanced over in Dillon's direction and said, "Well. It would appear you had a satisfying evening. You look like the cat that just swallowed the canary. Things went well last night?"

"Yes, a lovely quiet evening. I just ate some leftovers, read a book, and was asleep in bed just after 10:00."

"I thought you were off to the neighbor's house to help move something. You said she lived around the corner and was a great cook."

Damn it, Dillon thought. "Oh, yeah, but, umm, it was nowhere near as complicated as I thought it might be. I moved a couple of items for her, she offered me some crackers and cheese, and then I was home ten minutes later. I'm not sure what gave me the idea she'd be making me dinner and I'd be there for a few hours moving one thing and another."

Suel gave him a look for a moment, then turned on his computer and headed for the break room. "You want another coffee?" he asked as he passed Dillon's desk.

"No thanks. One is my limit. Enjoy your tea."

"If only," Suel said as he stepped through the door. They worked away at their desks over the course of the rest of the morning.

Dillon contacted Emily in the Tech Lab and Jim Burke in Facial Recognition. Neither one had been able to come up with any substantive clues in either robbery case. It was almost 1:00 when Dillon suggested he and Suel step out to lunch at the Hole in The Wall pub. "I think we both need to take a deep breath and start over on this investigation. We have to be missing something. I just can't believe these two are as stupid as they seem."

"Well, if they're not that stupid, they've done a pretty good job of convincing me they're as dumb as rocks. I think it's just a matter of time before they make some major mistake and we're able to nab them. They'll do some idiotic thing like lock themselves in a vault or park someplace and have their car towed away."

Dillon shook his head. "I only hope no one is hurt in the process. Come on, I'll drive over to the Hole In The Wall. What do you say?"

"Sounds like the best idea I've heard all morning."

They took the elevator down to the ground floor, then headed out to Dillon's car in the parking lot. It was a three-minute drive, and Dillon parked almost in front of the pub. A half-dozen runners were scattered around a couple of tables, drinking teas, and two of them were eating pastries. Dillon and Suel took a table at the opposite end of the patio.

A moment later, the waiter stepped over. "Hi, lads. Nice to see yous again. Teas? And would you like to see a menu?"

Suel shook his head. "I'll have a Hole Burger along with a tea."

The waiter nodded and looked at Dillon. "Coffee, black, and I'll take a Hole Burger as well."

"I'll be back with your drinks. Thanks."

When he was gone, Dillon asked, "Do you really think these two we're dealing with are as stupid as they seem?"

"Our bank robbers? Well, yes, I do, at least based on the facts thus far. I know they got a small amount of cash at AIB, but in the scheme of things, what in the world are they doing, even trying to rob a teller at a bank? Then that cluster at J&R, it's stupid from beginning to end. Now, I do agree with you. Based on their movements, they clearly had been in both places prior to the robbery or attempted robbery. I would even suggest they had been there a couple of times. Just checking the place out, getting the lay of the land. But that simply begs the question. What in the hell were they thinking in the first place? Both locations have total failure written across them."

The waiter returned with their coffee and tea. "Burgers will be up in just a couple of minutes. Anything else you'd like?"

"We're good, thanks," Suel said.

The burgers arrived a few minutes later. Dillon had just removed the top bun and was reaching for the catsup when his phone rang. "Do I dare answer that?"

"I have a strong feeling that would be a very bad idea. But you'd better all the same."

Dillon set the catsup down, pulled out his phone, looked at the screen, and said, "Oh shit." He took a deep breath and answered, "Marshal Jack Dillon." He shook his head and asked, "Bank of Ireland? Blackrock? Were there shots fired? Is everyone safe? I'm sure it's the same two that hit AIB last week and J&R Credit. Yeah, they did the same thing at AIB. I'm guessing it's a British Army training device. We've got the item number on record, 'A' something. If you would text me the address, please. I'm out of the office at the moment. I'm only twenty minutes from Blackrock. Yes, thank you," Dillon said and disconnected. "You should get the call in just a moment," Dillon said. As he signaled the water with a wave of his hand, Suel's phone rang.

"DI Suel," he answered.

"Everything all right?" the waiter asked as he approached Dillon.

"Unfortunately, we've been called away. Can you ring us up, and could we have two takeout boxes?" Dillon asked as he pulled a credit card from his wallet.

"Sure, be right back," the waiter said and hurried away with the credit card.

"What do you think the odds are it's our two idiots?" Dillon asked as Suel shook his head and returned the phone to his pocket.

"Another bank and interrupting our lunch. I'd say it's about a hundred percent certain it's these same two dumbasses. You can't make it up. You gave your man a credit card?"

"Yeah, but I'm just paying for me," Dillon said. Suel gave him a look, and Dillon started to laugh just as the waiter hurried back with the takeout boxes, Dillon's credit card, and the receipt.

"I got the tip, Dillon," Suel said and handed the waiter a two-euro coin.

They placed the burgers and fries into the takeout boxes. Dillon took a couple swallows of his coffee, and they hurried over to his car. He input the bank address on his GPS and pulled a U-turn at the next corner. He drove past the Hole In The Wall, An Garda Síochána headquarters, and across the Liffey on the Rory O'More Bridge. At least it wasn't end-of-the-day rush hour. The traffic was heavy, but then it always was in Dublin.

While Dillon drove, Suel ate his burger and French fries. Dillon raced past a number of drivers and even had Suel wide-eyed and hanging onto the dashboard for a moment. Eventually, they arrived at the Bank of Ireland building in the Blackrock section of south Dublin. There were three squad cars parked around the corner from the bank. Two uniformed officers were standing just outside the entrance to the bank.

Dillon pulled in front of the squad cars, pulled his lanyard with his ID from his pocket, and slid out from behind the wheel. The Bank of Ireland was a two-story building on the corner of a not-too-busy intersection. It was clearly half again as large as the AIB bank. The sidewalk in front of the bank widened into a large patio with two picnic tables, benches, and chairs. A number of people were seated out in front, drinking teas and snacking on pastries from the Centra Market next door to the bank. An Ulster Bank branch was just across the street.

Suel belched as they headed toward the front door. They held up their IDs, got a nod from the two officers at the door, and stepped inside. The inside of the windows appeared to be coated with residue from the smoke bomb. A fine dust residue covered the floor and every surface. Virtually all the desks were empty. Officers were seated at two distant desks interviewing two bank employees. The lobby was the standard layout, with a counter in the center holding a rack with deposit and withdrawal slips. At the moment, two officers were standing at the counter talking.

There were five stations at the teller counter. The entire counter was behind glass and obviously closed. Dillon looked at Suel and said, "Do you think it's strange that this robbery occurred over the lunch hour? That would seem to me to be one of the busiest times of the day."

"Yes, but then, believe it or not, you're actually thinking like a normal person. We haven't seen an image of the robber yet, but given the time, the fact that there are people seated out front with apparently no pressure to return to work or—"

"Just looking out there, it gives me the impression everyone is probably retired," Dillon said and nodded at the front window.

Suel nodded at the two officers at the counter in the center of the lobby. "That doesn't mean they wouldn't notice what was going on and may be able to give some identifying characteristics we won't pick up on the security tapes. Let's ask the two standing at the counter who we talk to and where they are."

THIRTEEN

As they approached, one of the officers said, "DI Suel, Special Branch?"

"Not to worry, he won't bother you. My job is to keep an eye on him. I'm Marshal Dillon, Special Branch. What can you tell us?"

The officer smiled and shook his head. "Two characters were in here just after 1:00. One of them waited over there at the counter, apparently keeping an eye on the four employees seated at their desks. The other one stepped to the teller's window. There were three tellers working at the time. Your man waited in line, passed a note to the teller, and showed his pistol but never pulled it out.

"Did they get any money?"

The officer nodded. "The teller he passed the note to emptied her cash drawer. One of the other tellers realized what was going on and pushed the alarm button. The two men fled. End of story."

"Are the employees still here?" Dillon asked.

"The tellers are back in the big shot's offices with a couple of people who were at the desks. The customers have been interviewed, they gave contact information, and they've left."

"Where did we meet? I know you," Suel said to the officer who recognized him.

"I'm Tommy Dempsey. I was involved in an arrest two years ago. A belligerent woman and her husband. There'd been a shooting, and as a citizen, she decided it was her right to take pictures and contaminate the scene."

"This was the shooting in a doctor's office, wasn't it?" Suel asked.

Dempsey nodded. "Yeah, a plastic surgeon, breast augmentation, actually."

"Right, and the shooter was a woman who was unhappy with her results, if I remember."

"Yeah, I was first on the scene. One for the books, as they say."

"We'd like to go back to the offices, talk to whoever is in charge, and request a copy of the security tapes. Unfortunately, we're probably familiar with the two idiots responsible," Dillon said.

"Interesting you put it that way," the other officer said. "They just updated their security systems here. They've got twice the cameras in the lobby. I think it was updated in the last thirty days. Look around. They've got six cameras in here," he said, pointing each one out. "There are four more outside, two covering the general area, one on the ATM, and the fourth covers the intersection."

"Who's in charge?" Dillon asked.

"DI Brennan Bancroft, not sure who he's interviewing back there, but you can't miss him. Bald as a cue ball."

"He's a good sort," the other officer said.

"Thanks, lads," Suel said, and they headed toward the door marked 'Offices.'

It was essentially the same layout as the office section at the AIB bank, only larger, more offices. Suel said, "Let me talk to this Bancroft, and maybe you could search out whoever covers the security tapes and get copies sent to us."

"I'll have him send tapes of the robbery and the week prior."

"I hate to say it, but maybe two weeks prior since we didn't see anything going back one week on the AIB tapes."

"I'm afraid you're right. You know it's too bad we have to sleep," Dillon said and headed down the hall. He stopped at the door labeled Security Services and knocked as he opened the door.

An overweight, curly-haired man wearing glasses with thick lenses turned around in his chair and said, "I think you have the wrong office."

"Is this Security Services? You're in charge of the video surveillance?"

"Yes, I am. Marcus O'Malley."

"Nice to meet you, Marcus. My name is Marshal Dillon. I'm with An Garda Síochána, Special Branch,"

Dillon held up the ID hanging from his lanyard, although he was too far away for anyone to read it, let alone someone wearing coke bottle glasses.

The guy actually smiled and said, "I was wondering when someone would want the tapes. You want me to run it for you now? It's short and sweet. One of our tellers set the alarm, and the two fled."

"Did they get any money?" Dillon asked and looked at the six computer screens mounted on the wall behind O'Malley.

This time, he grinned, "Oh, yeah, and at no additional charge, a dye pack."

"Red dye?" Dillon asked.

"Yes, we set the timer on the pack at twenty-five seconds. It's activated when the pack is removed from the magnetic plate. We have a transmitter at every door in the bank, so once they head out a door, they've got twenty-five seconds before the pack explodes. Usually, the criminal is in a hurry to leave, so twenty-five seconds should be enough to get them just far enough away."

"And your teller put a dye pack in with the cash?"

"Yes, she did. In a bundle of twenty euro notes, as a matter of fact. Just trying to make your job a little easier. Now, based on the security tape, they headed out a side door, but once the pack explodes, it's pretty standard that they get rid of what's left of the money. With any luck, you can be out there looking for two individuals with red dye on their faces."

"Can you run the security tape for me?" Dillon asked.

"It would be a pleasure. Here take a seat," he said and nodded at a chair in front of his desk. He turned around in his chair and began tapping on a keyboard, bringing an image up on one of the screens mounted on the wall. The screen was focused on two of the teller windows. A familiar man, once again wearing a disposable mask and sunglasses, suddenly appeared. He waited behind an older man getting some cash and then stepped forward. He passed a note and a white plastic bag across the counter. The bag looked like the kind you might get for small purchases in a grocery store.

The teller, a woman, filled the plastic bag with currency from her drawer and handed it to the man with the sunglasses. There was no sound on the security tape, but his sudden movement suggested that the alarm had just gone off. Interestingly, the two individuals did not head for the front entrance. The computer screen next to the one Dillon had been watching activated as they walked past the main door and out a side door. They were picked up on the next screen as they calmly walked across the parking lot, around a corner, and disappeared.

"So where do you think they were when that dye pack exploded?" Dillon asked.

"Twenty-five seconds, at the speed they were going, I would think they were just around the corner in that alley unless they had a vehicle right there and they'd climbed in. Actually, that would be ideal. Given the aerosol of red smoke and the fact that it burns at about 204 degrees Celsius, they would have to flee the car. If they didn't, there's a good chance they may have crashed it somewhere in the alley. Unfortunately, I haven't left this office, but I'm sure there have been officers out there."

"Has anyone been in here to look at the security tape?"

"Just one individual, DI Bancroft. But he had so much going on and people to talk to, he left once it was obvious which door they ran out."

"I may be back with my partner for another viewing. I'll check out that side door. Here's my card, Marcus," Dillon said, placing his card on the desk next to a half-eaten tray of what looked like macaroni and cheese. "If you would be so kind as to send those tapes of the robbery itself and the two weeks prior, it would be very much appreciated."

"Not a problem. You mind if I ask why two weeks prior?"

"With their faces covered, our facial recognition team is unable to identify them. This is the third robbery these two have been involved in. We think they check out the places they rob prior to committing the robbery, and we're scouring the tapes to try to find them. Thus far, we've come up empty-handed."

"Interesting. Yes, I'll send those tapes to your office in just a moment. Special Branch. Are you located in the headquarters building over by Phoenix Park?"

"Yes, we are," Dillon said and handed him a business card.

"Lucky you," O'Malley said.

Dillon thanked him and hurried out the door. He walked past an office where two men were talking with Suel. He debated stepping in and decided against it, eager to follow the route the two men had taken earlier. He crossed his fingers in the hopes that at least one of the robbers had been engulfed in red dye.

FOURTEEN

Dillon hurried out the side door, following the path the two robbers had taken a little more than an hour ago. He walked no further than ten feet from the building, and there it was, a large red stain across the asphalt and up the side, windows, and roof of what used to be a white Kia Optima. There was no indication that anyone had been coated with the red dye.

He hurried back to the door, but it was locked, and he couldn't open it. He jogged back across the parking lot and around the corner of the building next door, essentially taking the same path as the two bank robbers. He didn't see anything along the way that suggested they were coated with red dye. He stopped and checked three large dumpsters behind different businesses but couldn't find anything covered with red dye in the trash. He went around the buildings, walked back up the sidewalk, nodded a friendly hello to the same two officers at the front door, and stepped inside.

He went through the door leading into the offices and entered Marcus O'Malley's Security office. "Back so soon?" O'Malley said.

"I think we've got a problem," Dillon replied.

"A problem?"

Dillon went on to explain what he'd found and that a car was covered with red dye.

O'Malley whirled around in his chair, brought up the security tape, and fast-forwarded until the robbers were approaching the side door. He slowed the tape, and they watched as the two pushed the door open and stepped into the parking lot. They were missing for a second or two and then appeared walking toward the alley. There was no sign of red dye on them, and the white Kia Optima was nowhere to be seen. Apparently, there was a dead space on the tape of maybe ten or twelve feet before they reappeared. That would probably be where the Optima was parked.

"So there's a car that's covered with the dye?" O'Malley asked.

"Yeah. I'm thinking they removed the dye pack before it exploded and tossed it next to that car. If the timer is set for twenty-five seconds, would there be anything to stop them from removing it before the twenty-five seconds were up?"

"No, but they would have to know where the dye pack was."

"Euros from just one cash drawer. It's not like they had a number of bundles to go through. If they knew what they were looking for, it wouldn't take too much."

"I want to go out there and take a look. Maybe that car was theirs, and they left it behind rather than be identified as the bank robbers," O'Malley said, standing up from his chair. They hurried into the lobby and out the side door. The formerly white Kia Optima was right where Dillon had seen it five minutes earlier.

"Oh, damn it. Don't f'ing tell me. That's my wife's damn car."

Dillon shook his head. "You can't make it up. So, they pulled the dye pack and just tossed it here?"

"God, her car. I can't believe it," O'Malley said and ran a finger across the red dye covering the side of the car. His finger didn't make a mark on the dye, and when he glanced at his fingertip, it was clean. "Oh, no."

"So they had to know the dye pack was in there with the cash," Dillon said.

O'Malley nodded. "Not only that, but we installed a newer system at the same time we added more cameras. The new dye packs are about half as thick as the old ones, so they would be even harder to find. God, I can't believe this. She's going to go crazy," he said and ran his finger across the side of the car once more.

"Do you think they knew that was your car?"

O'Malley shook his head. "No, as I said, it's actually my wife's car. Mine's in the shop. Oh, God, she is not going to be happy."

"It's not common knowledge you have the dye packs here, is it?"

"Well, we don't advertise it, if that's what you're suggesting. But, if you were a bank robber, it would seem to me you'd want to approach every bank with the idea that they use dye packs. It's pretty standard,"

O'Malley said, then ran his finger over the side of his wife's car one more time and shook his head. "She's going to be really pissed off about this."

Dillon and Suel were talking in the hallway with DI Bancroft, the local officer in charge of the scene. Dillon had just finished telling them about O'Malley's wife's car, and they shared a quick chuckle.

Bancroft shook his head. "So they know enough to find and get rid of the dye pack, and yet they still rob the place at one of the busiest times of the day. That doesn't make any sense. There had just been a couple of large withdrawals at that window, so as near as we can estimate, there was maybe only a thousand or twelve hundred euros in the drawer."

"Now we've got three robberies from these two characters that don't make any sense. The fact that they knew about the dye pack and got rid of it is even more surprising," Dillon said.

"You think they're hitting these smaller places because there's just the two of them?" Suel asked."

"Yeah, sure, but why even take the chance? Did the teller say anything?"

Both Bancroft and Suel shook their heads. "Just the note, typed, and your man pulled his windbreaker back to show a pistol. The teller filled the plastic bag. As she's doing that, the fella working next to her sees what's happening, and he pushes the robbery button that sounds the alarm. The two idiots look at each other for a half-second; your man grabs the plastic bag and heads out the side door. No weapon was fired, and they didn't seem to be in any hurry. They let off that smoke bomb, which basically keeps everyone in place, and they're gone," Bancroft said.

"You think they could be bank employees?" Suel asked. "Not necessarily here in Blackrock, but maybe somewhere else, and they know the basics of the system."

"Yeah, but if that was the case, wouldn't they try to find a way into the vault? Maybe hold a bank officer's family hostage and have him empty a safe or something?"

"Other than not getting caught, yet, everything they've done thus far seems to be contrary to what any kid who's watched a crime movie would know to do," Dillon said.

"Well, keep us in the loop, Brennan," Suel said. "You mentioned your man O'Malley was going to send the security tapes?"

Dillon nodded. "Yeah, we can pop our head in on the way out. Do you have anything else we should look at?" Dillon asked Bancroft.

Bancroft shook his head. "Appreciate you lads coming out. If anything comes to light, we'll let you know. I'm just thankful no one was hurt."

Dillon and Suel stopped in to remind O'Malley to send the security tapes. He was on his phone at the time and said, "Just a moment, dear, Special Branch stepped in. No, it'll just take a moment, love," he said and placed the phone receiver on his lap. "I sent you the tape of the robbery along with lobby activity for the past two weeks. Any problem, give me a call," he said, then pointed at the receiver, shook his head, and mouthed the word 'wife.'

"Good luck," Dillon said, and they headed out to the car.

During the drive back to Special Branch, they re-hashed the same things they'd gone over uncountable times. The timing of all three robberies, the dye pack, the lack of acquiring any substantial funds now in two suc-cessful robberies, and the absolute stupidity in all three events.

Back at his desk, Dillon turned on his computer to find the security tapes Marcus O'Malley had sent. The actual robbery, including the time it took for the two in-dividuals to flee the scene out the side door, lasted not quite two minutes in total. The tapes covering the previ-ous two weeks were ninety-four hours long. Dillon phoned Jim Burke down in the Tech Department.

"Burke," he answered.

"Hi Jim, Jack Dillon. Say, I've got a bit of a head-ache, and I'm hoping you might be able to help."

"They don't have aspirin up in Special Branch?" Burke chuckled.

"So not funny," Dillon said, which only caused Burke to laugh louder.

"So what's the problem?"

Dillon went on to explain the two weeks of security tapes from Bank of Ireland they had to go through. "What I'm hoping is you might have some kind of program that could eliminate everyone except the individuals we're looking for."

"That would be wonderful if we knew who you were looking for. Unfortunately, the last I heard, these two were rather successfully disguised with a disposable mask, sunglasses, a wig, cap, and gloves."

"Yeah, and that's still the case in the images we have of them robbing the Blackrock Bank of Ireland. But is there a way you might be able to approximate weight and height? Eliminate anyone shorter, maybe set an age limit, and eliminate females, children, anyone with a cane. You get where I'm coming from? Hello, Burke? Are you still there?"

"Yeah, I'm here, just deep in thought. Tell you what, send me the tapes from all three robberies. I want to scan the images of the two individuals and then establish criteria, certainly approximate height and weight, along with some other standards. Interesting concept, Dillon. It's going to take some time, but I think we can eliminate a lot of what you would otherwise have to review. What sort of time frame are you under?"

"The sooner, the better, but as it stands now, we would have to review over ninety hours of security tape. Anything you could eliminate would be helpful."

"Okay, send the tapes down to me and give me a day or two. I think I might be able to come up with something that will help you."

"Thanks, Jim. I'll send them your way in just a moment," Dillon said and hung up. He brought the file up from Marcus O'Malley and sent it to Burke. Then sorted the additional files and sent them to Burke as well. Six files in all. When he'd finished sending the files, he felt as if a weight had been lifted from his shoulders.

FIFTEEN

Dillon walked over to Suel's desk just as Suel hung up the phone and turned toward Dillon with a frown.

"Problem?" Dillon asked.

"I was just on the phone with Bancroft. He was hoping they had a line on the vehicle these two knackers used to escape, but the CCTV camera around the corner had been conveniently taken out of service."

"What'd they do, shoot the thing?"

"No, nothing that high-tech. Someone spray-painted the lens. It's mounted on the corner of the Centra Market next door, out on the back of the building just above the loading dock. Apparently, no one in the market monitors the cameras, so they had no idea until Bancroft's team asked to review the security tapes."

Dillon shook his head, and as they headed for the break room, he asked, "Do you get the feeling this whole affair, all three of these robberies, are somehow cursed, and we're being paid back for some dreadful thing we did that we can't even remember?"

"Maybe you should think about going to confession and begging for forgiveness."

Dillon shrugged. "And yet, these two are still getting away with next to nothing. It's been one stupid operation after another right from the get-go. But they pull it off. How in God's name can the same two idiots who know enough to get rid of the dye pack and have the common sense to spray paint the CCTV camera on the building next door plan three different robberies that barely net them four thousand euros? Are they doing this for fun? Is it a big joke to them? Is it so they can let off one of those damn smoke bombs and run out the door?"

"They have to be two gob shites with experience," Suel said.

"I couldn't agree more, but then what in the hell are they doing robbing a bank teller? They should be focusing on something that will bring them millions of euros so they never, ever have to work another day in their lives. So they could live a life of luxury for their remaining years. Are we missing something here, Paddy?"

"We've checked, Dillon. There's been no effort to get into the vaults. No hostages have been taken. They have a note. They give it to the teller, and basically, if they get anything, it only amounts to chump change. I don't get it, either. You think they're maybe practicing for a bigger venue?"

Dillon shook his head. "Yeah, okay, but it's just the two of them. Well, unless they have a driver. But that still doesn't add up. A bigger operation is going to require more people. It's not like they can call a couple of pals, and suddenly, they'll be set to hit some major bank.

All right, enough of this. On a slightly brighter note, I spoke with Burke, our man down in facial recognition—"

"I thought he couldn't work with the images because of the masks and the sunglasses."

"That's still the case, but he thinks he might be able to come up with a program that he can run the ninety hours of security tape through and eliminate everyone except for figures that would be similar to the two idiots we're looking for."

"Oh, saints be praised," Suel said. They worked until after 5:00. Suel turned down Dillon's suggestion for a pint due to dinner at a cousin's home. Dillon headed home and let Lucifer out the door. He grabbed the leash hanging in the front entry, and they went for a walk in Albert Park. Once they were back, Dillon warmed a dish of hash brown casserole and settled in front of his TV. He searched the internet for a movie, couldn't find anything that appealed to him, and went upstairs to bed after the evening news. He woke up twice, briefly, in the middle of the night, after having nightmares of men in sunglasses and disposable masks. He was awake twenty minutes before his alarm was supposed to go off. He showered, shaved, and headed downstairs.

He had just poured his second cup of coffee when Lucifer appeared in the kitchen. He sent him out into the front garden and coaxed him back inside fifteen minutes later with a biscuit. He was planning to check the US news online but decided he was already in a foul mood and instead headed into Special Branch. He was surprised to find Suel already sipping his tea in the break room.

"What are you doing in at this hour, Paddy?"

"Well, Dillon. I suppose I could ask you the same thing. Are you just heading home from a romantic interlude last night?"

"I only wish. No, in fact, I had a boring night at home, a lousy night's sleep, and decided what better way to make the day complete than head in here early."

"Yeah, about the same for me."

"Things didn't go well at the cousins?" Dillon asked.

"Actually, no, on the contrary, it was a lovely evening. Seeing everyone's children with boys who've suddenly grown taller than me and girls who have become beautiful women. A very nice evening, all in all. Unfortunately, on the drive home, I couldn't get our two idiots out of my mind."

"Same for me. I woke up twice in the middle of the night after dreaming about them in those God-awful disposable masks and sunglasses. I'm hoping Burke will contact me this morning with a trimmed-down version of those Bank of Ireland security tapes, and we can start working our way through that. We have to find something, somewhere, on these two. I still have the sense we're missing something."

"I feel the same way," Suel said. "As a matter of fact, I'm going to start in on those tapes in just a moment, and if Burke can weed out the non-relevant figures, all the better. But if he can't, well, I'll already have an hour or two put to rest."

Dillon nodded and gave a sigh. "I don't see any other option at the moment. I'll start at fourteen days before the robbery."

"And I'll start at seven days. Good luck to both of us. Last one finished buys the first round tonight," Suel said.

"You got a deal," Dillon said. He filled his coffee mug and headed out to his desk. He checked to see if Burke had phoned in the last ten minutes. He hadn't, so Dillon brought up the security tape from Marcus O'Malley dated fourteen days prior to the Bank of Ireland robbery and began reviewing. He fast-forwarded through blank areas when no customers were in the bank lobby or when the figures visible were clearly not the two robbers. He noted the date and time on a legal pad for any images that might be either of the suspected individuals.

He'd been scanning security tape for a little over three hours when his phone rang. "Dillon," was how he answered and then proceeded to race through the images of an elderly, gray-haired man with a cane.

"Hi Marshal, Jim Burke here. Glad you're in. I've got a stripped-down version of those two weeks of security tape from Bank of Ireland. I'll be sending it your way in just a moment."

"Great news. First of all, thank you. Secondly, Suel and I have been going through the tapes for the past three, almost four hours. If you could send him a copy as well, that would really help. Anything stand out to you on the tapes?"

"Not particularly, but then, other than adult males under fifty, everyone else has been eliminated. I can tell you that the largest percentage of customers were senior citizens. I'm guessing women made up maybe sixty-five percent of that category."

"That doesn't sound all that surprising," Dillon said. "Can't thank you enough for taking the time to do this, Jim. It will really save us some time up here."

"Coming your and Suel's way in just a moment," Burke said and disconnected.

"Hey, Paddy," Dillon called over to Suel. "Burke down in the Tech Lab just phoned me. He's sending a stripped-down version of that Bank of Ireland security tape. Males fifty years or younger were his criteria."

"Thank God, I've had to pinch myself to stay awake," Suel said.

A bell suddenly sounded on Dillon's desktop computer, signaling an email. Dillon glanced at the alert in the upper right-hand corner. "My file just came through. You should see yours in just a moment.

"Got it," Suel said.

SIXTEEN

Dillon raced through the revised security tapes over the course of the afternoon. He was definitely making good time, but the bad news was he wasn't coming up with anyone who fit the general description. Women in skirts and dresses had been eliminated, but a number of women wearing slacks or jeans were still on the revised tape. A few teenage boys were on the tape. He eliminated the majority of the individuals actually conducting a transaction with the teller, thinking the odds of someone having an account in both the Bank of Ireland and AIB were slim to none. Individuals who were either too heavy or too slim were eliminated.

Toward the end of the day, he felt as though he had come up empty-handed once again. He was unhappy and slightly depressed and made a spur-of-the-moment decision to pick up his phone. Noreen Rooney answered on the third ring.

"Noreen Rooney," was how she answered.

"Hi, Noreen, Jack Dillon."

"Oh, Jack, how are you? I didn't recognize the number."

"I'm calling from my desk phone. Sorry for the last-minute call, but I'm hoping you might have time to meet me for dinner. I would gladly meet you out in Skerries or somewhere here in Dublin. Whatever you would like."

"Is everything all right? You sound, I don't know, maybe frustrated or something."

"Oh, it's just been another one of those days. We're working a case and not getting anywhere. I just felt I couldn't find a better day brightener than having dinner with you," he said, not adding his hopes for an erotic adventure after dinner.

"That's so nice of you. Oh, my, that sort of makes this our first real date, doesn't it," she said and giggled.

"Well, it's not like this would be our first get-together. I mean, we met at Paddy Suel's, and we had dinner at the Stoop Your Head out in Skerries."

"Well, yes, but this is the first time you've actually asked me out. So, first of all, yes, I'd love to join you for dinner, and I'm going to be dressed for work, so nowhere too fancy. Did you have a place in mind?"

"Not really. In fact, I hadn't even thought that far ahead. Name a place you'd enjoy, and that will make the night just that much more special."

"Oh, honest to God, you are just amazing. Okay, how about this, we could meet at O'Donoghue's. They've got session music, nice food, it's relaxing, and it sounds like you need to relax a bit."

"Yeah, among other things," Dillon said and just let that last comment hang out there for a bit.

"You know where they're located?" Noreen asked, not responding to Dillon's 'among other things' comment.

"They're on Merrion Row, aren't they?"

"No, not that O'Donoghue's. This is on Suffolk Street."

"Almost right across from Trinity? The building is white with black trim?"

"Yes, that's it exactly. Would 6:00 be too early? I'm just thinking, if we were there at that time, we could eat, catch up, and then take in some session music if you feel like it."

"Actually, it sounds like the perfect night. Of course, anywhere with you would be the perfect night," Dillon said, groveling now for some later evening festivities.

She laughed and said, "I'll look forward to seeing you there, and thank you so much for the date. Can't wait to see you in ninety minutes. Bye, bye, bye," she said and hung up.

"What are you all smiles about?" Suel called from his desk. "You find the knackers?"

Dillon shook his head, "No, unfortunately, but I'm going to have to miss out on a pint tonight. I'm having dinner with a friend."

"You know, normally I'd complain," Suel said. "But hopefully, an evening with a lady might just put you in a more positive mood. Anyone I know?"

Dillon shook his head. "No. It's actually an American, over here with her husband for a week. I'm just going to give them a list of places to see. They've rented a car and will be driving around the next few days."

Suel nodded and apparently took in the tall tale. Dillon waved goodnight while Suel was on the phone twenty minutes later and hurried out to his car. He drove home, let Lucifer out into the front garden, and grabbed a quick shower. He checked to make sure he had a wine bottle in the refrigerator, took four blueberry muffins out of the freezer, and coaxed Lucifer back into the house with a biscuit.

He was down at O'Donoghue's Pub ten minutes early, waiting for Noreen to show. She stepped in from the bar room twenty minutes later.

"Oh, God, thanks for grabbing the booth. It looks really busy. Have you been waiting long? I was just about to leave the office, and I made the mistake of answering the phone. I'll never learn," she said and slid into the booth across from Dillon.

Dillon slid out of the booth, leaned over, and gave her a kiss on the cheek.

"Oh, thank you. I didn't mean to not give you a kiss. I was just so frantic trying to get here and then with the traffic and trying to find a parking place and—"

Dillon raised his hand to stop her from going on as the waitress approached. "My princess is in desperate need of a glass of wine," he said to the waitress.

"Ma'am?"

Noreen grinned and said, "A glass of sauvignon blanc, please."

"Make it two and then menus when you have a moment."

The waitress nodded and headed for the bar.

"It sounds like we both had crazy days," Dillon said. "Let me just state for the record that your agreeing to meet me for dinner was like a ray of sunshine on an otherwise dreary day."

"Well, you calling me for our first real date has me all excited. Thank you. My day was just as crazy as yours." She went on to give a five-minute review of her day. She was right, it had been crazy, and her stories had Dillon smiling and laughing.

The waitress returned with the wine and the menus. Once she left, Dillon raised his glass to Noreen. They clinked glasses, and Dillon said, "Thank you for righting my ship. I was in a foul mood until you answered my phone call, and the world has become brighter ever since. Thank you."

"Oh, Jack, you should set your sights a little higher," she said, then laughed and took another sip of wine.

The food wasn't fancy, just pub grub, but it hit the spot. Dillon ordered a burger with fries, and Noreen ordered a beef stew that she couldn't finish. Dillon cleaned his plate and then, being the perfect gentleman, devoured the remainder of Noreen's beef stew. They had a pleasant conversation over the course of the meal and sat and listened to the session music for the better part of an hour after dinner.

It was during the break in the music that Noreen leaned across the table and said, "I've something to tell you, Jack." She did not look too happy. For a fleeting moment, he thought, *could she possibly be pregnant?*

"Are you all right? What is it?"

"First of all, I'm fine. Nothing is wrong. I have really enjoyed meeting and getting to know you and everything. It's just that I have this rule with myself."

"A rule?"

She nodded. "Yes, you're going to think I'm crazy, but, well, I, umm, I never do it on the first date."

"Never do it? What are you talking about?"

"Sex," she said a bit louder than she intended. The woman in the booth across from them looked over. "This is our first real date, and I just have this kind of crazy—"

"Noreen, there's no 'kind of' about it. We slept in bed together at my house and then at your house. We enjoyed ourselves. Well, at least I did, very much, I might add. You're wonderful. But, that's not the reason I called you this afternoon. I called because I was having a lousy day after a lousy yesterday, and I thought you have a way of making my day just so much better, and I really enjoy everything about you, and—"

"So, can you put up with my stupid rule?"

"Well, if it's so stupid, why are you doing it?"

"I just need to, okay? It's our first real date, and I—
"

"Okay, I don't get it, but if that's what you want. Okay. Will we have more than this first date, or is this your way of telling me you're moving on to a better guy?"

"Oh, no, it would be nothing like that, honest. I just, I've always been like this and well—"

"Okay, but for your information, I happen to think you're worth the wait. I just want to be on record as saying that this is very hard for me to do. But if that's what you want, okay. You about ready to head back to Skerries?"

She nodded but didn't say anything.

"Let me pay the bill, and I'll walk you to your car. If there's a guy waiting for you in your car, he's as good as dead," Dillon said and then smiled.

"Thanks for understanding," she said and squeezed his hand.

Dillon paid the bill and walked Noreen to her car. He opened the door and gave her a kiss. She almost looked like she would change her mind, but then she climbed in behind the wheel and started the engine. Dillon watched her drive down Nassau Street and shook his head. *Damn it,* he thought, *it just doesn't end.*

<h1 style="text-align:center">SEVENTEEN</h1>

It was heading toward 9:00. Dillon had been home for almost an hour feeling sorry for himself. He'd almost stopped at the Grape Vine on the way home from O'Donoghue's but decided, given his mood, now was probably not the best time to buy alcohol. He had a lousy movie on the TV, and his date, Lucifer, was asleep next to him on the couch. It was times like this he wished he subscribed to a magazine but then wondered if you could even do that in today's world. It was probably too late to phone Suel and link up tonight, although he had no doubt Suel would do it if called. He hadn't seen a car parked in front of Tara's just across the lane, and he was debating the wisdom of that thought when the doorbell rang.

The way the past few days had gone, it was no doubt someone asking for a donation to help wayward women pay for an education. He smiled, thinking about asking whoever it was if they had a list of names and phone numbers. He was hoping whoever it was had left when the doorbell rang again.

"Oh for the love of God, it figures," he groaned as he made his way to the front door in his stocking feet. As he opened the door, he said, "I don't have any—Noreen?"

"Would it be all right if I came in?" she asked. It wasn't lost on Dillon that she was carrying what looked like an overnight bag.

"What? Well, yes, please, please come in. It's so great to see you. Did you drive all the way home to Skerries?"

"Yes, kicking myself all the way there and back, if you must know. I'm so sorry. I used to think it was funny when I gave my first date excuse. It would mean the second date would be wonderfully wild and crazy. It suddenly dawned on me that the two times we'd been together had already been wonderfully wild and crazy, and I had made a very big mistake. I'm sorry, Jack. Really, I am."

"You don't have to—" he couldn't finish whatever it was he was going to say. She pushed him back against the wall, wrapped her arms around him, and kissed him hard until they both had to come up for air. "I'm just glad you're here, Noreen. Thank you. This has to be a sign that my luck is finally changing."

She kicked off her shoes, took him by the hand, and led him upstairs to the bedroom. Eventually, they both laid back on the bed to catch their breath.

"Would you like a glass of wine or maybe a tea?" Dillon asked.

Noreen glanced past Dillon and said, "It's almost 11:00. I probably shouldn't have the wine, and I definitely should not have the tea. Can we just talk?"

"Sure, I'd like that," Dillon lied, fearing she was going to drop something on him like she was either pregnant or dying from a mysterious contagious disease. Instead, she just told him about her day and then gave him more information about herself in between asking Dillon questions about himself.

Eventually, they drifted off to sleep. Dillon woke once. Noreen was sound asleep with a smile on her face, which brought an inner peace to him, and he drifted back to sleep in about fifteen seconds. He turned off the alarm just a few minutes before it was set to go off and tiptoed out of the room. He brought her overnight bag upstairs from the entryway and set it on top of the chest of drawers. He got a clean towel and washcloth from the linen closet, set them out in the bathroom for her, and then went down to the kitchen.

He heard the shower come on fifteen minutes later, and five minutes after that, Lucifer appeared in the kitchen. Dillon let him out into the front garden and then turned on the kettle for tea. Noreen came downstairs twenty minutes later and stepped into the kitchen, dressed and looking beautiful.

Dillon handed her a fresh mug of tea and an eye dropper he'd found in the back of his silverware drawer. "Here, you can use this, so you don't add too much milk."

"Oh, thank you. This will be perfect," she said, not realizing he'd been joking. She partially filled the eye dropper from the small glass of milk he had set on the counter.

He scrambled up eggs and bacon rashers for breakfast and served them along with the blueberry muffins.

"Oh, this is so nice. Thank you."

"Well, just in case you didn't hear me last night, thank you so much for driving all the way from Skerries. All of a sudden, it's a sunny day. I have a smile on my face, and I feel ready to deal with whatever the day has in store for me."

"I'm going to apologize one more time for my 'first date' routine. It never dawned on me before that it was such a stupid—"

"Noreen, quit beating yourself up. That part is over, and you gave me, no, you gave both of us such a wonderful night. I can't thank you enough," he said, then leaned over and gave her a kiss. "I mean it, thanks. Now, eat up before that breakfast gets cold."

"Yes, sir," she said and shoveled a large forkful of scrambled eggs into her mouth.

They chatted over breakfast, and then Dillon walked her to the door. They kissed, he waved goodbye as she drove down the street, then ran up the stairs and jumped in the shower.

He pulled into the secured parking lot at An Garda Síochána headquarters and took the elevator up to Special Branch. He input the code on the keypad and stepped inside, hoping he'd beat Suel into the office. One look down the row of desks told him that would not be the case. Suel was at his desk and talking on the phone.

Dillon made his way to his desk. He gave Suel a friendly nod, got a wave in return, settled into his desk chair, and turned on his computer. He'd just finished answering a couple of emails, one from Jim Burke asking how the revised security tapes had worked and another from Emily in the Tech Lab saying she hadn't had any luck.

"So, how was your evening with your American friends?" Suel asked.

"What? Oh, yeah, it went just fine. They're all excited about their trip. First time in Ireland and all that. Would have loved to see more of them, but they're off to somewhere else today and booked every minute until they hop on a plane and head back to the States."

Suel nodded and asked, "Oh, so where'd you go to dinner?"

"Dinner? Oh, I met them at the Trocadero," Dillon said. Mentioning a trendy restaurant in Dublin that he knew and was aware that Suel was familiar with.

"The Trocadero? Oh, interesting. You enjoyed yourself?"

"Yeah, you know, always a good time there."

"Yeah, see, it's kind of funny because a mate called me last night and casually mentioned that he thought he saw you at O'Donoghue's enjoying the company of a gorgeous red-haired woman. Just the two of yous, laughing and kissing and the like. I figured, nah. That wouldn't be Dillon. If he was out having dinner with a gorgeous redhead, say, for example, Noreen Rooney, he would have told me. Am I right?"

"Oh, God, I can't get away with anything in this town."

Suel burst out laughing. "Serves you right, you bollox. Great that you're seeing her. Was this your first time out with her?"

Dillon shook his head. "It's complicated. You have time for a tea outside the office?"

Suel glanced around. No one appeared to be paying any attention to them. "I do, and you're buying," he said.

Dillon nodded. He'd been caught, and he didn't care.

EIGHTEEN

Dillon paid for his coffee and Suel's tea at one of the food trucks in Phoenix Park. They were walking back toward the Headquarters building. Suel took a loud sip and said, "I should do this every day. It's so great."

"You mean coming out here and getting a decent tea instead of forcing yourself to drink that poison in the break room?"

"No, I meant making you pay for it. It's a wonderful way to make any day that much more special."

"Well, thank you," Dillon said.

"So, I believe you were going to give me an update on your evening with the lovely Miss Rooney."

"Well, only that we got together for dinner."

"Don't kid a kidder, Dillon. I need the details."

"Okay. So, this is the way it went down," he said and went on to tell Suel about the dinner date, Noreen's first date rule, and how she drove to Skerries and all the way back to Dublin and rang his doorbell.

"I'd say you're one lucky bollox for deciding to answer the door. Someone calls me after 9:00 or, God forbid, rings the doorbell. It can almost never be for a good reason."

"I'm not kidding when I tell you that I opened the door, and it was like an instant ray of sunshine on an otherwise stormy day. I didn't realize how depressed I was getting from our lack of progress on these bank robberies until I opened the door, and there she was, looking beautiful and wanting to see me."

"So, based on the way you're explaining this, I have the sense that this wasn't your first get-together, am I right?"

"Well, we may have met up a time or two prior to last night. I'm just so happy to have someone in my life. She's patient, attractive, and fun to be with. It's been so long since I've been with someone like that, that I'd actually forgotten how nice it is. My history is they're around for a few weeks, and then they drop me like a hot potato."

"Well, that may be due in part to the job we have. We're essentially on call twenty-four-seven. We're not necessarily dealing with the upper crust of society, and at the end of any day, we've been involved with some pretty awful situations."

"Oh, and don't forget to add, we're not making a lot of money," Dillon said.

"That goes without saying," Suel replied.

"I'd appreciate it if you'd keep this quiet, Paddy. I don't want Noreen to have to deal with all sorts of questions from her friends. Or worse, someone telling her they know a woman who dated me, and she had finally had enough and dumped me."

"Yeah, women dumping us, that list is long and continues to grow. They're pretty much all nice people who eventually seem to come to their senses," Suel said.

"Yeah, what's wrong with them? Who wouldn't want to be with a guy who has to leave dinner at your parent's home and investigate a grisly murder?" Dillon said just as his phone rang. He shot a glance toward Suel.

"Answer it. Maybe it's Noreen, and she wants to have a quick meet-up with you over the noon hour."

"If only," Dillon said and pulled out his phone. He mouthed the 'F' word. "It's Emergency Response, Paddy," he said and answered his phone. "This is Marshal Dillon. Time? Really. Yes. In Palmerstown? Anyone injured? I can be there in five minutes." He disconnected and looked at Suel. "Let's take my car. You'll no doubt get the call in a minute. The Ulster Bank in Palmerstown, the robbery happened just a few minutes ago. Someone injured in an explosion."

"Let me drive. I know exactly where it is, Lucan Road," Suel said. He dumped the tea from his cup onto the grass. They hurried around the corner of the building and into the secured parking lot. Suel's car was in the far corner of the lot. As they approached, his phone rang, and he answered, "DI Suel. Yes. Just got the word, and

I'm already on my way," he said and disconnected. He pulled out his car keys and pressed the fob. The lights flashed on the car just one row away.

Dillon was in the front seat and buckling up as Suel slid behind the wheel. He tossed his empty paper cup into the back seat and turned the engine on. He buckled his seatbelt as they pulled out of the parking lot and sped toward Lucan Road.

"Did you say someone was injured in an explosion?" Suel asked.

"That's what they said. I just told them I was on my way, and they hung up, so I don't know anything else. This might be the break we've been looking for, Paddy. It will be just minutes by the time we arrive. Be interesting to see if the explosion they mentioned was another one of those smoke bombs," Dillon said as Suel swung into the oncoming traffic lane. He raced past two cars and veered back into the proper lane just as the driver of an oncoming truck leaned on the horn, and his passenger gave Suel the finger.

"Must have been someone who knows you," Dillon said.

As they approached the scene, an ambulance was just pulling away. Two squad cars were already in front of the Ulster Bank building. Based on their position in a 'no parking' area, they'd obviously screeched to a stop and hurried up the stairs to the front door. Suel pulled in next to one of the squad cars, slipped on his lanyard, and hurried out of the car. Dillon was right behind him.

The door to the bank was propped open, and clouds of gray smoke were drifting out of the bank lobby. A number of people were standing outside, clearly in recovery mode from the smoke bomb. A couple of people were bent over, coughing and spitting. In the distance, Dillon could hear a siren.

An officer stepped out of the lobby, leading an older woman by the arm. They were both coughing, and he led her toward the half-dozen people, all watery-eyed, coughing and spitting.

"DI Suel, Special Branch," Suel said. "How can we help?"

The officer coughed for a moment, then pointed toward the door. "Two more in there," he said and started another coughing jag just as an officer stepped out leading a woman by the arm.

Dillon hurried into the lobby. The smoke was gradually clearing out the door, and the bottom three feet from the floor offered better visibility. He bent over and moved in the direction he thought might be the teller counter. He heard coughing off to his right, spotted a woman on the floor ten feet away, and headed toward her.

"An Garda Síochána. Let me help you out of here. Keep your eyes closed, and I'll lead you out," he said and then couldn't stop coughing. He helped her to her feet. They crouched and slowly made their way toward the open door.

Once outside, the woman coughed violently and said, "Oh, oh, my God. Thank you. I can't . . ." Her coughing got the better of her.

"Just take your time and breathe in some fresh air," Dillon said and left her taking deep breaths with her eyes closed. He headed back toward the door just as Suel stepped out, coughing. "God, but that's awful, and I was only in there for half a minute. I didn't see anyone. Are you aware of anybody still in there?"

Dillon shook his head and said, "No. I'm going to give it a quick check. Back in a minute." He stepped back into the lobby and bent over. He covered his nose and mouth with his hand and made his way through the lobby. It appeared to be a version of the AIB and Bank of Ireland lobby, with a counter in the middle of the room and three windows at the teller counter. Fortunately, he didn't see anyone lying on the floor, and after making a thorough inspection of the lobby, he hurried out of the cloud of smoke.

He was leaning against the front of the bank, blinking his eyes clean and breathing in fresh air as two more squad cars pulled up. The opposite side of the street had lovely-looking two-story attached homes, clearly a notch up from Dillon's place. As far as banks went, this Ulster Bank appeared to be slightly smaller than the other two that had been robbed. The building was just one story with a railing around the flat roof. Two glass panel windows, four feet wide, were next to the front door. There was a box holding a rolo above the door and windows that would be lowered at night to cover them after business hours. An ATM was about six feet away from the entrance. Five steps led up to the entrance. Just now, four people were sitting on the steps breathing in the fresh air. Next to the steps was a back-and-forth handicap access ramp, a portion of which was covered with what looked like red dye. Dillon crossed his fingers and prayed that the dye pack had exploded on the robbers.

Two more vehicles pulled up. An ambulance and a black car. A familiar-looking guy in a suit stepped out of the car, but Dillon couldn't remember his name.

"Oh, well, if it isn't DI Thomas Kehoe. Finally decided to join us, Tommy?" Suel asked.

"Paddy Suel, never one to miss an event. Are you the Special Branch officer they contacted?"

"Lucky you, Tommy. My partner Dillon and I are here. That's him breathing deeply and leaning against the building."

Dillon gave a wave as Kehoe said, "I appreciate you being here. I think we've got one of them. An ambulance took him down to James's hospital."

"Was he shot?" Suel asked.

Kehoe chuckled. "No, although he looked like he'd been shot more than a few times. Turns out he had hold of the bag with the bundle of euros when the dye pack exploded. Blistered the lad's hand and covered his head and arms with the dye. It happened just down there at the base of the wheelchair access ramp. Get this. He was making his getaway on one of those skateboards like the kids use."

"A skateboard? How old is he?"

"Just turned twenty."

"You have a name?"

"Eamon Walsh. As I said, he's being admitted into James's. The man insisted he had nothing to do with the robbery, but there he is covered in red dye with euros covered in dye scattered all around him."

"You've someone watching him?"

"The knacker is going to be handcuffed to the hospital bed, and he'll be locked up first thing tomorrow morning once he's released from James's. Until then, there's an officer stationed right outside the door to his room. I'll place a call, and you're free to go over and interview him. We've got our hands full here at the moment."

"That would be wonderful, Tommy," Suel said and gave Dillon a thumbs-up.

NINETEEN

As Suel drove to St. James Hospital, he said, "All I can say, Dillon, is you sure as hell weren't kidding. We've got one of them under lock and key. It's like Noreen Rooney came into your life, and suddenly, things are looking a hell of a lot better in all directions. Once we talk to this muppet, I'm going to send her a bunch of flowers and tell her thanks for eliminating the bad vibes we were all getting from your dark soul."

"My dark soul? Listen, no one is happier with the arrest of this Eamon Walsh than me. No one has worked harder on these robberies than the two of us. Something had to give sooner or later. I just didn't think it would be some kid on a skateboard."

"Well, at twenty years old, that knacker's not a kid anymore," Suel said as he turned onto St James Hospital grounds. He parked just off to the side of the main building, directly in front of a 'No Parking' sign. An older couple was just walking past. The woman was using a walker, and the guy had a cane. They gave Suel a disgusted look.

"Reach into the glove box there, Dillon, and pull out the An Garda Síochána sheet. I don't want to come back out only to learn we'd been towed."

Dillon pulled the sheet out of the glove box. It had the An Garda Síochána logo with a phone number below it. "Let's go," Dillon said. "God, I can't wait to start to get these cases behind us. It feels like we've been dealing with this for a year."

They headed into the hospital and took the elevator up to the third floor. They made their way along a circuitous route through a series of halls and eventually ended up at the nurse's station in the Burn Center. Two doors down from the nurse's counter, a uniformed officer was seated in a chair, reading a book.

"I've met your man before," Suel said. "I just can't remember his name."

They headed toward the officer. He looked up as they approached and smiled.

"Well, look who got the plum assignment for today," Suel said. "How's it going? Long time no see."

"Nice to see you, Suel. I got the call from Kehoe saying you were on your way." He looked over at Dillon.

"Oh, this is my partner, Jack Dillon. Introduce yourself, Dillon. He's American, and I'm still having to teach him manners." Suel and the officer laughed.

Dillon held out his hand and said, "Jack Dillon, nice to meet you."

"Pleased to meet you," the officer said, smiled, and shook hands.

Suel waited a moment, but the officer never mentioned his name. "So, it's all right if we check on your man?"

"You can. He's a sight. The staff has been in and out a few times, testing to see if they can remove the dye. I don't think they've had much luck. The lad swears he's innocent. To be honest, from the staff response here, I'm ready to believe the poor soul."

"This is the fourth robbery this pair has done, and we've finally got one of them," Suel said.

"They were able to toss the dye pack when they hit the Bank of Ireland in Blackrock, and my guess is the timer was set to go off just a wee bit sooner today at Ulster Bank. That's why your man ended up here. It's about time we caught a break in this case. With any luck, we'll be able to shut the two of them down. What do you say, Dillon? You ready to meet this bollox?"

"You kidding? I've been waiting for this for over a week. Let's do it."

"Good luck, and try not to laugh too loud," the officer said.

Suel opened the door, and they stepped into the room. The young man handcuffed to the bed was dressed in a white hospital gown. His face, both arms, and his formerly black hair looked like they had been dipped in a bucket of red paint. He had white areas around his eyes, no doubt from the sunglasses he had been wearing as part of his disguise. Dillon found it interesting there was no suggestion that he'd been wearing a disposable mask.

The young man watched as they approached and said, "Are yous here to unhook me? This is crazy." He lifted his left arm, displaying the handcuff attached to the bed rail. "I didn't do a bleedin' thing. I'm a customer of the damn bank, and when I get out of here, I'm going to get me a solicitor and have him sue the arse off the damn bank and you lot, too."

Suel nodded and said, "We're here to find out what happened. Can you tell us what you—"

"You're playing with me. I've talked to three or four of yous already, and no one wants to believe me."

"Talk to us, Eamon. We're with Special Branch, and we want to know what happened," Dillon said.

"Jasus, at least you know my name. Did you happen to check me out? I'm in my third year at DCU. Computer programming. I live in Palmerstown. I've had an account at the Ulster Bank since I was fifteen years old. I was in there getting twenty euros on account of I was supposed to meet some lads for lunch, and then we were going to do some skateboarding in Phoenix Park. The next thing I know, I'm handcuffed to a bleedin' hospital bed, and they can't seem to get this shite off me skin."

"How did it get on there?" Dillon asked.

"I'll tell you what I told all the others. I'm in the bank. I get a measly twenty euro note from my account, so I can buy a lunch with me mates. I step outside, go down the stairs, and I'm about to get on me skateboard, which, by the way, has been confiscated. So, I'm about to step on me board, and your man says, 'Here, lad, a little present just for you,' and he hands me a paper bag from Arnotts. You know the type? It's got handles, and it says Arnotts on the bag."

"What was in the bag?"

"That's the real crazy part. He's walking away, him and his mate are laughing, and I'm thinking those two just gave me a bag of dog shite or something. I look in the bag, and it's filled with all sorts of euros. I'm thinking, what the hell? I look in the bag again, and all of a sudden, the damn thing pops, and this red cloud covers me. I fell down and hit me head on one of the handicap railings going up to the bank. Next thing I know, I'm in an ambulance, handcuffed to the damn gurney. What did I do wrong? I'm the damn victim here."

Dillon suddenly had a very bad feeling that Eamon Walsh was telling the truth. "What shirt were you wearing?"

"Oh, that's another thing. A Six Nations short sleeve jersey from two years ago. That's ruined. Got that red shite all over it. I'm sure it's not going to come out in the wash. What the hell is going on here? Are you lot listening to me?"

Suel looked at Dillon, and Dillon could tell they were both thinking the same thing. They'd essentially been set up. "Paddy, can you call Tommy Kehoe and maybe bring him up to date? They should be able to spot Eamon on security tape at the teller's window. Mention the Six Nations jersey and have them check his account."

Suel nodded and hurried out of the room.

"Check my account?"

"Just routine, Eamon. We just need to confirm what you're telling us, and then we'll get you squared away. Are you feeling any pain from the dye on your skin?"

He shook his head and said, "I just want to get the hell out of here and get me skateboard back."

"We're trying to speed that up now. While we're doing that, what can you tell me about the two guys that gave you the Arnotts bag?"

"Crazy old guys. Dressed funny. They'd sunglasses and those COVID masks. But they were old. Your one that talked and handed me the bag had this raspy old guy voice, and even though he had long blonde hair, his eyebrows were bushy and gray. Not old like you but more like me granddad. It was funny; as soon as they gave me the bag, they picked up speed. Not running, but they weren't wasting time either. Then this woman come out of the bank, coughing and wheezing, and before I could say anything, boom, the damn bag exploded, and I hit me head on the railing. Next thing I know, I'm in the ambulance and under arrest for robbing the bleedin' bank. What the hell happened?"

Dillon asked a number of questions attempting to catch Walsh off guard. But he stuck to his story. He even mentioned the faded caps and the brown cotton gloves the two men were wearing. By the time Suel returned ten minutes later, Dillon was positively convinced Walsh was telling the truth. In case he had any doubts, Suel, shaking his head, convinced him otherwise.

"They spotted him on the security tape, getting twenty euros from the teller. In case that isn't enough, the exterior camera has the two handing him the bag just before the dye pack explodes."

"Jesus," Dillon groaned.

Suel continued, "Mr. Walsh, the officer out in the hall will be receiving instructions to remove the handcuffs in just a moment. They would like you to remain here for the time being. They want to make sure you're okay, and the hospital staff is working to find an antidote to the dye."

"Is there anything we can get you?" Dillon asked

"How about some lunch and the name of the bollox whose ass I intend to sue?"

TWENTY

Suel shook his head as he drove out of the hospital grounds. "Incredible. On the way over, I was thinking we finally got a break, and now, I'm wondering if there's any way we could look more stupid?"

"Here's a basic problem," Dillon said. "We've got a wonderful, sunny day. There occasionally is still someone who will wear a disposable mask. But when two men enter the bank wearing disposable masks, sunglasses, and gloves, wouldn't that be a wakeup to the tellers or anyone else that this isn't going to go well? Shouldn't that send a red flag to security, bank employees, and even to oblivious customers? What does it take? Are the banks so stupid that, after three robberies, they still haven't presented a description to their employees? And what is with these two handing the bag of stolen money to Eamon Walsh? Did they know when the dye pack was going to go off?"

Suel shook his head. "So we're thinking they're pulling off these things, but they're getting hardly any cash. Now, the little they got today, they give away to someone."

"I'm guessing they gave it away because they couldn't find the dye pack," Dillon said.

"Okay, but then why did they apparently hang onto the cash from that AIB bank on Hanover Quay?"

"Maybe they were convinced there wasn't a dye pack. I don't know. Maybe they knew there wouldn't be a dye pack. You think they might have some link or relationship to some way of knowing which banks use dye packs and which ones don't?"

Suel seemed to think for a moment, then said, "Okay, so let's say the robbers know which bank does and doesn't have dye packs. But then, why are they robbing banks with dye packs? Why not direct your effort toward the banks without them? It would be one less problem you'd have to deal with. It seems like one more thing that makes us think they're idiots, but all along, maybe we're the ones who are the idiots. Something's just not right with this whole thing."

"Which reminds me of something else," Dillon said. "Walsh described the robber who handed him the bag as old, like his granddad. Said he had white eyebrows. When we looked through the tapes that Burke adjusted using men fifty or younger as the guide, did you find anyone you thought might be a robber checking the bank out?"

"Maybe a couple, but I get what you're saying. We apparently were looking in the wrong place. What about you? Did you spot anyone who might be a robber?"

"No one, there were a few, but they just didn't look right. Plus, the ones I saw, I think in every case, and I'm talking maybe only four or five guys, they were all making deposits. Are you going to rob the bank that handles your accounts?"

Suel drove around to the back of Ulster Bank and parked in the parking lot. There was a uniformed officer at the door who let them in once he checked their IDs. DI Kehoe was standing outside an office talking to a bank employee. He nodded as Dillon and Suel approached and said, "Gentlemen, this is Kevin Bennett. He's in charge of Security Services at Ulster Bank."

Dillon and Suel shook hands with Bennett as they introduced themselves. He looked to be in his early thirties. Already bald with dark hair on the sides and bright blue eyes.

"You're the Special Branch officers who were just at St. James's talking to the dyed customer?"

"Yeah, Eamon Walsh, not a very happy guy at the moment. They're hoping to keep him in the hospital until they can figure out a way to remove the dye. His arms and head were covered with it," Suel said.

"You contacted the officer at the door and told him to take the handcuff off Walsh?" Dillon asked.

"Yeah, as soon as we got your call and saw him on the security tape in that Six Nations jersey. He apparently made a withdrawal of twenty euros."

"Yeah, just a warning to the bank and the department," Dillon said. "He wasn't what you'd call happy and was threatening a lawsuit."

"Any good news?" Kehoe asked.

"He told us the robber that gave him the Arnotts bag had bushy gray eyebrows and a voice like his granddad. We've been thinking all along that these two had to be younger individuals."

"Yeah, they've got long hair. One's blonde, and the other—"

"Has black hair," Dillon said. "It's our opinion they're both wearing wigs. Does your tape show them wearing gloves?"

Bennett nodded. "Gloves that look to be standard brown cotton work gloves. Then the disposable masks, sunglasses, caps, and blue windbreakers."

"You've just described them as they appear in each and every security tape. Did you receive anything like an alert from the powers that be regarding the description of these two? Something that mentioned the disposable mask, the sunglasses, and cotton gloves?"

Bennett shook his head. "Nothing that I can recall. We were alerted to be on guard, but nothing specific other than the robberies were committed by two males."

"Incredible," Suel said and shook his head. "You didn't receive copies of security tape from AIB or Bank of Ireland?"

"No, nothing like that."

Dillon glanced over at DI Kehoe. "Anything on exterior surveillance?"

"We're lining that up now. It's being forwarded to our station, and we've instructions to forward it to Special Branch."

"Can we take a look at what you have here?" Suel said, not really asking permission.

"Are we finished?" Bennett asked Kehoe.

"By all means, take a look at the tape and touch base with me before you leave. I'll probably be out in the lobby."

"My office is just back this way," Bennett said, and they followed him down past the restrooms to a door simply labeled '105.' Inside, the office was the same as the other security offices they'd been in, only a little smaller. Once again, there were six screens mounted on the wall displaying two black and white images of the lobby, the teller counter, the hallway, the back parking area, and the front of the building.

"Let me just bring it up for you. The robbers entering will be on the lower right screen, and as they move across the lobby, they'll appear on the screen next to that and eventually on the screen recording the front of the building," Bennett said. He leaned over the desk and quickly typed on the keyboard.

A moment later, the two men stepped into the lobby. Just like the previous robberies, one stopped at the counter in the center of the lobby, and the other man stepped up to the teller window. At the moment, he was the only individual at the teller counter. Dillon checked the digital clock in the lefthand corner of the screen. The robber's interaction with the teller, a dark-haired woman who appeared to be in her mid-forties, lasted all of thirty-five seconds.

He slid the brown paper Arnotts bag with the note on top beneath the glass. She read the note, glanced up with a surprised look on her face, and he pulled back the front of his windbreaker and lowered his right hand over the pistol. She quickly filled the bag, then halted for just a second or two and pulled out the final small bundle of euros. It seemed obvious to Dillon that this would be the bundle containing the dye pack. The man nodded but did not appear to say anything and walked toward the door, followed by his partner, who looked left and right.

As they stepped out of the bank, the partner pulled the pin on the smoke bomb, leaned down, and rolled it across the floor. Suel counted out loud and got to just four seconds before the smoke bomb burst, and the screen immediately clouded.

They reappeared on the exterior screen hurrying down the five steps. The man holding the bag opened it, glanced inside, and handed it to Eamon Walsh, who had just skateboarded down the wheelchair ramp.

Walsh stopped, said something, and looked in the bag. He appeared to shout as the two hurried away. He looked in the bag again just as the cloud of dye was released, knocking Walsh off his skateboard. As he fell backward, his head bounced off one of the steel railings, and he was apparently unconscious on the ground as the cloud of red dye gradually settled around him. Once the red cloud cleared, the two men were just rounding the corner and disappearing from sight.

They watched the tape four more times. In total, from the moment the two entered the bank until the dye pack exploded and they disappeared around the corner, the entire event took two minutes and fifty-three seconds.

Dillon left his business card with Kevin Bennett. They thanked him for his time and met up with DI Kehoe out in the lobby. Once again, Dillon could smell a slight odor from the smoke bomb, although he wasn't sure if it was coming from the lobby or off his clothes. They exchanged cards with Kehoe and headed back to Special Branch.

They each got two large slices of pizza from a food truck in the park and then headed up to the break room in Special Branch.

TWENTY-ONE

Suel took a large bite of pizza and asked, "So, where do you figure we stand?"

"I think we should basically start over. One of the first things we should do is send an email to financial institutions with images of the bank robbers and a brief description mentioning the clothing, their procedure, and the timing. This latest one today was at an earlier time than the others, but we've still got four robberies. Let's get the information and descriptions out there. My next thought is, what if we send the information to the news outlets? If we could get them to show facial shots, while I doubt anyone would be able to identify these two, it might alert everyday customers or clients to watch out for these idiots and sound the alarm if they see them."

"Let's get on that this afternoon. Why don't you talk to Maeve Byrne, she's the PR person with all the contacts, and I'll try and assemble some images that—"

"Paddy, if she's the PR rep, let's send her the tapes from the robberies. They can isolate whatever images they want and send them out. If you and I do it, we're liable to screw something up."

"Yeah, the more I think about it, the more that makes sense. Hard to believe," Suel said and took another bite of pizza. "Why don't you talk to her, and I'll send her a copy of the tapes."

"I'll go down there when we're finished eating and set it up. You have her email address?"

"Yeah, somewhere. Grab her card if you remember. Otherwise, I can look it up. Honest to God, something has to start working for us on this."

"You're telling me," Dillon said.

They finished lunch, and Dillon went down to the first floor and into the PR office. It was just off the main lobby. Unlike the rest of the building, there was actually a reception counter with a woman seated behind it. She reminded Dillon of his mother, although she was obviously younger. But she had the same 'no nonsense' look about her.

"Good afternoon," she said as Dillon approached.

"Hi, I'm Marshal Jack Dillon. I'm assigned to Special Branch. I'm here to see Maeve Byrne."

"Do you have an appointment?"

"No, I don't, but we're working a case, and we need to get some information out to a variety of news outlets."

"Let me see if Maeve can spare a moment. You can take a seat over there," she said and nodded toward four chairs arranged around a coffee table.

As Dillon headed toward the chairs, he heard, "Yes, Maeve, this is Sinéad out in the lobby. I have a gentleman who would like to see you. He says he's with Special Branch, but apparently, he doesn't have an appointment. Oh, really? Are you sure? Very well. Yes, thank you," she said and hung up. "Miss Byrne will be out shortly. In the future, it might be best if you made an appointment."

"Thank you," Dillon said, then smiled and bit his tongue so he wouldn't respond any further.

The door off to the side opened a couple of minutes later, and a nice-looking, dark-haired woman stepped into the lobby. Sinéad, still seated at her desk, gave a disapproving nod in Dillon's direction.

The woman ignored her and hurried over, extending her hand as Dillon stood. "Hi, I'm Maeve Byrne, and you are?"

"Jack Dillon with Special Branch," he said as he shook her hand.

"Please, come on back to my office. You're the American we've heard so much about," she said.

"Well, don't believe any of it. I'm really a nice guy."

She looked at him and laughed as they walked through the door and into a hall with a number of offices. She led Dillon into the second office, which was labeled manager. "Please have a seat," she said, pointing to one of the leather chairs in front of her desk.

Dillon settled into the chair, one of the more comfortable office chairs he had ever sat in. She stepped around the desk, sat down, and said, "So, how can we help you?"

"My partner and I have been working on a series of bank robberies that have been happening. As of this morning, we've had four. Are you familiar with them?"

"Only from what I've heard on the news, which isn't much. If I recall, there was one at AIB on the Hanover Quay and another down in Blackrock. You said there were four?"

"Yes, the most recent was this morning in Palmerstown, and then there was the robbery of J&R Credit in Coolock, not a bank, obviously, but nonetheless robbed by the same two individuals. We have a couple of problems we think you may be able to help us with. The first is we're having a difficult time making any progress on catching these two individuals. Part of the problem is that, amazingly, information about the two suspects, like a basic description of what they look like, has not been distributed to the financial institutions. Or, if it has, no one is paying any attention, and the robberies continue to be successfully completed. Thankfully, they're not getting away with large amounts of cash, but sooner or later, someone is going to be killed. We do know that the robbers are carrying guns."

"So what would you want us to do?"

"We were wondering if you could send out a news alert to various stations, along with an alert targeted to financial institutions at the same time, with images of the individuals involved. They've worn the same get-up in each robbery," Dillon said and went on to describe the sunglasses, face masks, gloves, and the like. "We can send you images we have from the security tapes. The get-ups are unique enough that they would attract people's attention, and it might also force the institutions to alert their staff, which, surprisingly, they don't seem to have done."

She seemed to think about that for a moment, then smiled, nodded, and said, "I can't see why we wouldn't. This sounds like exactly the sort of thing we like to be involved in. Clearly, it will be of interest to the public and certainly spread a note of concern among the financial industry. When were you thinking of sending these out?"

"The sooner, the better," Dillon said. "I can have my partner send you images taken from surveillance tapes of the individuals and would be happy to work with you or whoever is providing details."

She nodded and said, "Yes, I agree with you. The sooner we can get this information out there, the better it will be. What you're asking for sounds simple enough, and I'm thinking our creative team could have something ready in an hour or so."

"Excuse me, but you have a creative team?"

She smiled. "Officially, they are our production department, but they provide the creative service to put something like this together and send it out. Our recipients are busy on a number of different levels, and in order to attract their attention, we need the creative talents of our production department. I don't mean to sound unkind, but if we send out a version of what we receive

internally, well, you can imagine the percentage of recipients who wouldn't even bother to open the email."

"I get it. What do you need from us?"

"The images, first and foremost. You want people
to see them, to focus on them, and to remember them,
don't you?"

Dillon nodded and said, "Yes, exactly."

"Along with the images, if you could provide a basic
description. Height, weight, eye color. Do they have an
accent, are they armed, does one of them limp? Obviously, anything that would make them unique and iden-
tifiable. Does that make sense?"

"It does. Would you happen to have a card with your
email address?" Dillon asked.

"I'll trade you one for one of yours," she said and
grinned.

Dillon handed her a card. She gave him two of her
cards in return. "You mentioned a partner. What's the
name?"

"DI Paddy Suel. We're both in Special Branch. Are
there any unique technical requirements for these images? Computers and technology are not much of a
strong point with either one of us."

"If you'll just send the images, our people will handle the rest."

Dillon stood and extended his hand. "Thank you.
We'll get these images off to you as soon as possible.
Very nice to meet you. Please feel free to contact me

with any concerns," Dillon said and nodded at his card on her desk.

He hurried back up to Special Branch. "Everything go okay?" Suel asked as Dillon approached.

"Yeah, just fine. Here's her card. Send her the images, and I'll write up descriptions of both individuals and send that off to her. Make sense?"

Suel nodded. "I've got some facial close-ups, as well as three shots of the two of them standing together. When you're writing up that description, make sure you mention the smoke bomb."

"I'll get started on it now," Dillon said and settled in at his desk. Fifteen minutes later, he had the page of descriptions typed up. He included the height and weight approximations and the fact that one of them had bushy white eyebrows. He mentioned the brown cotton gloves and the suspected latex gloves underneath. His final point was Eamon Walsh's description of one of their voices, which he put in quotation marks, 'Raspy old guy voice like me granddad.'

He read through the list three times, then emailed it to Maeve.

TWENTY-TWO

An hour and a half later, both Dillon and Suel received an email from An Garda Síochána Production Department. The email was succinct and exactly what they hoped it would be. Dillon emailed an approval, and it was sent out to various news stations and a laundry list of banks and financial institutions at 3:45. Nine minutes later, Dillon received a response from a news station thanking him for the email and asking if there was an approximate age on the two individuals. As he was writing his three-sentence response, he received two other emails. He sent his response and opened one of the two emails just as three more emails came across. He was suddenly receiving six to ten emails per minute. Many were clearly auto responses thanking him for the email and stating that it would be reviewed as soon as possible. But they still had to be opened in order to read the response.

It was a little after 5:00 when Suel turned off his computer and strolled over to Dillon's desk. Sounds like you're a popular fellow with all the noise your computer has been making. Did you post on a dating site?"

"No, Paddy, I didn't post on a dating site. I think I've received over forty emails so far, just in the last couple of hours. A lot of them are automatic replies, but I still have to open the damn things to see if that's the case."

"Anything from your new friend, Maeve Byrne?" Suel asked and laughed.

"Don't even go there. Paddy. I got more than I can handle with Noreen right now. The last thing I need is to start chasing another woman."

"Just thinking she's pretty attractive, and it might not be a bad idea to have someone, you know, waiting in the wings, as it were."

"Oh, please, don't even suggest that."

"You have time for a pint tonight, or are you going to be racing out to Skerries and do whatever task Noreen wants done?"

Dillon shook his head. "Against my better judgment, I'll join you for a pint. Let me just deal with the rest of these emails, shouldn't be more than twenty minutes."

"That will be perfect. I'll stop on the way to the Autobahn and get some petrol. First one there orders two pints. Deal?"

"Yeah, count me in."

Suel headed out, and Dillon went through the last of his emails. On the way out to his car, he stopped by the PR office to thank Maeve Byrne and to joke with her about all the email replies he had received, but the office was locked. Probably just as well, he decided and made his way out to his car.

Since Suel was going to stop and gas up his car, Dillon headed home and let Lucifer out into the front garden. He coaxed him back into the house with a biscuit and then drove over to the Autobahn. As he drove up the street, he saw Suel climb out of his car and head into the pub. Dillon waited in his car for five minutes to give Suel enough time to order their pints and then hurried into the pub.

Suel was seated at a corner table, and Dillon spotted him just as a waitress was setting two glasses of Guinness on the table. Dillon waited a half-minute and then headed over to the table.

"Oh, it figures. Perfect timing on your part," Suel said as he slid a pint across the table to Dillon.

"Thanks, here's to both of us," Dillon said and raised his pint. They clinked glasses, and each took a hearty sip.

"So, despite all the responses you received, what do you think of the email the PR department sent out?"

Dillon nodded. "Right off the top of my head, I would say it's better than not having anything out there. The more I think about it, the more I can't get my head around the fact that these two individuals have been able to walk up to the teller's window, pass a note, display a gun, and walk back out with a bag full of cash. This latest one, well, virtually all of them took little more than a couple of minutes, and they've committed a robbery, let off a smoke bomb, and disappeared. With any luck from here on in, they'll be spotted before they even enter the lobby."

"One can only hope," Suel said. "Of course, that's if they maintain the same routine. If they catch something on one of the news stations, it wouldn't take much for them to change their costume. You hear anything else on your man, Walsh?"

"Eamon Walsh? No, I haven't. I've been thinking about him looking in the bag and seeing the cash. He calls something out to the two of them and then opens the bag just as the dye pack goes off, and that cloud envelops him. It would be funny if it didn't cover the poor guy, and he banged his head on that metal railing," Dillon said.

"You think he's going to sue the bank?"

"He won't have a problem finding a solicitor who would be willing to give it a try. In the end, it's unfortunate, but the bank didn't do anything wrong. Same thing with suing the Palmerstown Gardai. Yeah, they could have moved a little faster getting the handcuffs off him, but they'll argue he was injured, apparently unconscious, and they brought him to James's to get checked out. As soon as they determined he wasn't one of the robbers, they uncuffed him and let the hospital see if there was a way to remove the dye."

"Honest to God, you can't make it up," Suel said.

They chatted on for another hour and a second pint. Dillon was home, sitting in front of the television with his laptop literally on his lap. It wasn't quite 8:00, and he pulled out his phone and called Noreen. She answered almost immediately.

"Hi, Noreen. Just checking in. How was your day?"

"Oh, thank you for calling. I survived, so all in all, it was a good day. What about you?"

"Unfortunately, more of the same," Dillon said and gave her a brief synopsis of the Ulster Bank robbery.

"Speaking as someone who is not involved in your line of work. I have to wonder what in the world these two men are doing. You've told me they're not getting very much money, and now, in that event this morning, they didn't make as much as a farthing. I just don't get it."

"Well, if you ever come up with an idea of what their thought process might be, please let me know. Because I sure can't figure it out."

They chatted for fifteen minutes, and then Dillon asked her out to dinner for tomorrow night. "I'd be happy to take you somewhere in Skerries or here in Dublin, whatever you would prefer."

"Oh, decisions, decisions. I tell you what. If we went out somewhere in Skerries, then I could cook us a leisurely breakfast the following morning. How does that sound?"

"It sounds wonderful," Dillon said.

"Why don't you plan on meeting me here tomorrow evening at 7:00. You pick where you'd like to have dinner and—"

"That sounds great, except for me deciding where we have dinner. Obviously, you have a better handle on places to eat out there. You pick a spot, casual. If it's the Stoop again, that's fine with me, whatever you'd like."

"All right, I'll see you here tomorrow night at 7:00. Looking forward to it," she said.

"Me too, thank you," Dillon said. They disconnected a minute or two later.

TWENTY-THREE

Dillon was up a couple of minutes before his alarm went off. He showered, shaved, and was in the kitchen watching a US news show from the night before on his laptop when Lucifer entered the kitchen. He let him out into the front garden and filled his food and water dishes. Once he let him back in the house, he went upstairs and laid out a shirt and trousers for the evening with Noreen. He packed an overnight bag and then closed the bedroom door on his way downstairs so Lucifer wouldn't hop onto the bed and take a nap on his clothes.

He tossed Lucifer a biscuit and headed into the office. The morning was uneventful other than a brief phone call from Maeve Byrne in the PR Department. She asked about any feedback from the blurb her department had sent out on the bank robbers.

"Quite a few email responses," Dillon said, "and a good deal of those were automatic responses, thanking me for the email. Still, I had to open them to see they were automatic replies."

"Unfortunately, I'm familiar with that," Byrne said. "I believe they're programmed to arrive when you have a half-dozen projects up in the air and no time to spare."

"That sounds about right. Have you gotten any response?" Dillon asked.

"Nothing out of the ordinary. It will be interesting to see if anyone reports these two individuals. It never ceases to amaze me when we run a project like this that there are people out there who will be completely unaware. They'll end up giving the robbers a ride to the train station or the airport and calmly phone us three days later describing the event."

"Maybe they're the lucky ones instead of waking up in the middle of the night like us trying to remember if we covered all the bases. Or worse, getting the call on something in progress just as you're about to step out for a nice relaxing dinner."

"Well, if we can be of any further help, please don't hesitate to contact me," Byrne said. They disconnected just as Suel stepped over from his desk.

"I'm thinking some Thai stir fry from the truck in the park might hit the spot for lunch. Interested?"

"Perfect," Dillon said, and they headed out of the building and into Phoenix Park. Today there were a half-dozen food trucks in the park. It was a gorgeous sunny day, and there was a line at every truck. The Thai truck was parked the furthest away, not that it mattered with the lovely weather. They waited in line for five minutes, slowly moving forward. The closer they got to the truck, the better it smelled. Dillon ordered basil stir fry with chicken and spring rolls. Suel got his usual seafood curry and curry puffs.

They settled in at a picnic table in the sunshine and ate. They discussed the bank robberies. Both of them were convinced it was only a matter of time before the next one occurred.

"I'm taking Noreen out to dinner tonight in Skerries. Which probably means we'll get the call right around 5:00, and I'll have to cancel."

"Things are going well with the two of you?"

Dillon nodded. "Yeah, I think we're both taking our time. No pressure on one another. She seems to understand the craziness of our business and is okay with that. We'll see how it goes."

"Well, I wish the both of you good luck. She's a nice woman and not hard on the eyes."

They were back in the office thirty minutes later. Dillon had basically started over at square one and was reviewing the security tapes of the four robberies along with all the interviews with the various tellers, staff, and customers. He found it interesting that the one person who provided the most information was Eamon Walsh, the skateboarder who got covered with dye outside the Ulster Bank.

Dillon kept glancing at the time in the upper right-hand corner of his computer. The clock seemed to slow right around 2:30 and then apparently came to a complete stop around 3:00. He was tense for the next two hours, expecting his phone to ring at any moment announcing another robbery, but nothing happened, and after what felt like twelve hours, it was suddenly 5:00.

He turned off his computer, locked his desk, and gave Suel a wave as he headed out the door. Once home, he let Lucifer out, shaved, took a long hot shower, and changed into the clothes he'd set out that morning.

His drive to Skerries was uneventful, and the gate was open at Noreen's, so he drove in and parked next to her car. He grabbed his overnight bag from the back seat and headed up the front path. She opened the door as he approached, looking gorgeous in a very short grey skirt and a sleeveless white top.

"At no surprise, you're right on time," she said and grinned.

"A very long afternoon. I had to check and make sure the clock was ticking. It was moving so slow."

"Mmm-mmm, don't I know." She gave him a quick kiss on the lips and then moved to the side so he could step in. "Now, we could have a glass of wine here, or we could go to the restaurant. Whatever you would like."

"Doesn't matter to me," he said, setting his overnight bag on a bench in the front hall. "It's just nice to be with you. What would you prefer?"

"If it's okay with you, I think I'd like to go to the restaurant. We will be dining this evening at Piccolo Trattoria. It's a quaint little Italian place, great food, lovely staff."

"What are we waiting for? If you give me directions, I'll drive."

He held the passenger door open for her and then hurried around to the driver's side. It was only a five-minute drive, and he parked almost in front of the two-story building with blue trim. The name PICCOLO was painted in white letters above the door and in gold letters on the windows on either side of the entrance. Two small, round tables were on the sidewalk in front of the restaurant, with couples eating and drinking at both tables.

"Oh, this place is just what I needed," Dillon said. They stepped into a room painted white with stained wooden beams across the ceiling. Lights hung down from the ceiling, casting a series of bright lines down the walls. There was a beautiful wooden floor that looked to be a hundred years old. Wooden chairs with cushioned seats were arranged around white tablecloth-covered tables placed against the walls. In the middle of the room were two large wine barrels standing on a wheeled base with a number of different wine bottles on top of the barrel.

"Two of you?" a man with a mustache and wearing a short sleeve white shirt asked.

Noreen nodded as Dillon said, "Yes, just the two of us."

He led them to a table in the corner, pulled the chair out for Noreen, and placed a menu on the table in front of them. A server stopped a half-minute later. Noreen already knew what she wanted, and Dillon said he'd have the same. He ordered wine. A bottle, not a glass, and when the server left, he asked, "So what are we eating?"

"You ordered it, and you don't know what you ordered?"

"Well, I figured whatever you were getting would be good, so, yeah, I didn't know. I can't believe they have a bad meal in this place. It's really lovely. Great choice," he said as he looked around.

"We're having Filetto di Manzo," she said.

"Oh, well yeah, of course. That's just what I was thinking of ordering. What is it?"

She smiled and said, "I'm pretty sure you'll like it. It's beef fillet, with a sautéed mix of mushrooms, beef jus, and roast potatoes."

"How did you know that would be what I would have ordered? God, I hope I got the right wine."

"Oh, you did. Hey, thank you for doing this. I didn't want to pressure you. I know you've got a lot on your plate at work and—"

"Here's the thing with me, Noreen. I'm always going to have a lot going on at work, and it will be the rare day that it's something nice. So, if I don't tell you a lot about what I'm involved in, it's not that I don't think you care. It's just that oftentimes it's pretty awful, and a lovely person like you shouldn't have to be exposed to it. I don't know, am I making any sense?"

"I get what you're trying to say, and that's very kind of you, but you can tell me. Okay?"

The server returned with their bottle of wine. Dillon nodded at Noreen to take a sip and nod approval, which she did. The server filled their glasses, and they chatted for ten minutes until their dinners arrived. The beef fillet was wonderful, and Dillon had almost cleaned his plate while Noreen wasn't even halfway through. He set his silverware on his plate and chatted away while she continued taking small forkfuls of food, smiling and laughing.

Once she finished, Dillon insisted she order a dessert for them. She ordered Belgian chocolate tarts with walnuts, and Dillon ordered two glasses of dessert wine. He paid the bill, and they were back at Noreen's by 10:00. They had a final glass of wine in her kitchen and then went up to bed. They drifted off to sleep sometime after midnight.

TWENTY-FOUR

Dillon woke just as Noreen stepped out of the bedroom. The sun was up, and he remained in bed, hoping she'd return and join him. After a few minutes, he heard what sounded like plates being arranged on the kitchen counter downstairs. Eventually, he climbed out of bed. He pulled on the white terrycloth bathrobe she'd set out for him last night and headed downstairs.

"Oh, I hope I didn't wake you," she said as he stepped into the kitchen. She was wearing a short version of the robe he had on. "Can I make you some coffee? I have some instant in the cupboard. It will only take a minute."

"No, don't worry about it. Can I help you in some way?"

"Yes, you can take a seat and stay out of the way. Would eggs and rashers be acceptable for breakfast?"

"I can't think of anything better. Thank you for a lovely evening. That restaurant was wonderful. Great choice on the dinner and dessert."

"Well, thank you for picking up the bill."

"You more than paid me back, thanks. I needed that."

She looked at him for a moment, smiled, and said, "Me too. Thank you."

They chatted over breakfast, reviewing last night's dinner, the Piccolo restaurant, and some of the people at the other tables. Dillon offered to help clear the dishes, but Noreen said no and suggested he could go upstairs and get dressed. Which, without saying, meant any physical interaction would be limited to a goodbye kiss.

Dillon thought about that for a moment and then gave her a kiss on the cheek and headed upstairs. He dressed and checked his phone. Thankfully, no calls or messages. Since it was Saturday morning, the chance of a bank robbery was somewhat lessened. He crossed his fingers and hoped the robbers planned on a quiet weekend. He carried his overnight bag down into the front hall, set it on the bench, and went back into the kitchen.

Noreen was at the kitchen table, reading what looked like the morning paper on her computer and sipping a tea.

"Okay, hot number, I'm going to get out of your hair. I've got some things I have to attend to. You have a great day, and thanks again for a wonderful evening. I really enjoyed it."

She grinned and said, "I'm the one who should be thanking you for coming all the way out here." She stood and walked him to the door. They kissed, and she opened the door. They kissed again, and he headed to his car. As he climbed in behind the wheel, the gate to the parking area opened. He backed his car up, gave Noreen a wave as she stood in the open doorway, and drove out onto the road.

Twenty-five minutes later, he pulled into his drive. It was almost 9:00 when he unlocked the front door. Lucifer bounded past, assumed the position alongside the car next to the driver's door, and did his business.

Dillon stepped inside, prepared to clean up whatever mess Lucifer had made, but surprisingly, everything appeared to be in order. He went upstairs expecting to find a feather pillow torn apart or the duvet in bits and pieces, but again, everything appeared to be just as he had left it. He filled Lucifer's food and water dishes and coaxed him inside with a biscuit.

He went online and checked his emails. Nothing he had to respond to, and since he didn't need life insurance, cremation services, a new roof, or a host of other things, he eliminated the emails in about thirty seconds. He did feel the need for a coffee, and he set his coffee maker for four cups.

He sent Noreen an email thanking her once again for a lovely evening and then searched the local news for anything suggesting the work of the two bank robbers. He breathed a sigh of relief when he didn't find anything. He puttered around for the rest of the morning, eventually grabbed Lucifer's leash, and they went for a walk in Albert Park. Being Saturday, there were two soccer games and one rugby match being played on various fields, not to mention plenty of people doing exactly what Dillon was doing, walking.

Saturday afternoon consisted of a light lunch, a review of some online files, and a nap. The nap ended with his cell phone ringing. He glanced at the clock as he reached for the phone. It was after 3:00, and virtually all the banks, if they were even open on Saturday, closed precisely at noon. He silently swore and glanced at the screen on his phone, hoping it wasn't Special Branch. It was Suel.

"Please don't tell me something's happened," was how Dillon answered.

"How can you be so crabby on a gorgeous day like today? Did I interrupt you? Is Noreen there?"

"Yes and no. Noreen is not here, although we had a really great night. You did interrupt my nap, but it was time for me to get out of bed anyway. So what's up?"

"Calling because I know you can't get enough of me during the week and wondered if you have dinner plans."

"As a matter of fact, I don't have any plans, and I'm sure I could give you proper direction on whatever you need."

"What do you say to grabbing a pint and some pub grub at Brannigans?"

"Yeah, I can do that. What time are you thinking?"

"How 'bout we meet around 7:00, have a pint, and get some food? They close at 11:30, so it won't be a late night."

"Perfect, I'll see you down there at 7:00," Dillon said.

"See you then. Now, you're free to get back to your beauty sleep, which you desperately need. Sweet dreams," Suel said and disconnected.

Dillon remained in bed for another ten minutes before he got up. Lucifer was asleep on his pillow at the foot of the bed, and Dillon quietly tip-toed out of the room and went downstairs. He was back online for a few minutes, double-checking to make sure there wasn't an incident at a bank. There wasn't, and he wondered if alerts from the PR department were actually having an effect.

At 6:15, he headed out the door and walked over to the Ballymun bus stop just outside of Albert Park and Dublin City University. He hopped on the number thirteen bus. All the buses in Dublin were double-deckers, and after using his Leap Card, the pay-in-advance Dublin Bus card, he took the stairs up to the top level.

On a Saturday night, the bus was usually full of people heading into the city center. Tonight was no exception, but he was able to find a seat next to a young woman busily sending a text message. She got off on Dorset Street Upper, and Dillon got off two stops later on O'Connell Street and walked back a block to Brannigan's on Cathedral Street.

TWENTY-FIVE

The pub was a three-story brick building with wooden letters painted gold announcing the name BRANNIGAN'S above the door. There were a half-dozen tables out front, actually on the street. The tables were fenced off by planter pots filled with flowers.

Dillon was twenty minutes early when he walked into the crowded pub. He hadn't taken five steps into the place when a familiar voice called, "Hey, Dillon, you right plonker. Over here." He glanced over, and there was Suel, already seated at a table with a glass of Guinness in front of him.

Dillon headed over and said, "I was sure I was gonna beat you here. Have you been in here long?"

Suel glanced at his pint of Guinness, nearly full, suggesting he'd been there only long enough for a sip or two.

"Get you something?" a server asked as Dillon sat down.

"Yeah, thanks. I'll have a pint of Guinness. Paddy?"

"Good for now, mate," Suel said.

"God, I can't believe it's shaping up for us to have a quiet Saturday," Dillon said as he glanced around the place."

"Don't say that too loud, or all hell is bound to break," Suel said. "You think it might be because of the alerts they sent out?"

"It would be nice if that was the case, but I don't know."

"Well, I know they ran on RTÉ 1, Virgin Media, TG4, and Sky News for about a minute and a half, complete with the images of your two favorite knackers. That's potentially a lot of viewers."

Dillon nodded. "Even just running on one of those stations would be a huge increase in awareness. I guess I'm looking at it like this; no matter how many or how few saw it, that's more than before the broadcast. Now, if the banks will just cop on and alert their employees, you'd think they would be the first to want that information."

The server arrived with Dillon's pint. He handed her a ten euro note and said, "Keep the change."

"There you go again, Dillon. Spoiling it for the rest of us."

Dillon shook his head. "As I was saying, now, if the banks would alert their employees."

"Yeah, I know what you mean. I just expect these two knackers to change what they've been doing up until now. Maybe they'll dress up like women or even Garda officers."

"Mmm-mmm, I think you're right, but if they do that, we'll send out another press release. They keep this up, and sooner or later, we have to be able to nail their ass."

"One can only hope. So how did last night work out for you?"

"Good, we ate at a really nice little restaurant in Skerries called Piccolo. Delicious Italian food, nice and quiet, then back to Noreen's for a glass of wine and the main event."

"I'm glad it seems to be working out," Suel said with a nod.

"Yeah, me too. Obviously, if you're dating you or me for any length of time, your patience is going to be sorely tested."

"Yeah, true, and that's just dealing with our personalities, to say nothing of us working in Special Branch," Suel said and raised his glass. They clinked glasses and began to look at the menu. Suel ended up ordering a lamb stew, and Dillon went for the Beef and Guinness casserole. The server was back with their dinners ten minutes later. They ordered two more pints of Guinness and dug into the food. Over dinner, they discussed what they could be doing differently in the investigation and decided to go through a list of formerly convicted individuals. Based on the comment by Eamon Walsh regarding the man with bushy gray eyebrows, they would focus on that characteristic. Dillon offered to check on Walsh to see how he was doing and hopefully calm him down and dissuade him from suing Ulster Bank and An Garda Síochána. They had another pint after dinner and left Brannigan's.

"You thinking of stopping somewhere for one more?" Suel asked.

Dillon shook his head. "No, I think I'll head home. I just have this inner sense that things are going to get crazy this coming week, and I want to take it easy while I can. Besides, I'm still exhausted after my major league workout last night."

"Yeah, right. I'd like to hear Noreen's version. She'd probably tell me you fell asleep in front of the telly, and she woke you up in the morning and told you to get the hell out of her house."

"Are you kidding? She was calling to me as I left. Begging me to stay. Saying she'd do anything I wanted, and—"

"Really?"

"You think? No, we had a great night, and we were both in recovery mode this morning."

"Still sounds great. Okay, hopefully, I won't have to see the likes of you until Monday morning," Suel said and held out his hand. They shook, and Suel headed in the opposite direction toward the parking ramp where his car was parked. Dillon hurried across O'Connell Street and picked up the 13 bus in front of Buddy's Diner. He climbed the stairs to the upper level. At this hour, there were only five other people seated. He grabbed the first empty spot, looking out the front window of the upper level. It was dark outside, and as they passed apartments or pubs, he could glance into the occasional lit window and see the interior for a second or two. Eventually, they rounded the corner and went up Ballymun Road, past his wine store, The Grape Vine. Dillon pressed the button for the next stop. He went down the stairs, stepped off the bus, and walked back to St. Pappen's Road. The only place open on the commercial corner was Macari's Take Away. Dillon walked another block and then took a left down Dean Swift Road and into his place.

Lucifer met him at the door, accepted a head scratch, then stepped outside. Dillon made a mental note to pick up the various deposits in the morning before he stepped in one of them. He let Lucifer back in the house, and they went upstairs just after 11:00.

TWENTY-SIX

Since he didn't have to work on Sunday, Dillon woke up thirty minutes before his alarm would normally go off. After ten minutes, he gave up trying to go back to sleep and climbed out of bed. He dressed quietly and went downstairs. He was on his second cup of coffee and watching last night's American news on his laptop when Lucifer made his appearance. Dillon gave him a good head scratch, then let him out into the front garden.

Lucifer was back in the house twenty minutes later. After breakfast, Dillon grabbed the long-handled scoop and proceeded to pick up Lucifer's deposits. Based on the number he picked up, he decided it was more like deposits from the past two weeks. He dutifully placed them in the trash bin and rolled the bin closer to the Tuesday morning pick-up point. He phoned Noreen just before noon and left a message. He took Lucifer on their walk after lunch, came home, and took a nap. Noreen returned his call just before the dinner hour. After eating, he began reading a new book, then went to bed.

He woke Monday morning a few minutes before the alarm went off. He was actually eager to get to work, and he chalked that up to not having to work over the weekend. He had Lucifer settled in and was on his way to Headquarters just after 8:00.

When Suel arrived at his desk just before 9:00, Dillon had been reviewing security tapes from the robberies. This time, looking for older men, particularly one with bushy gray eyebrows. So far, he hadn't found any.

Suel took a sip from a paper cup and stepped over to Dillon. "You didn't get enough of that last week? Now you're back for more?"

"Same thing, different angle. I'm looking for two older guys, one of them with bushy gray eyebrows."

"Let me guess," Suel said and took another sip, "you haven't found anything yet."

"Well, yeah, but I've only been on this for thirty minutes."

"Which tape are you looking at?"

"Ulster Bank," Dillon said.

Suel shook his head. "It's shaping up to be a long day, and I only just got here. I'll start in on Bank of Ireland."

Three hours later, both of them had basically come up empty-handed.

"I'm thinking of stepping out and grabbing lunch. You interested in one of those big taco things?" Suel asked.

"I think you mean a burrito."

"What? Oh yeah, those big ones. You interested?"

"Yeah, get me one with no beans and mild sauce."

"Anything else? You want the tomatoes peeled?"

"Not funny," Dillon said and laughed.

"Back in ten minutes," Suel said and hurried out of the office.

Dillon continued scanning the tape, and five minutes later, he came across two individuals that fit the bill. There was just one problem. The guy with the gray-ish hair and the gray bushy eyebrows was in a wheelchair and pushed by another man, a redhead. Dillon pegged their ages at late-fifties to mid-sixties. He watched as they entered the bank, and the guy pushed the wheelchair over to the counter in the middle of the lobby. He handed a slip, Dillon guessed deposit or withdrawal, to the man in the wheelchair. They both took their time filling out the slip, casually glancing around. After a minute and a half, the guy pushed the wheelchair out of the lobby. Someone about to enter held the door open for them, and they disappeared. Dillon wrote down the time and date and then fast-forwarded the tape to see if they reappeared. He had run through the next thirty-eight minutes, and they hadn't reappeared when Suel returned. He backed the tape up as Suel approached.

Suel had a brown paper bag and a tray with two paper cups, one with tea and the other with coffee. "Join me in the break room," he said as he passed Dillon's desk.

"Hold up, I think I found them," Dillon stopped him.

"You're kidding, really?" Suel hurried around the desk and stood behind Dillon in his desk chair.

"Check this out," Dillon backed the tape to the time he'd written down. "This is about forty-eight hours before they hit Ulster Bank." He started to run the tape.

"Your one is in a bleeding wheelchair," Suel said as the wheelchair rolled into the bank lobby.

"Yeah, exactly. But look at him. He looks fit. He's wearing runners on his feet. Now watch and see what they do. They're only in there for a minute and a half."

They watched the tape. When the one guy turned the wheelchair around, and they headed out the door, Suel said, "Wait a minute. They didn't get any cash or make a deposit."

"Yeah, and I ran the tape forward for more than a half-hour. They don't come back in, so it's not like they forgot a check or something out in the car."

"Okay, can you isolate that portion and send it to me? I'll look at the Bank of Ireland tape and—"

"What if we do this? We send the image down to Burke. With any luck, he can do facial recognition on these two and run them through all four tapes. If they show up on the other tapes, it would seem to me to be a pretty strong indication that we just may have located our bank robbers."

"Yeah, give Burke a call and join me in the break room. God, if this works, I should have gotten a dessert for us as a celebration."

"If this works, Paddy. I'll buy us each an ice cream cone."

"There you go, always the big spender. Give Burke a yell, and then drag yourself over so we can eat."

Dillon punched in the three-digit extension for Burke down in the Tech Lab.

He answered on the third ring, "Burke."

"Hi, Jim, Dillon. Calling again for another favor."

Dillon heard him exhale, suggesting Burke was not looking forward to whatever Dillon wanted. "I'm going through the security tapes, and I found something that might be our two bank robbers, two days before the last robbery at Ulster Bank."

"Was this on the tapes I sent you focusing just on men fifty or younger?"

"Actually, no, it wasn't." Dillon went on to explain the brief 'bushy gray eyebrow' description they got from Eamon Walsh, the dye pack victim.

"That sounds a little thin, Dillon."

"Yeah, at face value, but when you look at the tape, it's just a minute and a half long. Your man looks in good shape, except he's in a wheelchair. Anyway, if you could just take a look and see what you think. I think the tape is clear enough that you could possibly run it for facial recognition."

"Hmmm." Burke didn't sound too excited, but he said, "Okay, send it down, and we'll take a look. No promises, but we'll see what we get."

"Thanks, Jim, coming your way in just a moment."

TWENTY-SEVEN

Suel shoved more chicken burrito into his mouth, chewed and said, "I'm thinking if Burke can get facial recognition on one of these two, we might be looking at the beginning of the end."

"I just hope the guy in the wheelchair isn't some poor soul who injured his back moving a box of books, and he'll be back to normal in forty-eight hours. I probably would have blown right past the two of them, except that they basically just looked around, and after filling out the deposit slip, they up and left. Thank God Eamon Walsh mentioned the bushy gray eyebrows."

"Yeah, well, your one in the wheelchair certainly had those. Let's just hope the two of them are the real deal."

Dillon took a sip of his coffee. "Hey, thanks for getting lunch. It's my turn next time."

"Not to worry, I won't forget," Suel said just as his phone rang. They both looked at one another. "Oh, please, God. Don't tell me it's another lunchtime robbery by our two idiots." He looked at the phone screen, swore, and then answered. "DI Suel. Yes. When. Where? In Tallaght? Let me just repeat it, twenty-five Donomore

Avenue. Got it. I'm on the way," Suel said and disconnected as he shook his head.

"That didn't sound like a bank?"

"No. More like a couple's confrontation that's now turned into a hostage situation. Tallaght Garda are there. The Emergency Response Team is on the way."

"The ERU? It's that bad?"

"I think it's more of just a caution. Your man has a record and—" Dillon's phone rang.

"Marshal Dillon," he answered as Suel stuffed the remainder of his burrito into his mouth and stood. "Yes. In Tallaght. Got it, heading out now. Thank you," he said and disconnected. "What a pleasant change from a bank robbery that doesn't involve a lot of money."

"Keep it up, Dillon. You'll be driving yourself. I'll drive. We were out there once before. It's right alongside Killinardan Park. Hopefully, they can talk this knacker down."

"You never know. A lot of stress. You have the name of the suspect?"

Suel shook his head. "No, just the address. ERU is on the way. Hopefully, they'll have everything calmed down by the time we arrive."

Dillon wrapped the remainder of his burrito in the foil and set it on his desk. He slipped on his protective vest, attached his pistol to his belt, and sipped his coffee as he followed Suel out the door.

Suel signed out a Garda vehicle and climbed in behind the wheel. Dillon buckled up and took another sip of coffee as Suel backed out of the space. He turned on the flashing lights and pulled out of the parking lot. They took Lower Road to the M50, raced down to the N81 and into Tallaght. It took a little more than fifteen minutes with the flashing lights on the vehicle.

As they rounded a corner, they saw the Emergency Response Unit van parked up ahead. Suel slowed down, turned off the flashing lights, and parked thirty feet behind the ERU van.

There was an officer standing next to the van. He turned around as they approached and asked, "Are you the negotiators?"

"That's the last thing you'd want. The two of us negotiating," Suel said.

"We're with Special Branch. Just got the call and hurried out here," Dillon said.

The officer nodded. "We've got someone in there with a gun. There's a woman he's been arguing with. Not sure if there are children, but there's a tricycle in the front of the house and a bike with training wheels. We're just keeping things buttoned up until the negotiation team arrives, and then we'll hand things over to them. They're on the way. That's why I thought it might be you."

"How can we help?" Dillon asked.

"If you wanted to step out into the park area, you'll see the ERU lads up against the wall. If you could move further down, just in case your man goes over the back wall, into the neighbor's garden, and out their front door.

We've kept it pretty quiet, no sirens or loudspeakers, and the like. So, with any luck, we'll be able to defuse the situation, and you can get back to whatever yous were working on."

"That would be nice," Dillon said.

They headed toward the gate at the end of the lane and just across the street from the house where the man was holding up. The gate led into Killinardin Park, a massive open area with walking paths. They gave a nod at the nine-man ERU team lined up along the eight-foot stucco garden wall of number 25 as they walked past and took up a position at the end of the next street, Donomore Avenue.

"So here we are for the rest of the bleedin' day," Suel groaned.

"Look at it this way, it's sunny, we're not in a bank parking lot trying to determine how the robbers disappeared, and we've got this gorgeous scenery of green grass and trees in the distance. It's been worse, Paddy."

"Oh, so suddenly now you're Mister Positive."

"That's who I've always been," Dillon joked.

It had been close to five hours since they took up the position opposite the end of Donomore Avenue. They were vaguely aware that the negotiators had been working back and forth for most of that time, but apparently, nothing had changed. The walking paths had been closed down due to the current situation, so there was no one passing by. Dillon was tempted to phone Burke in the

Tech Lab but didn't want to interrupt him in the event he was working on their project.

They were currently discussing the odds of Burke matching one or possibly both individuals on the security tape and keeping their fingers crossed. Suddenly, there was movement among the ERU team leaning against the garden wall. The officer in charge had given the word, and everyone looked like they were ready to charge. They suddenly began moving around the corner and into the front garden of the house. They weren't running, but it wasn't a casual stroll either.

"You think we should follow them?" Suel asked.

Dillon shook his head. "No, let's stay here just in case your man all of a sudden appears."

Five minutes later, they heard what sounded like muffled shouting but couldn't make out what was being said. Maybe a minute after that, a blue nylon bag flew over the wall and landed about five feet away from them. Dillon signaled with his hands that they spread apart and leaned against the wall. No sooner had they done that, standing ten feet apart and against the wall, when they looked up just in time to hear a groan as a pair of hands were visible on top of the wall. A figure suddenly appeared, facing the wall, and dropped to the ground. The guy took four backward steps in an effort to regain his balance before falling to the ground. He seemed to catch his breath for a half second, which was all the time Dillon and Suel needed to land on top of him and pin him down. They rolled him over onto his stomach, and Dillon slapped a pair of handcuffs on him.

"An Gardai Síochána, you're under arrest," Dillon shouted.

The man looked at the two of them, took a deep breath, and half-shouted, "Oh, what the hell?"

He wasn't what you might call muscular. He was lean without an ounce of fat on him, and Dillon thought he would probably have been able to outrun both of them if he had been turned around before dropping to the ground.

"You can't arrest the likes of me. I ain't done nothing wrong."

"Then we'll just check that out and let you go," Suel said. They raised him to his feet just as two heads appeared looking over the wall.

"Looking for anyone in particular? We'll see you out front," Dillon shouted. They took a couple of steps, and the man began to twist side to side in an effort to break loose. He suddenly kneed Suel in the groin, causing him to let go and drop to his knees. Dillon kicked the man hard at the back of his ankles, sweeping his feet out from underneath him. He seemed to levitate in midair for a moment, then landed on the ground, knocking the wind out of him.

"You okay, Paddy?"

"I'm going to kill that bollox once I recover. Yeah, I'm fine. Oh, God," he groaned and curled into the fetal position.

Dillon rolled the man over and placed a knee on his spine for a long minute until Suel gave him the nod and stood. Three men from the ERU team hurried around the corner. They grabbed the man by his arms and yanked him onto his feet.

"You two okay?" the sergeant asked.

"Bastards tried to crack me head open. Said they were going to kill me," the handcuffed suspect exclaimed.

"Damn it, I knew we got here too fast," the sergeant replied, and the other two ERU men laughed. "We'll take him from here. Nice work, lads. LT Crowley will want a word and to thank you. He's in the house talking to your woman." They led the man back around the front of the house. Dillon grabbed the blue nylon bag, and they followed, with Suel setting the pace. He took some deep breaths and gradually came back to something close to normal.

"Probably a good thing they took that bastard away, or I would have paid him back," Suel said.

"Maybe enough excitement for one day," Dillon said. He handed the nylon bag over to one of the ERU members, and they stepped into the attached house. It was about half the size of Dillon's place. At the moment, a woman with red, puffy eyes and a bruised jaw was seated on a worn couch. She held a little boy, maybe three, and next to her was a little girl, no more than five or six, with both her arms wrapped around the woman's arm.

An officer was standing in front of her, talking in a soothing tone, telling her she was all right and the children were okay.

"Special Branch?" a voice from behind asked. Dillon and Suel turned around, and the ERU officer introduced himself, "I'm Lieutenant Crowley. Let's step outside, and we'll give them some room."

TWENTY-EIGHT

When they stepped outside, Dillon suddenly noticed that there were three times as many vehicles out front as before. Most of them were squad cars, but two were clearly unmarked Garda vehicles.

"I want to thank you for grabbing this knacker. There's a chance he could have made a getaway, and that wouldn't have made me very happy," Crowley said.

"Not a problem," Dillon replied. "We would like to put it on record that after we identified ourselves as Gardai, he assaulted my partner. Kneed him and sent him to the ground."

Crowley smiled. "So noted, we'll add it to the list of charges. You're both with Special Branch?"

They nodded, and Suel said, "I'm DI Paddy Suel."

"Marshal Jack Dillon," Dillon added.

"Nice to meet you both, and we appreciate you being here. Dillon, you're the American in Special Branch?"

"Yeah, apparently, they could only deal with one of us."

"I've heard about you. Were you the one out at Terminal Two in the airport a few years back?"

Dillon nodded and said, "What can you tell us about your man here? Was it a break-in? Some sort of domestic?"

"Basically, a domestic disturbance, although we've been looking for him for a while. You may have heard of him, Callum Gannon. He's wanted in an attempted bank robbery and was hiding here. The woman wanted him out, but he wouldn't leave. He kept her and the two kids locked in a room for a couple of days. He's got a record. Hopefully, they'll charge him with kidnapping, the attempted robbery, your charge of assaulting an officer, and anything else they can find."

"Tell me about the bank robbery. We're working a bank robbery case."

"Well, I can start by saying he wasn't successful. Claimed he was going to make a citizen's arrest on those two clowns that have been pulling these crazy stunts at banks lately."

"You mean the two guys robbing the tellers and making off with maybe a thousand euros?" Suel asked.

"Yeah, those are the guys. Talk about amateur night. Can you imagine being locked up for a half-dozen years for stealing a thousand euros? You have to wonder what in the hell they're thinking."

"You've got him in the ERU van?" Dillon asked.

"Yeah, we've got a nice cold cell waiting for him at the station. Soon as we're done checking the house and making sure it's safe for your woman and the two children, we'll lock him up. It would be just like this idiot to leave something that's going to go off around midnight or to pierce a gas line or something."

"You mind if we talk to him for a minute? It would be interesting to see if he actually knows anything about those two idiots pulling the bank robberies."

"Be my guest. Just a warning, his history suggests he's pretty impressed with himself, and he'll tell you anything you want to hear. But, whether or not it's the truth is another question."

"Thanks, LT. We'll chat him up for a minute."

"Let me just give the word," Crowley said. He stepped over toward the ERU van and said, "Special Branch is going to have a bit of a chat with Mr. Gannon."

There were two officers, one was leaning against the front bumper, and the other was standing next to the passenger door. Dillon and Suel walked over to the van, and the officer who had been standing led them around to the rear doors. "He's handcuffed to his seat, but best to leave your weapons here. We'll keep an eye on them."

Dillon said, "That was our pair of handcuffs on him, any chance of getting them back?"

"They're with me mate, in the front. Grab 'em when you're finished."

Suel said, "That's my vehicle just over there. I'll lock our weapons in the trunk, and yous won't have to bother. Back in a minute," he said and held out his hand for Dillon's pistol. He hurried down the street to the car he'd driven, opened the boot, and placed the pistols inside. He hurried back to Dillon and the officer.

"Okay, I'm sure Mr. Gannon would love to plead his innocence to you. I'm guessing we're going to be leaving shortly, so best to make it quick."

"You're heading back to Tallaght station?" Dillon asked.

"Yeah, been a long day."

"I'll say," Suel said as the officer opened one of the rear doors, and he climbed up into the van. Dillon was right behind him.

Callum Gannon had his hands handcuffed behind him and attached to a ring bolted to a steel bar on the side of the van. He was seated on a bench with manacles around both ankles and attached to the floor. He focused in on Dillon and Suel as they climbed into the van. The ERU officer left the rear door open.

"Yous can't be doing anything to me. I didn't know you was the Gardai. I thought you were going to rob me."

"Shut up before you find yourself in real trouble," Suel said. "Now, along with all the charges you're facing, and there's quite a number of them, I'm thinking I'm going to file an assault charge against you. Assaulting an officer of the law. I think the penalty for that is about to change and will become an automatic twelve years behind bars."

"But I didn't know you were the Gardai, and besides, I was handcuffed. I didn't really assault yous anyway."

"Oh really, because we've got it on film," Dillon said. "We told you, you were under arrest. Who did you think we were? A couple of guys walking through the park?"

"Okay, okay, I'm sorry, Jasus. There, does that make the two of yous happy?"

"Just want you to know you're liable to be locked up for somewhere between twelve and twenty years. With your record, you won't get a job, and you'll be on the dole, taking dogs for walks or washing cars just to get enough money for food. No woman will want you."

"I'm sorry, okay? I didn't mean to—"

"Let us know when you're done lying, and maybe we can help you. Come on, let's go," Dillon said.

"No wait. I'll do whatever yous want. Don't leave me here with this lot. Please."

"Think about telling the truth, and we might get back to you," Dillon said and hopped out of the van. Suel followed.

"Wait, wait. I won't lie to yas, I promise. Come on. I know shit you could use. Come on back. Hey, did yous hear me? Hello?"

"Everything okay?" the ERU officer asked.

"Yeah, you were right. He's full of himself. Can I get those handcuffs back?" Suel asked.

The officer, still seated on the front bumper, reached behind his back, pulled out a pair of handcuffs, and handed them to Suel.

"Thanks. Stay safe, lads," Suel said, and they headed down the street to their vehicle. They crawled back to the headquarters building through rush hour traffic. Once back in the Special Branch section, the room was basically deserted. Dillon checked his computer for email messages. He deleted all but two and left a message for those two individuals to call him in the morning.

Suel approached and said, "I think I'm going to take a pass on grabbing a pint tonight. I'll see you in the morning."

"You sure you're okay? It's not from the knee that Gannon prick gave you, is it?"

"Yeah, I'm okay. The knee was just a momentary thing. It's just been a long day."

"Okay, mind yourself, and I'll see you in the morning."

"Have a good night. Give my best to Noreen if you see her," Suel said and headed out of the office.

Dillon watched him leave, hoping he was just tired and not dealing with some deeper injury he didn't want to mention. The more he thought about it, the more the idea of heading home sounded pretty good. He tidied up his desk, locked the drawers, and headed home. He spent a quiet night with Lucifer, the two of them watching the telly until it was time to head upstairs to bed.

TWENTY-NINE

O nce again, Dillon was in the office a half-hour early. He placed a call to LT Crowley in Tallaght, mentioned that he'd like to have a chat with Callum Gannon at some point during the day, and if Crowley could call and let him know a time that would be best for whatever Tallaght had scheduled for Gannon today. As he hung up the phone, he half-jumped when he saw Suel standing behind him.

"Oh, my God. You just scared me half to death. You feeling better this morning?"

"Yes, I think I was in bed last night at 8:00. Nothing that a good night's sleep couldn't cure, so stop your fretting. You're driving the likes of me crazy. Did I hear you say you wanted to meet up with this Gannon bollox at Tallaght station today?" Suel asked.

"Eventually," Dillon said. "I'm hoping a night behind bars may have helped to get him on the right track. I'm not interested in playing games with him. If he starts to try to work us, I'll walk out and let him do twelve years for kneeing you."

"I'd settle for five minutes in the cell with him," Suel said.

Dillon turned on his computer. There was an email from Burke down in the Tech Lab. He held his breath and clicked on it. There were a total of six different images of the two men. Four of the images had them using a wheelchair. But they were apparently taking turns pushing one another around. Those four images were at AIB, J&R Credit, Bank of Ireland, and Ulster Bank. In addition, two more images were from the Bank of Ireland. In those two instances, both men were in the bank lobby but acting separately, waiting in different lines.

An accompanying email from Burke stated that, although the images were sufficient to locate the additional images on the security tapes, they were not accurate enough to use in facial recognition for purposes of identifying the individuals. Burke finished by stating he would attempt to adjust the images and that he was still working on them.

Dillon phoned him and ended up leaving a message. "Hi, Jim, Dillon here. Just wanted to thank you for the work you've done locating these two in the banks prior to the robberies. Please let me know if there is anything we can do to help. Thanks." He hung up and called over to Suel. "Did you get an email from Burke?"

"Let me check," Suel said and, a moment later, shook his head. "No, I'm not seeing anything."

"Come over here and take a look at what he sent me," Dillon said.

Suel hurried over and stood behind Dillon as he brought up the various images. "Interestingly, they were all roughly forty-eight hours before the robbery. So they were in the AIB branch roughly ten minutes before close, Bank of Ireland at 12:47 and the Ulster Bank at 10:35. It makes sense," Dillon said.

"To a degree," Suel responded. "I get checking the times, but a noon on, say, Wednesday may not be as busy as a Friday noon or the noon before some sort of a holiday."

"Burke's email said he's adjusting the images to try and get facial recognition. Just now, they're too blurry to work with the program. Still, we know a little bit more about these two, and our initial thought was correct. They've visited the lobby and checked it out before performing the robbery."

Suel shook his head. "So I feel as though we've come full circle again. They're checking the place out. Theoretically, they have a sense of what they're dealing with as far as layout, lack of security staff, and the number of customers in the place at a specific time, and yet, they rob a teller for a fraction of what they could get if they hit the vault. It still doesn't seem to make a lot of sense."

"I don't know, Paddy. Maybe we should count ourselves lucky that they haven't figured that part out yet. One other thing I noticed. I'm thinking there's a similarity between the two. Your one appears slightly younger. He's got bushy eyebrows too. But more red hair than gray. I'm wondering if they may be related. Brothers or maybe cousins."

"Possibly, although I don't want to jump the gun on that. I'll give them this much. Despite not leaving with a large amount of cash, they do seem to be working well as a team."

Dillon nodded. "I had the sense they enjoyed trading places in the wheelchair. Which reminds me, hang on while I make a call."

The phone rang twice, then a voice answered, "Yeah."

"I'd like to talk to Eamon, please."

"This is me. Are you that American that talked to me up in the hospital?"

"Yeah, Jack Dillon. I wanted to check on you, see how you're doing," Dillon said and nodded at Suel.

"Well, a bit of the dye is still with me, but they got a good deal of it off. Actually, it's made me pretty popular at the skateboard park. I was even giving autographs to the kids. A couple of pals made up a story about me grabbing the bag of cash from the bank robbers instead of them just handing it to me, and there've been a couple of girls who found that interesting," he said and just let that last line hang out there for a minute.

"Still pissed off about them handcuffing me, but on the other hand, it adds to the story. I'm going back and forth to James's every two to three days, and they're checking my skin and doing some removal work."

"Removal work? You mean like surgery?"

"No, they've come up with some mix they apply and let it set for a bit. It's gradually removing the dye. Then they apply a cream and send me home. I have to apply the cream three times a day to protect my skin."

"Okay, so it sounds like slow, but sure, you're making a recovery."

"Yeah, not going as fast as I'd like, but it's getting better little by little."

"Well, I wanted to tell you that, based on the information you gave us, remember you told me an old guy with a raspy voice and bushy gray eyebrows handed you the bag?"

"Yeah, he was the one what handed me the bag and said, 'Here, lad. A little present for you.' Just before that cloud of dye exploded from the bag."

"Yeah, well, we've found images of both of them on security tapes, without the sunglasses. All because you gave us the bushy eyebrow clue. We may be able to track them down, so I wanted to tell you thanks, and I'm glad you're doing so well."

"Yeah, okay. Thanks for making the call, sir. It's nice to talk to you."

"Well, you got my number. If you think of anything else, feel free to call me any time. Deal?"

"Yeah, I'll do that. Thanks."

"Thank you, Eamon. All the best," Dillon said and disconnected.

"Why in the hell are you sucking up to that bastard?" Suel asked.

"I'm not sucking up to him, Paddy. I was thanking him for giving us a clue and maybe, without saying it, but maybe he'll think twice about suing the department."

"He'd never win a case like that. Covered with the dye, arresting him was the right thing to do. The only thing that could have been done."

"Yeah, sure, and then some news knacker gets ahold of the story, and it becomes another tale about police brutality or some damn thing. Wouldn't it be better that, if he told the story, he'd add that one of the officers called to check on him and thanked him for his help? We're going to nail these two sooner or later. I still think they're on to something bigger. I just can't figure out what the hell it is."

"Well, when you do finally figure it out, you can share it with the rest of us."

Dillon's desk phone suddenly rang. "Oh, God. Please, not another robbery."

"If that was the case, they'd contact you on your cell," Suel said.

Dillon seemed to relax. He looked at the screen on his desk phone and nodded toward Suel. "Hi, Jim," was how he answered. "Thanks for returning my call. I didn't get your email until this morning. We were out working a domestic yesterday afternoon into the early evening."Dillon shook his head. "No, down in Tallaght, as a matter of fact. Fortunately, everything went well. Hopefully, I'm going to talk to the suspect later today. He spent the night compliments of Tallaght Station." Dillon glanced at Suel and said, "Yes, both Suel and I went through the tapes. Interesting, especially the two of them taking turns in the wheelchair. We were wondering if you'd had any luck coming up with names via facial recognition? Oh, damn it, I was afraid of that," Dillon said, looking over at Suel and shaking his head.

Suel mouthed an expletive.

"One other thing. Did you think there was a similarity in appearance between the two?" Dillon asked.

"Yeah, okay. Keep us posted. If we learn anything, we'll let you know. Yeah, you too. Thanks, Jim," Dillon said and hung up. He looked at Suel and shook his head. "He thinks the images are too blurry for any facial recognition."

"What'd he say about a similarity between the two?" Suel asked.

"He didn't seem too impressed, just said maybe."

"Okay, then. I guess it's back to work," Suel said.

THIRTY

L T Crowley phoned Dillon later that afternoon.

"Thanks for returning my call, LT. I'm wondering if Callum Gannon is still under your loving care. If so, would it be possible to come over and talk to him yet today?"

"Well, you can if you want to. I'll be honest. We haven't gotten much from him. He's telling us he was the one kidnapped and held in the bedroom for the past couple of days. Said the woman called us only because he wanted to leave. According to what he said, she wanted him to pay her some outlandish fee for the room she supposedly rented to him. None of it makes any sense. I'll be honest. I think you're going to be wasting your time, but he'll be available if you still want to come over. He's going to be here for the foreseeable future, so there's no rush on this end."

"I'll head out shortly. Should I ask for you or someone else?"

"Go ahead and ask for me. First name is James, by the way. It will just make it easier for you once you get here."

"Alright, I'll head over in just a bit. Thanks in advance, much appreciated."

"Not a problem. Just glad you two were there to grab him. God only knows what he'd be up to left to his own devices," Crowley said and hung up.

Dillon brought up the four images from Burke of the two suspects pushing each other around in the wheelchair and printed them off. He put the printed copies in a manila folder, shut down his computer, and locked his desk. He stopped at Suel's desk and said, "I just got off the phone with Crowley down in Tallaght. I'm going to talk to your friend Callum Gannon. See if he knows anything about our two idiots."

"I don't think that bollox has spoken the truth in months, no, make that years, Dillon. He's just going to lie his scrawny ass off and hope he can get you to cut some sort of deal for him. He knows he's going away, so he's got nothing to lose playing the likes of you for some soft-hearted plonker."

"I wish I could disagree with you, Paddy. But I'm afraid you're right. Still, we're grabbing at straws, so I'm going to give it a shot."

"Let me know how it goes. You feel like meeting up later?"

"Let me see how this goes. I'll give you a call once I've finished. Enjoy the rest of your afternoon," Dillon said.

"I'm counting the minutes," Suel said with a smile.

Dillon took the same route Suel had driven the day before, the Lower Road to the M50, then down to the N81 and into Tallaght. Of course, he was driving his car, so there were no flashing lights, which meant the drive took about three times as long. He finally pulled into the Tallaght Station parking lot, showed his ID to the officer at the gate, and mentioned that he was meeting with LT Crowley. He parked and then had to walk around to the front of the building because he didn't know the keypad code for the parking lot door.

"Hi, Marshal Dillon with Special Branch. I'm here to see LT Crowley. He's expecting me," Dillon said to the desk sergeant in the lobby. He raised his ID hanging around his neck to give him some credence.

"I'll give him a call. If you'd like to take a seat," the sergeant replied.

The lobby had a handful of people seated in it. Dillon settled onto a black plastic chair away from everyone and waited. He'd looked at the clock on the wall a number of times and was about to ask the desk sergeant if Crowley was even in the building. Suddenly, the security door opened, and Crowley called, "Dillon?"

He hurried over to Crowley. They shook hands as Dillon stepped into the hallway. "Sorry it took so long," Crowley said as they headed down the hallway. "Like everywhere, we're a bit short-staffed, and it took a while to get him escorted into the interview room. Would you mind if I joined you? I don't plan on saying anything. But I think it would be wise to have two of us present and to record the interview. We're familiar with Gannon, and he would like nothing better than to set you up and then file a harassment lawsuit or bang his head on the table and accuse you of hitting him."

Crowley opened a door, and they went up a set of stairs. "Gee, he sounds like a wonderful person," Dillon joked. "Yeah, if you wouldn't mind, I would appreciate you being there. I'll be honest. I've got a couple of specific questions and four different images of two guys for him to look at. If he starts to play games, I'll end it right then and there."

"Tell him that at your introduction. He's aware he's going to be looking at some serious time. So that may be a nice way to get his attention. It may be dawning on him that he's looking at years. A lot of years."

They walked down a hallway on the second floor toward an officer stationed just outside an interview room. "Thanks, Colin. Is the recorder on?" Crowley asked.

"Yes, sir. Thus far, he's looked around the room and flashed his middle finger to the camera up in the corner. No surprise." The officer chuckled and opened the door.

Dillon stepped in with Crowley behind him.

Gannon was seated at a metal-topped table, dressed in an orange nylon jumpsuit. He was handcuffed, and the handcuffs were attached to a ten-inch chain that was bolted to the table.

Two chairs were on the opposite side of the table. Dillon pulled out a chair, sat down, and placed the folder on the table. Once Crowley sat down, Dillon said, "Callum Gannon, my name is Marshal Jack Dillon. I'm with An Garda Síochána Special Branch. Lieutenant James Crowley is with An Garda Síochána, Tallaght Station. Are you in the room of your own free will?"

"You mean did I want to see the likes of your lousy ass? Not—"

"Let me warn you right now, Mr. Gannon. You pull a stunt like that again, and we're finished. I've got a couple of questions to ask you. If you choose not to answer them, that is your right. If you do that, it is my right not to present you as a cooperating witness, in which case, since you're looking at some major sentences, you'll probably serve them consecutively."

"But I didn't do anything. I already told you. I—"

"I don't have anything to do with the pending charges against you, your court appearances, or your sentencing. That will be left to the legal system and the courts. Do you understand?"

"So what the hell are you doing here?"

Dillon flashed a quick smile. "I'd like to ask you a couple of questions. If you provide honest answers, I would be able to put in a good word to the court saying that you were cooperative and helped. If you choose not to provide an honest answer, that is your right to do so, as it is my right not to put in a good word. Your choice."

"How do I know you'll put in a good word?"

"Maybe look at it this way. If you don't answer my questions, don't cooperate, then obviously, I won't put in a good word. However, if you do help me out, well then, at least you have a chance."

"I don't see how that's going to help me."

Dillon took a deep breath and stared at Gannon for a brief moment. "Okay, your choice. Enjoy the rest of your afternoon," Dillon said. As he stood, he picked up the folder, tapped it on the tabletop, and pushed his chair in.

"Hey, wait a minute. I didn't say I wouldn't help you. I just need to know that you'll put in a good word for me, so they'll let me go."

Dillon shook his head. "That's not going to happen. You're facing some serious charges, possession of a firearm, kidnapping, attempted murder, attempted robbery, assaulting a Garda officer, and probably drug use. I'm guessing we could throw rape on top of that."

Gannon shook his head. "That bitch is lying to yous. I didn't do none of that."

"Did you have a gun?"

"He did," Crowley said.

"Did you threaten to kill the woman?"

"He did, and the two children," Crowley said.

"But I didn't mean it. I was just trying to—"

"Doesn't matter. You threatened to kill them, and we have to take that threat seriously. You get the picture I'm painting here, Callum? You're in deep weeds. Now, I don't have time to waste. Do you want to try to help, or

are you gonna play games? If you even think about playing me, I'm out of here, and you can get ready for a very
long time behind bars."

"Okay, okay, what do you want me to do?"

"I want you to look at some pictures and see if you
recognize the men. You think you can do that?" Gannon
seemed to think for a moment and then nodded. "I need
to hear your response."

Gannon started to give Dillon a look but then nodded and said, "Yeah, I'll look at the pictures."

"Okay, let's get started," Dillon said and sat back
down.

THIRTY-ONE

Dillon opened the file and took out the four images of the robbers trading places and pushing each other in the wheelchair. He turned them around and pushed them across the table toward Gannon.

Gannon glanced at the images, gave a quick look at Dillon, and then slid them closer, studying them for a couple of minutes without saying anything. Eventually, he looked up and said, "Yeah, I recognize them. What's with the wheelchair?"

"Just something they're doing, taking turns giving each other a ride. Do you know their names?"

Gannon seemed about to say something, then shook his head. "I don't know them, okay? I just know who they are. Your one, the red-haired one, he called me a piece of shite. Told me if he ever saw me around again, he'd give me something to remember him by."

"Why'd he tell you that?"

Gannon shook his head and wouldn't look at Dillon. "They thought I was following them. I wasn't. We just ended up in the same couple of places one night. They used to be big names around Dublin, then disappeared for a while. Well, actually, a number of years. I heard they were living in Spain. Costa del Sol, but I don't know that for a fact. They were legends, you know, way back before my time, and then I guess they disappeared."

"So what're their names?"

"You mean you don't know who they are? I mean, they're famous," he said, looking over at Crowley.

Crowley slid one of the images over, studied it, and shook his head.

"It's the Meehan brothers, Liam and Rory. They're bleedin' legends," Gannon said.

"The Meehans? They've been dead for over twenty years," Crowley said.

Gannon shook his head. "No, that's them there. Honest, they've been back in Dublin for almost half a year."

"No. They were both murdered in Spain back in 2001. A car bomb." Crowley said. "What was left of their bodies was photographed by the Policía Nacional, the Spanish police. They were cremated, and their ashes are in a plot in Glasnevin Cemetery. I've been there. I've seen the gravestones."

"Well then, I guess it was a pair of ghosts that I followed that night."

"If they were back in the country, believe me, we would have heard about it. As a matter of fact, the Meehans were bank robbers. Yeah, so of course, these two knackers told you that's who they were. Such famous bank robbers that they're robbing the likes of AIB for eleven hundred euros, and they get chased out of J&R

Credit without a cent. I don't know who these two are, but they sure as hell aren't the Meehan brothers."

"But that's who they told me they were. Honest, I'm not lying to yous. I got everything to lose by not telling yous the truth. Now, maybe they made it up, but that's who they said they was."

"And why did they tell you their names?"

Gannon hung his head and said, "Because I told them I wanted to work with them. Told them I wanted to be famous, just like the two of them. That's when they laughed, and your man, Rory Meehan, the one with the red hair, he told me he'd give me something to remember them by if I didn't leave."

"Oh, for feck's sake," Crowley said.

"Where did this happen?"

"In a pub named Dirty Dick's."

"You know it?" Dillon asked Crowley.

Crowley nodded and said, "Haven't been there in years. Not the nicest place in town, has a bit of a reputation."

"There were two big guys at the door, security types. They patted me down when I stepped in."

"Patted you down?" Dillon asked.

"Yeah, for real. They patted me down and then ran a wand over me before they let me in. I was in there for all of five minutes. I ordered a pint I never got because Rory Meehan was going to kick my arse if I didn't leave. But I remember the bartender, some old guy. He gave 'em both a pint and said it was on the house 'cause they was so famous. So then I said I wanted to umm, well, you know, and—"

"So, let's just say for a minute this was the Meehans, and you're looking to link up with them in some way. Why?"

"Why? Well, because they were famous and umm, well, the word kind of out on the street was they were going to do something really big," Gannon said and gave a quick glance over at Crowley.

"Oh, for the love of God. So word on the street is, or rather was, they're planning something big. Amazingly, no one ever bothered to mention it to us. We never heard about it, oh, and guess what? It never happened. But then, how could it? If the two of them are robbing bank tellers for a measly thousand euros and then handing the Arnotts shopping bag to some guy on a skateboard just before the dye pack goes off. Honest to God."

Gannon looked at Crowley and shook his head. "Look, I don't know anything about your Arnotts bag with a dye pack. Besides, Arnotts doesn't even put dye packs in their shopping bags. All I know is, them two is Liam and Rory Meehan. Okay, now, can I get my things and get out of here, please?"

Crowley held up his hand and said, "If it's okay with you, Dillon. I'll summon the guard, and he can escort Mr. Gannon back to his cell."

"Back to my cell? I just told you who those two are. You said you were going to put in a good word for me, and then I'd get out of here."

"That's not what—"

Dillon gave Crowley a look and said, "I'll put in a good word for you, Callum, but these things take time. Go ahead, LT, call the guard."

Gannon shook his head as Crowley headed for the door. "I knew yous were gonna screw me. I just knew it."

Crowley opened the door, and the guard stepped in. He unlocked Gannon's ankle manacles from the floor chain and then unlocked his handcuffs from the chain on the table. "I'll be back in a minute, Dillon. Just going to help with the escort," Crowley said as he led the way, followed by Gannon with the guard behind Gannon.

"Thanks for your help, Callum," Dillon called.

Gannon raised his handcuffed hands over his head and flashed Dillon the finger using both his hands.

Dillon shook his head, silently laughed, gathered up the print images, and returned them to the folder.

"Sorry for the waste of time, Dillon," Crowley said, stepping back into the interrogation room a few minutes later. "I was afraid something like this was going to happen. God, the Meehans. Hell, they'd both be somewhere in their fifties by now. You just can't make it up."

"So you're convinced he's lying?"

Crowley seemed to think about that for a moment and shook his head. "No, I'm pretty sure he followed those fellas. Said something to them. They may have even told him they were the Meehan brothers. He clearly believes it. The only problem is that's not who they are.

The Meehan brothers were killed, cremated, and they're buried over in Glasnevin Cemetery. Like I told you, I was out there with a couple of mates shortly after the ashes were buried, just to be sure they were there," he said and chuckled.

"Damn it, another dead end in this case. Well, looks like we're once again back to square one, and not for the first time."

"I'm sorry about that, Dillon, really I am. Tough luck."

"What's that old country song? If it weren't for bad luck, I'd have no luck at all?"

Crowley gave him a funny look.

"Okay, LT, let me get out of your hair. I appreciate you taking the time and letting me talk to Gannon."

"Oh, I get it. We've got to cover all the bases, and well, it can make for a long day, sometimes."

"You got that right," Dillon said and followed Crowley out of the room, down the stairs, and into the lobby. They shook hands. Dillon apologized once more and headed out to his car. Once in his car, he placed a call to Suel.

"Hey, Dillon, I was just thinking about you. What did you learn?"

"Just that we're back to square one, and I could use a pint. You up for one?"

"I could do that," Suel said. "The Autobahn?"

"Sounds good. I'm just leaving Tallaght, so no need to rush over. I'm a good thirty minutes out, given the traffic at this hour."

"I'll see you there. First one in buys the round," Suel said and disconnected.

THIRTY-TWO

Dillon pulled out of the Tallaght Station parking lot and headed toward the Autobahn. Forty minutes later, he pulled into a parking place on Collins Avenue and parked. He thought he spotted Suel's car parked down the street, so he stepped into the lounge expecting to spot Suel. Unfortunately, he didn't see him.

He grabbed an empty table just opposite the restrooms. A server arrived a couple of minutes later, and he ordered two pints of Guinness. She brought them to the table, and Dillon took a sip from his pint, looked around the room for the umpteenth time, and wondered where Suel was. He had just decided that it couldn't have been Suel's car parked down the street when the door to the men's room opened, and Suel peeked out.

"Are you f-ing kidding me?" Dillon called out, attracting the attention of folks at more than one table.

"Oh, I was just combing my hair and making sure I looked nice for your arrival. Mmm," Suel said, taking a sip, then setting his pint back on the table. "Well worth the wait. So, you said things didn't go well down in Tallaght. Tell me about it."

Dillon proceeded to fill him in, ending the tale with Crowley's suggestion that Gannon didn't necessarily lie. He just was duped by the two who pretended to be the Meehan brothers.

"I get what he's saying, Dillon. There's only one problem."

"Yeah, they're not the Meehans, and we're no further ahead than we were two weeks ago when they robbed the first bank, that AIB over on Hanover Quay."

"No, not that, the murder of the Meehans in Spain. They were killed in a car bomb. Their bodies were completely destroyed. They were identified by documents listing the car as belonging to them. Their remains were cremated within twenty-four hours at the request of a family member who just happened to be visiting. Yes, the remains are buried in Glasnevin Cemetery, but to my knowledge, they've never been genetically tested to confirm that it is indeed Liam and Rory Meehan."

"Wait, so there's never been any test—"

"Hold on. I get where you're going, but the other side of that is that the Meehans were wanted for not just robberies but big robberies, Dillon. I'm talking at least three that I can think of that would add up to over six million euros. But having said that, they were in Spain because, at the time, they couldn't be extradited and returned here to face the music. So, suddenly, in 2001, when Spain changed their law so that extradition was no longer forbidden, and the Meehans could be extradited, they were killed in a car bombing and cremated. Now, here's the question. If they are still alive, what have they been doing? There has never been one iota of information involving them for almost twenty years. No one has reported seeing them. Former contacts have not gone someplace to possibly visit them. If, indeed, they are back in Ireland, how, in God's name, did they get here without raising a flag when passing through passport control? Did they take a rowboat across the Irish Sea?"

"If they were involved on the level you say, it would seem to not be that big a deal to establish fake identities, get fake passports, even have some cosmetic surgery done that would alter their appearance," Dillon said.

"You know you're right, and then they could get back into the country and carry out their robberies at various small institutions where they net one or two thousand euros. Dillon, it would be nice if it was them, but this can't be the Meehans. You know, in a way, it's one more thing that seems to add credibility to the idea that they were killed in the car bombing almost twenty-five years ago."

Dillon shook his head and signaled a waiter.

"What can I get for you?"

"Two more Guinness, please," Dillon said.

They went back and forth, taking both sides of the discussion, whether or not the Meehans were responsible for the slew of amateur robberies. In the end, Dillon paid the tab, and they headed home in opposite directions.

Dillon let Lucifer into the front garden, tossed him a biscuit outside, and gave him another biscuit fifteen minutes later when he came back in the house. He microwaved half an order of Thai stir fry he found in a plastic tray toward the back of the refrigerator. He dozed off in front of the telly just as the evening news came on and joined Lucifer, already stretched out on the bed, just before midnight.

The alarm woke him the following morning. He went through his morning routine and arrived at Special Branch just as Suel was getting out of his car.

"Dillon, a late start for you. Did you drive out to Skerries from the Autobahn last night?"

"God, no. In fact, I fell asleep in front of the telly and wandered upstairs to bed when I woke up. I think the negative result from my meeting with Callum Gannon knocked the wind out of my sails. It's just time to take a deep breath and start back at square one once more."

"Well, with any luck, we won't hear about those two today."

"Don't even say that, Paddy. You'll just encourage a phone call alerting us to the next robbery."

For the past half-hour, Dillon had been going through the file on the AIB robbery, the first of the four. All the while, in the back of his mind, he kept thinking about the Meehan brothers. He brought up the files on them, starting with time served as juveniles, and began to read. They had attended St. Mark's Community School in Tallaght, and their first recorded involvement with the Gardai was after they were caught breaking into the school in an effort to change their grades in a teacher's notebook. They were caught breaking into the local GAA club while in the process of stealing team jerseys. One year spent in a juvenile detention center only served to educate them about the criminal world.

They were suspected of participating in a series of office robberies but were never charged. Their first known bank robbery occurred at the Core Credit Union in Monkstown, an area in south Dublin. The robbery itself was successful, but the Meehans were arrested after crashing the stolen getaway car into a city bus. They served three years of a six-year sentence at Mountjoy prison, which basically served as a finishing school for up-and-coming bank robbers. It was the last time they were arrested, although they were suspected in the three largest bank robberies in the late 1990s. They were apparently killed in the car bombing and hadn't been heard from since.

Dillon picked up the file folder with the Meehan brothers' images and walked down to Jim Burke's office in the Tech Department. He pushed the intercom button next to the door.

A moment later, a voice growled, "Tech Department."

"Marshal Dillon from Special Branch. I'd like to see Jim Burke."

"Do you have an appointment?"

"No, I don't."

"Just a mome—" the voice replied, cutting himself off.

The door buzzed a half-minute later, and Dillon stepped in. Burke's head suddenly appeared over the wall of his cubicle. "What impossible mission do you have for me today, Dillon," he grinned and then laughed.

"Just a couple of questions and a possible lead."

"Oh, a lead? Really?"

Dillon stepped into the cubicle, and Burke slid a chair on wheels out from a counter. "Take a seat and tell me what you got."

Dillon sat down and opened the folder. "These are copies of the images you sent to me," he said, handing the printed sheets of the men with the wheelchair to Burke.

Burke nodded and asked, "Were they of any help?"

"They may have been. It's sort of a fifty-fifty shot." He went on to tell Burke the story of Callum Gannon and his insistence that the images were the Meehan brothers.

Burke nodded and said, "I think I've heard of them, but I'm not familiar. We'd have facial shots of them if they were arrested." He spun around in his chair and ran his fingers across the keyboard. "Give me one of their names again,"

"Rory Meehan. M, double e, h, a, n," Dillon responded.

"Humph, an old shot almost thirty years ago. Okay, it will take me about a half hour to compare his image to the security tapes, and I've got a couple of projects ahead of it. Can I give you a call later this afternoon?"

"Yes, please. In the images you sent me, Rory's the one with the red hair. I've got copies of the images here if you want them," Dillon said and held out the file.

"No thanks, I'll pull the images from my file, and we'll see. I can tell you, given the quality of the security tapes, we won't be able to get a hundred percent match, but if we can make it to, say, a seventy percent match, that would be close to a sure bet."

"I appreciate it, Jim. Thanks," Dillon said as he stood.

"Happy to help," Burke replied. He handed the file back to Dillon, spun his chair around to his keyboard, and began to type.

Dillon left and headed back upstairs.

THIRTY-THREE

Suel was out of the office, so Dillon grabbed an order of fish and chips from one of the food trucks for lunch and wolfed it down in about five minutes. He was back at his desk reviewing the file on the car bombing of the Meehan brothers. There were three photos of what remained of the burned-out hulk of the car. He found it interesting that the car was off to the side of what appeared to be a rural road. Remnants of the burnt bodies were apparent in the images, which only convinced Dillon that they couldn't be visually identified as either one of the Meehan brothers. There was no record of DNA testing having been performed, and both bodies were cremated within twenty-four hours of the explosion. The ashes were escorted back to Dublin the day after cremation by Evan Meehan, a relative of Liam and Rory, who just happened to be visiting at the time of their deaths.

Dillon was highly skeptical and also aware of the fact he had other things to do besides investigating a car bombing from over twenty years ago and in a completely different country. It was just after 4:00 when his desk phone rang, Jim Burke.

"Hi, Jim. Were you able to find anything?"

"Yes, just slightly better than the seventy percent match I mentioned. Both images of Liam and Rory Meehan came up with a seventy-two percent match. I would say there's a good chance, a very good chance, it's the two of them trading places on the wheelchair."

"Thank you, Jim. I can't believe it. Actually, some good news in our investigation."

"Probably a good idea not to get used to that. I'll talk to you later." Burke laughed and hung up.

Suel still wasn't back from wherever he had gone. Dillon googled Dirty Dick's pub, the place where Callum Gannon followed the suspected Meehan brothers. It was located along the Liffey River on Sir John Rogerson's Quay. Dillon found it interesting that the pub was within easy walking distance of the AIB bank on Hanover Quay, the site of the first robbery they were investigating. He left a quick note for Suel, letting him know where he was headed. He removed the four prints of the Meehans with the wheelchair, stuffed them in his pocket, and headed out the door.

The drive wasn't all that far, but given the hour of the day, rush hour was in its early stages, and Dillon seemed to catch every other red light along the way. He pulled into a parking place alongside the pub. The lot was barely half-full, with nothing resembling a newer vehicle. Dillon wondered for half a second if the cars had been recently parked by people heading home from work or had they been parked there by all-day drinkers. He removed his ID from his pocket and locked it in the glove compartment. Double-checked his pockets for anything suggesting he was with An Garda Síochána and climbed out of the car. He pressed the fob on his key to lock the car door and headed inside the two-story brick building.

Illegible, black spray-painted graffiti was along the corner of the building for about ten feet. From the look of it, the writing had been there for a couple of years. The name Dirty Dick's in neon lights was along the top of the building, but the apostrophe and the final 's' were apparently burnt out. Dillon pulled open the steel door and stepped inside. Two large men in black short-sleeve shirts with the embroidered word 'Security' stood just inside the door.

"Good evening, sir. Would you mind if we gave you a quick pat down?" one of them asked.

"What would happen if I said, yeah, I would mind?" Neither one smiled, and Dillon said, "Please, go ahead." He spread his legs and stretched his arms out.

One of them gave him a quick pat down, and when he finished, his partner ran a hand-held metal detector over Dillon. "Thank you, have a nice evening," the man said, and Dillon stepped into the dingy bar. There were about a dozen people in the place, a table of four, two couples in separate booths, and four guys seated two or three stools apart at the bar. No one looked like the sort of person you'd want to chat up for a few minutes. The barman was an older guy with glasses. At the moment, he was leaning against the counter behind the bar and eyeing Dillon.

Dillon walked over to the end of the bar and settled onto the stool that was the furthest away from anyone else at the bar. The barman waited for a long moment and then walked over.

"What can I get you?" he asked as he half-tossed a coaster labeled Dirty Dick's in front of Dillon.

"Pint of Guinness," Dillon said.

The barman walked down to the end of the bar, filled a Guinness glass three-quarters full, then let it sit for a minute or two. He topped it up and set it on the coaster in front of Dillon. "Eight euros."

Dillon reached into his pocket, pulled out a ten euro note, and handed it to him. The barman waited, apparently expecting to keep the change. When Dillon didn't say anything, he shook his head and walked down to the cash register. He wandered back after five minutes. Dillon had taken two small sips from his glass. The barman set the two euro coin on the bar next to Dillon's glass.

"Oh, go ahead and keep it. I'm supposed to meet a couple of pals here tonight."

"Oh, yeah. Who's that?"

Dillon studied the barman for a moment and said, "Rory and Liam."

"They got a surname?" the barman asked.

Dillon pretended to think and then just said, "Yeah."

The barman nodded and walked away.

Dillon kept an eye on him. He stood for a few minutes, leaning against the back counter. Eventually, he stepped over to one of the men seated at the bar and said something to him. Dillon was too far away to hear what was being said, but at one point, the guy looked down the bar at Dillon.

Dillon took another sip of his pint, waited a couple of minutes, and then slid off his stool and headed toward the men's room. There were two wooden stalls that looked about ninety years old. He stepped into one, closed the door, then slipped under the interior wall and into the other stall. He had just partially closed the door on the other stall and was standing on the toilet seat when someone stepped into the restroom. He heard footsteps walk across the tile floor and stop in front of the stall with the closed door. Suddenly, there was a loud bang as the door was kicked open. "Who the hell do you—"

Dillon swung out of the stall, holding onto the door, and kicked both feet into the man's lower back. There was a quick groan cut off by his shaved head bouncing off the porcelain tank attached to the upper wall. He fell backward, and his head bounced off the tile floor. A red welt was forming across his forehead, where he had slammed into the porcelain tank. Dillon thought for half a second about checking the pockets but then decided the better idea would be to just get out of there.

There was a window on the exterior wall. He hurried over, turned the brass sash lock, and raised the window. Thankfully, it opened, and he was able to hop up into the window, gradually turn around and drop four feet to the ground. There wasn't more than a two-foot space between Dirty Dick's and the next building over, but that was all the room Dillon needed. He angled his shoulders slightly sideways and hurried toward the back of the building and the parking lot.

He slowed and peeked out. The parking lot appeared to be empty, and he hurried over to his car, slipped in behind the wheel, backed up, and drove out of the lot. As he left, he glanced in the rearview mirror but didn't see anyone.

He pulled to the curb a few blocks away and phoned Suel. "Oh, Dillon, got your note. You up for a pint? I suppose I could meet you at Dirty Dick's."

"The Autobahn would probably be better."

"You okay?"

"Yeah, interesting place. I don't think I'll be going back there anytime soon."

"But you're okay?"

"Yeah. I'll see you at the Autobahn," Dillon said and disconnected.

THIRTY-FOUR

Suel had a pint waiting on the table for Dillon when he stepped inside the Autobahn. "Oh good, you've already combed your hair," Dillon laughed as he sat down.

"Just wanted to look my best for you," Suel said. "So, tell me, what happened at Dirty Dick's?"

Dillon told him the story, starting with the pat down after entering and ending with his jump out the men's room window.

"Oh, so just an average night for the likes of you," Suel grinned, then raised his glass in a toast. "Here's to you. Nice move." They clinked glasses, took a healthy sip, and Suel asked, "Who do you think your man was?"

"The guy kicking in the bathroom stall? I don't know. The best answer would be someone maybe planning something with the Meehans. The more logical answer is he was probably just a local barfly, and me telling the barman I was waiting for Liam and Rory just pissed him off, and he figured I'd be an easy hit."

"Amazing, so you're thinking it really was Rory Meehan who told Cullen Gannon he'd give him something to remember him by?"

"Let's just say I'm still not convinced he was lying to me. I do have another bit of information that adds some credibility to Gannon's story. I got a call from Jim Burke this afternoon. In fact, it was his call that convinced me to pay a visit to Dirty Dick's. He did a face match on the two with the wheelchair. He had told me that if it came up seventy percent possible, given the blurry image, that would be a pretty strong indication it could be the Meehans.

"And did it come close to seventy percent?"

Dillon shook his head and then smiled. "No, it came up seventy-two percent."

"So, you're saying those images with the wheelchair are likely to be Liam and Rory Meehan?"

"Yeah, based on the facial recognition that Burke ran."

"And does Burke know that they're legally listed as dead?"

"Paddy, based on what we know, there's a pretty good chance that was a bogus pronouncement. I'm not suggesting it was intentionally made. But given the two individuals, it's entirely possible that it was a setup right from the get-go. The car bomb exploded on a country road in Spain. The bodies couldn't be visually identified. It could have been anyone in the car. Then a relative just happened to be in Spain visiting, and he requested an immediate cremation. The ashes are buried in Glasnevin cemetery within days. Oh, which reminds me, I'm going to be a little late coming in tomorrow."

"Oh, are you planning a night in Skerries?"

"I only wish. No, just checking on something that shouldn't take more than a half hour or so. Anyway, tell me about whatever you were up to this afternoon."

"I went back over to Ulster Bank in Palmerstown. Talked to DI Kehoe to see if he had anything new and then stopped at the bank itself and spoke with Kevin Bennett, the security man at the bank."

"Anything new?"

Suel shook his head. "Not as far as the investigation. I did find it interesting that the bank now has a security man in the lobby, supposedly keeping an eye on things."

"I guess that's an improvement of sorts."

Suel nodded and said, "Possibly, at least until something happens, say, another robbery by someone with a gun, and then he'll be raising his hands and lying on the floor with the rest of them."

Dillon shook his head and said, "I just wish we could get a lead on these two and figure out what they're up to. Why in the hell would the Meehans fake their deaths, hide for twenty years, and then come back to do what they're doing? It's crazy."

"You think those images could be relatives? Nephews, cousins, or maybe even their kids, and that's why Burke got the seventy-two percent reading?"

"He was pretty sure the seventy-two percent was due to the blurry images. Besides, the guys look like they're in their mid-fifties in all the tapes before the robberies when they're just checking the various places out."

"Would another pint help us solve this problem?" Suel asked.

Dillon shook his head. "Not that I wouldn't like one, but I think I should probably head home."

"Preaching to the choir, unfortunately," Suel said. "I'll see you in the morning. Whenever you get in, just stay safe. That knacker at Dirty Dick's was enough."

"Yeah, I wonder if he's still on the floor."

"It's the kind of place no one would think twice seeing someone on the floor. They'd just step over him once they checked his pockets."

"I'll see you in the morning," Dillon said as they stepped outside and headed for their cars.

Dillon was home two minutes later. He let Lucifer out, picked up the mail inside the door, and stepped into the kitchen. There was some cold pizza on a plate in the refrigerator, and he set that out on the counter. Both pieces of mail were addressed to the occupant, and he tossed them into recycling. He phoned Noreen and left a message, got Lucifer back in the house and gave him a biscuit, then settled in with the plate of pizza and watched the American news for fifteen minutes before he turned the station to a movie he didn't like.

THIRTY-FIVE

As usual, Dillon was up before his alarm went off. He let Lucifer out into the front garden less than an hour later and ate a leisurely breakfast. He wanted to make a stop on the way into the office, and the place didn't open until 9:00, so he grabbed the leash and took Lucifer on a short walk in Albert Park. They did two laps, which added up to a little over two miles, and then headed home. He tossed a biscuit to Lucifer, who hurried into the sitting room so he wouldn't have to share.

He backed out of his drive and took a round-about route over to Glasnevin Cemetery, probably the closest thing Ireland has to Arlington Cemetery in the US. Glasnevin Cemetery was initially known as Prospect Cemetery and was opened to the public in 1832. Dillon pulled into the parking area next to the contemporary administration building and souvenir shop. He walked into the building and over to the counter, where a young man was seated, working on his computer.

"Good morning," Dillon said.

The young man smiled and said, "Oh, American?" Dillon nodded. The young man quickly gathered four separate sheets of historical information and handed them to Dillon. "The Michael Collins grave site is just out the door and to the right. Daniel O'Connell's grave is at the base of O'Connell Tower."

"Thank you, I won't be needing that," Dillon said. "Could you give me directions to the graves of Liam and Rory Meehan, please? I believe they were installed in 2001."

"Umm, yes, sure, just a moment while I log onto the directory," he said, sitting down in front of his computer and typing. "I'm sorry. Could you give me those names again?"

"Last name is Meehan," Dillon said, spelling the name for him. "The two men are Liam and Rory."

The young man nodded as he typed, waited a moment, then tapped a key. The printer next to him suddenly started up. A sheet of paper fell out of the printer and into a tray. He grabbed the sheet and stepped back to the counter. He placed the sheet in front of Dillon and then marked the Administration building with an 'X.'

"This is where we are. You can walk to the site or drive a little further down Finglas Road to gate four and drive in. You'll take the second left, and the sites are located in the third section on your right," he said and circled an area.

"Is it all right if I leave my car out in the lot and walk down there?"

"Oh, yes, certainly. It's a long walk, but if you don't mind, well, yes, by all means."

"Thank you. Oh, one other question. Can you tell me when the burial plots were purchased?"

"Purchased?"

"Yes. I don't need a price or anything like that. I'd just like to know when the plots were purchased."

The young man seemed to think about that for a moment, and just as Dillon was about to pull out his ID, he said, "Sure, just a second." He sat back down in the desk chair. His hands flew across the keyboard, and a moment later, he half-turned in his chair and said, "Both plots were purchased at the same time, back in January of 2001."

"Okay, thanks for your help," Dillon said and headed toward the door.

"Enjoy your day," the young man called, and then watched Dillon as he stepped out of the building and walked down a path.

Dillon was aware that over eight hundred thousand people were buried in Glasnevin Cemetery. Many of them in unmarked graves during the years of the Irish famine. The gravestones were very close together, and in the area where he began walking, most were very old. So old that the letters carved in the granite stone were often illegible. As he gradually made his way through the cemetery, there were fewer and fewer tall Celtic crosses and more standard gravestones. He double-checked the area marked on the map and saw it up ahead. Not too far beyond where the Meehans were supposedly buried was an open area with no gravestones, presumably representing available plots.

The Meehan graves were opposite a rather large oak tree. They were side by side with identical black granite gravestones with gold-colored letters. With the exception of their names, Liam and Rory, the stones were virtually identical. The dates were 1966-2001 for Liam and 1968-2001 for Rory. There was nothing else on the gravestones like the words "God Bless" or "Rest in Peace." Dillon photographed both stones using his cell phone.

Not surprisingly, there was nothing that indicated a recent visitor, like wilted flowers or a small stone resting on the gravestone. He made note of the fact that, other than a government plot he passed a few sections back, the Meehan gravestones were some of the smallest in the cemetery.

He took a casual walk back to his car, comparing the Meehan plot with others along the way. Yeah, definitely smaller gravestones than every other personal plot he looked at. He climbed into his car, thought for a moment, and then headed to Headquarters. Suel was at his desk when Dillon stepped into Special Branch.

As Dillon passed Suel, he asked, "Can I talk you into a tea outside?"

"Yeah," Suel replied, drawing out the word. "Is everything okay?"

"Oh, yeah. No problem. Let's grab a tea and a coffee in the park, and I'll tell you about my visit."

"Noreen didn't tell you she was finished with you, did she?"

"What? No, nothing like that. I just had an interesting look at something, and I want to bounce it off you."

"Something about the robberies?"

"Yeah, come on, I'll tell you over a tea, and I could use a coffee."

Suel pushed his chair back, and they stepped out of the office. Since Dillon was buying, Suel got a pastry along with his large tea. Dillon got a medium-sized coffee. He paid the fourteen euro tab and tipped the woman behind the counter with a euro. They settled in at a table just vacated by a couple.

"Okay, so fill me in," Suel said over a mouthful of chocolate pastry.

"So, I keep thinking about the Meehans dying in the car blast, and I did a little history investigation. On December thirty-first, 2000, at 11:00 pm, the European Arrest Warrant stopped applying in its current form. The Dahl was planning to debate it over the coming months, but it was a pretty sure bet it would pass. It meant that if you were a criminal living in Spain, you were going to be looking at potential extradition at some point in 2001. The burial plots in Glasnevin cemetery for Liam and Rory Meehan are next to one another. They were purchased in January 2001, which turned out to be a good thing because they were supposedly killed in the bomb blast a month later in February. Their bodies were cremated twenty-four hours after the bomb blast."

"Sounds like pretty good timing," Suel said.

"Yeah, no kidding. Now tell me if this lines up with what you know of the Meehans. Other than a government site burying soldiers and those killed in the 1916 Easter Rising, the two gravestones are the smallest that I have seen in Glasnevin cemetery. They list their names, Liam and Rory Meehan, and the supposed years they lived. That's it. Nothing like rest in peace or God bless or anything."

"So what are you thinking?" Suel said.

"I'm thinking it's a setup. They manufacture their deaths. There's no way to identify the bodies. No one is going to dig up the bones and do a DNA test, and given the millions they've stolen, they live a quiet, comfortable life."

Suel nodded and took a sip of tea. "Which leaves us exactly where we were before. So, if, indeed, it's them acting like amateurs and robbing these little banks. What's their endgame? On top of not getting any serious cash, not only are they risking getting caught, but if they're caught, they will definitely be sentenced to life. What's the point?"

"If I knew that, we would probably be able to catch them in the act. Whatever the act is going to be. We just don't know what it is."

"I think what we need to do is check and see if there is something major that is scheduled to happen. A large bank moving to a new location, a major transaction, maybe some sort of government thing where they would be moving cash. God, do they even do that anymore? Move cash. Hell, even I'm using my credit card on a three or four-euro purchase. I'm not disputing your idea," Suel said. "I'm actually on board. I just don't know where this is headed. A retirement plan or something?"

"More like some kind of a retirement scheme. Maybe we check with some financial folks, see what's going on. Is the government doing some kind of trade deal with another country? Maybe they're setting something up with the UK after their Brexit fiasco." Dillon shook his head. "Are we at least together on the thought that the Meehans are still alive and most likely in Ireland cooking up some sort of scheme?"

Suel nodded. "Yeah, I'd say it's a pretty sure bet."

"Thanks for the support, Paddy. I just wish I knew what it was they're up to."

"Let's draw up a list of potential people we can at least talk to. My sense is that, in today's world, we're not looking at something that might be a couple million euros. I'm thinking it's more like ten or twenty million or more."

"Yeah, but back to your earlier point, just think of transporting something like that. Are they going to rob someplace using a semi-truck?"

"I don't know, maybe a helicopter?"

Suel shook his head. "It still doesn't make any sense."

"Let's go back and start talking to people," Dillon said.

THIRTY-SIX

They started making phone calls talking to individuals at the Irish Central Bank, three major real estate developers, the finance guy at EU Google, a hospital, and Ryan Air. Suel went out and got burritos for lunch. They worked the phones throughout the afternoon and still came up empty-handed.

Dillon had just gotten off the phone with someone from Amazon Ireland, who basically laughed at his suggestion and asked for a phone number to call back just to make sure Dillon was actually with An Garda Síochána. Toward the end of the day, his cell phone rang, and he took it out of his pocket, praying it wasn't an alert to another robbery. Fortunately, the screen displayed Noreen's name.

"Hey, how are you?" was how he answered.

"I'm good. More importantly, how are you? I saw the call from you the other day and meant to call back, but we've just been crazy here at work. I hope you aren't mad at me. I'm sorry that I didn't—"

"Noreen, relax. There's no problem other than it's just been yet another day from hell with no end in sight."

"Oh, dear, it sounds like we could trade stories."

"You aren't kidding. Say, would you have time tonight to get together? Right now, I feel like you are one of, if not the only bright spot in my life, and I would love to see you."

"Oh, that is so sweet. Yes, I would love to see you, too. How about this? I'll meet you at your house, so you don't have to drive out to mine. I'll pick up something for dinner, probably Thai. Your job will be to get the wine. I want it just to be the two of us. No one else, and then you can cook me breakfast."

"That sounds wonderful. Would half-past six work for you?" Dillon asked.

"It would work wonderfully. I'll see you then. Don't forget the wine. Later, darling," she said and then made a kissing sound on the phone and disconnected.

Once Dillon set his cell phone down, Suel called over, "We're not being summoned to another robbery, are we?"

"No, just a dinner invite with Noreen. God love her. You talk to anyone with an idea?"

"Not really, just a number of folks who thought I was wasting their time. What about you?"

Dillon shook his head. "Pretty much the same thing. As a matter of fact, I spoke to a guy at Amazon who wanted my number so he could call me back. He thought I was someone working a scam."

"Unfortunately, not far from the truth."

"Well, when he called back, we had about a two-minute conversation, and he said he had nothing to tell me and hung up."

Suel laughed at that.

Dillon left the office just after 5:00 and hurried home to get things ready for Noreen's arrival. He took Lucifer on a brief walk, bought wine at the Grape Vine, changed the sheets on the bed, showered, and arranged crackers and cheese on a plate for hors d'oeuvres. He was peeking out the window when Noreen pulled up in front. He opened the front door as she stepped out of her car. "Oh my, the perfect host."

"No, you're just the best thing to happen since the last time I saw you."

"Oh, thank you," she said, looking stunned. She hurried into the front garden carrying a little overnight bag and stepped onto the stoop. She gave him a lingering kiss, then handed him a paper bag. "Here, I worked all afternoon making this stir-fry dinner."

Dillon peeked in the bag, "Oh, wow. Good thing you had those two plastic trays to put it in and the two little white boxes for the rice."

"Let me in. It's been one of those days where I might need more than one glass of wine."

"Oh, don't get me started. Come on in, grab a seat, and let me wait on you."

He got another kiss for that last comment. They unloaded about their days over a glass of wine. Eventually, Dillon placed the rice and stir fry in two bowls, warmed them in the microwave, and placed them on the kitchen counter. He refilled the wine glasses, and they chatted about everything and nothing over dinner. He opened a second bottle of wine for dessert. They talked as Dillon loaded the dishwasher and twice ordered Noreen not to help with the cleanup.

They had a final glass of wine upstairs in bed before he turned off the lights. They had an exhausting interlude, then fell asleep with their arms wrapped around one another. Dillon was up before the alarm went off. He tiptoed out of the bedroom and headed down to the kitchen to get ready for breakfast. He organized the makings of French toast and then went onto his laptop. He let Lucifer out into the front garden and turned on the kettle for Noreen's tea. Once he heard her turn off the shower, he brought a tea up to the bedroom.

She was downstairs twenty minutes later, looking gorgeous and handing him the empty tea mug. "Oh, thank you. That was just what I needed."

"Well, you were, or rather are, just what I needed. The world appears to be a little bit brighter today. Thank you. Now, do you have time for breakfast? I was going to make French toast. It will only take a couple of minutes."

"I'd be foolish not to make time. Could I coax you into making another tea for me?"

"Happy to do so. I'll let you add the milk," he said and handed her the eyedropper he'd used earlier. He turned the kettle on and turned on the stove for the French toast.

Noreen made her tea, and Dillon served up the French toast a few minutes later. They had a pleasant chat over breakfast. Noreen casually mentioned she left a couple of things on his dresser. Dillon walked her to the door, where they had a three-minute round of kisses, and then she thanked him again and went out to her car. Dillon stood in the doorway, watching until she drove out of sight.

He let Lucifer out into the front garden, quickly cleaned up the kitchen and then hurried upstairs to shave. As he stepped into the bedroom, he stopped and stared at the bottles and containers of powders, lipsticks, facial creams, skin creams, moisturizing soap, eye makeup, perfume, two brushes, two combs, and a makeup mirror. It all brought a smile to his face, and he made a mental note to start looking for a makeup table.

He let Lucifer back in, tossed him a biscuit, and headed to Special Branch. He had just settled in at his desk when Suel entered the office. He walked toward his desk and then stopped and stared at Dillon.

"From the look on your face, I'm going to make a wild guess and suggest that you met up with Noreen last night."

"I did, and it was wonderful. We were both exhausted from work, and it was so nice just to have a pleasant conversation with a very nice lady who seemed just as happy to be with me as I was to be with her."

"You better watch it, Dillon, or you're liable to fall in love."

"I got news for you, Paddy. I think I may already be there."

THIRTY-SEVEN

Dillon had spent most of the morning making more frustrating, worthless phone calls. His cell phone rang. *Perfect timing*, he thought and pictured beautiful Noreen on the line. He glanced at the screen only to see that the call was from Emergency Response. "Marshal Dillon," he answered. "North Wall Quay? Shots? Hostages? How many? Jesus, over twenty? Got it. On my way," he said. He glanced over at Suel and shook his head. He was about to say something as Suel placed his cell phone next to his ear.

Dillon stood and attached the holster with his 9mm pistol to his belt. He opened the bottom drawer on his desk, pulled out his protective vest, and began to strap it on. He draped his lanyard with his ID around his neck, turned on the radio attached to the vest, and stepped over to Suel.

Suel shook his head, tossed his phone on the desk, and stood. "I think our questions about what their plan is have just been answered."

"You think it's them? The Irish Central Bank, and they've taken at least twenty hostages? For starters, the bank has security."

"I'd guess there's more than the idiot Meehan brothers involved. The other thing is due to budget cuts, Central Bank recently hired outside security," Suel said as he strapped on his vest.

"Budget cuts and they reduced security? You gotta be kidding me."

"I wish I was, but sorry to say it's the real deal."

"Are they armed, this security?"

"I hope so, but I don't know that for a fact. Maybe we'll find out on the way. Let's go. I'm taking a vehicle from the motor pool."

As they headed out the door, two more officers were pulling on protective vests. Dillon figured there was a good chance all of Special Branch would be called out. They hurried down to the motor pool. Suel signed out a squad car, and fifteen minutes later, they were driving out of the parking lot. Four more Special Branch officers were in the motor pool as they left.

"You think this is the Meehans?" Dillon asked again as Suel pulled out of the lot with the lights flashing and the siren going.

"I think there's a pretty good chance. We haven't heard from them for a few days, and now this, the Central Bank and hostages. This isn't just another little bank. This is the Central Bank for the entire Republic. They're bound to have a hundred of us called up."

"I'll make some phone calls while you're driving to see what we can find out about the security."

Dillon ended up leaving two messages with people and then, on a whim, phoned Maeve Byrne in the PR department.

"Maeve Byrne."

"Hi, Maeve, this is Jack Dillon. Hey, I've got a question for you."

"Another blurb to post and send out to news stations?"

"No, thankfully. I heard something the other day about the Irish Central Bank facing a budget cut, and they hired an outside security agency. Do you know anything about that?"

"Only what I've heard on the news. Which is, yes, they did have to hire an outside agency. In fact, I believe this may have gone into effect just this week. You just have to shake your head and wonder. I guess we're spending too much on five-star hotel suites when our politicians go to Brussels."

"Probably not far from the truth, okay, sorry to bother you."

"Not a bother, Dillon. Call any time."

Suel drove along the Liffey River, zipping left and right past vehicles as they pulled over. They were listening to the radio traffic. There had been a perimeter established around the Central Bank Building. Nothing was mentioned regarding bank security except that they were among the hostages taken. Suel slowed as three men strolled across the street and onto the O'Connell

Street Bridge. He leaned on the horn, causing one of the men to jump out of the way.

"Bleedin' knackers," he shouted as he sped through the intersection. They drove past four more bridges but, thankfully, didn't have a problem. They sped past the Famine Memorial and the Jeanie Johnston ship that played a part in over a million people fleeing the country back during the Great Famine. The road was blocked up ahead, just past the Samuel Beckett Bridge. Suel turned off the siren and pulled over to the side. Four officers were in the process of diverting traffic.

Suel lowered his window as an officer approached and said, "I'm sorry, sir, but you can't park here."

"Yeah, I hear all sorts of chatter on the radio. Is there anywhere we're supposed to check in?"

"Take the Beckett Bridge across the river and head down Rogerson's Quay. Someone will direct you over there. Leave the siren off and keep your flashers on."

"Okay, thanks, and stay safe," Suel said.

"Yous too," the officer said. He held up his hand, stopping three cars to give Suel a chance to back up and turn onto the Beckett Bridge. As they crossed the Liffey, Dillon glanced out the rear window and saw squad cars blocking the street on either side of the eight-story Central Bank building. He leaned forward to look past Suel and out the driver's window. Two police boats were on the Liffey River, theoretically blocking any traffic heading down the river and out into the Irish Sea. Suel took a left at the end of the bridge onto Rogerson's Quay and headed toward two squad cars in the middle of the street two blocks down.

"You find it interesting that we're close to Dirty Dick's pub where Callum Gannon supposedly met the Meehan brothers? By the way, we're just two or three blocks from the AIB bank on Hanover Quay, where the Meehans pulled their first robbery."

"Maybe that's where they saw the Central Bank and decided they should hit it."

"I got a feeling they were well aware of the Central Bank long before they hit AIB," Dillon said.

Suel pulled alongside the two squad cars blocking the street. "Any idea where we're supposed to go?" he asked as an officer approached.

"Take a right and head up Forbes Street. Take your first left, that's Horse Fair, and everyone is meeting up in the parking lot."

"I get the feeling we didn't have to rush down here," Dillon said as they pulled away.

"They'll probably have us out in front of one of these apartment buildings making sure residents don't step outside. What an absolute mess."

Suel pulled into the parking lot, where a couple dozen officers were milling around, all in protective vests. He parked in the first space he saw, which turned out to be the last available parking spot in the lot, and they climbed out of the car.

"Welcome, Suel," someone called, and they headed toward a group of four officers.

"Donny, good to see you. Hey, this is my partner, Jack Dillon," Suel said.

Dillon nodded and said, "Hi."

"What the hell is going on? Is anyone in charge?" Suel asked as he looked at all the officers milling around the parking lot.

"Not that we can tell. We've been here for over twenty minutes. More officers keep arriving, but no one seems to have any idea of what we're supposed to do."

"We're clear across the Liffey from the Central Bank. If the plonkers ran out the front door, we'd never be able to catch them," Suel said.

"Yeah, I don't know if they've got teams in the back of the bank. We've heard they've been slowly getting employees from the upper floors out of the building."

"We heard they have hostages," Dillon said.

"Yeah, we heard that too. More than twenty, but we don't know how many more. One, two, ten? We're thinking if we don't hear something soon, we'll walk back over and set up a perimeter around the back of the place. They can always use more men."

Suel looked over at Dillon and said, "Sounds like a plan rather than wasting our time standing around back here."

Fifteen minutes later, a sergeant climbed up on a two-foot brick planter and signaled with his hand for conversations to stop and for everyone to move in closer. A moment later, he grabbed the microphone on his vest and said, "We're going to form into four groups. We'll cross the Beckett Bridge on foot, and the team over there will direct us to man a defensive perimeter along the sides and the back of the Central Bank Building. Leave a two-minute interval between groups. I'll direct the crossing from the corner of Rogerson's Quay. We just received word that five hostages have been released. I believe they are all part of the new bank security team. Cross your fingers, and let's hope we can get more individuals released. All right, form up in four ranks," he said and hopped down from the planter.

"Nothing like flying by the seat of our pants," Suel said as they lined up.

THIRTY-EIGHT

Once in line, they headed out of the parking lot and walked down to Rogerson's Quay. The sergeant was leading and stopped once they reached the quay. "Don't run, lads, but don't drag your asses either. They'll direct you on the far side of the bridge. We have a team on the phone with them now. First team, maintain a distance between one another. Questions? All right, stay safe, gentlemen. Go!"

They walked quickly, not quite running, and keeping a ten-foot distance between each other for a block and a half to the Samuel Beckett Bridge. The bridge was a contemporary cable-stayed structure for both cars and pedestrians. Dillon kept his eye on the Central Bank building as they moved across the bridge. Not that he could do anything other than run if someone started shooting. They were met on the far side of the bridge by an individual who led them to Mayor Street Upper and then over three blocks to the rear of the Central Bank Building.

There were three Early Response Units stationed behind the building. Barricades had been erected along the street so no vehicles would be able to enter or leave. Dillon, Suel, and the rest were spread out across a small side street that was more like an alley on the far side of the Central Bank Building.

Two hours later, five more hostages were released, this time two pregnant women and three elderly individuals. One of whom was a man with a walker. Helicopters were continually flying over, not all of them An Garda Síochána. There were two that appeared multiple times and were with the Home Defense Force, the Irish Army. One helicopter, painted red, was from a news organization. It appeared only once and then was escorted away by an An Garda Síochána chopper. The afternoon dragged on, and nothing happened, at least where Dillon and Suel had been stationed.

Toward the end of the afternoon, Dillon's stomach growled, not for the first time.

"You and me both," Suel said.

They were able to take restroom breaks in the building behind them, and later that evening, Dillon wandered into the building, paid a visit to the restroom, and went back outside. Instead of taking up his position again, he walked in the opposite direction toward two squad cars blocking the street. As he approached, an officer stepped out of the squad car and called, "What can we do for you?"

"I'm with close to a dozen guys, and none of us have had anything to eat or drink. You have any idea what's going on?"

The officer shook his head. "I feel your pain, literally. We're in the same situation. They're still talking with these plonkers. I guess that's the good news. But other than that, we're in the dark, just like your lot. I wish I could help you, but we've been told to stay put."

"Okay, thanks for the update," Dillon said. As he hurried back to his spot, it was beginning to turn to dusk. He wondered if maybe the Meehans or whoever was in the bank would try to make a break once it was dark. But that would be next to impossible. There had to be close to a hundred officers stationed around the building. He settled into the same place he had been for the last nine or ten hours.

"What'd you do, take a nap or get something to eat?" Suel asked.

"I only wish. No, I talked to some guys stationed down on the corner. They know about as much as we do, which is nothing."

"Some of the men were talking. Rumor has it they're about to give up."

Dillon shook his head. "If it's the Meehans in there, and I'm pretty sure it is, that doesn't sound like them."

"Well, unless they can fly, there's no way out for them. Even then, the choppers would get 'em," Suel said just as a chopper slowly passed along the Liffey with a large spotlight illuminating the area in front of the Central Bank Building.

"I have a very bad feeling we are going to be here all night," Dillon said.

"We should have brought sleeping bags," Suel replied.

Dillon dozed off more than once for ten or fifteen minutes before he was back awake. He counted four large spotlights now illuminating the front and back of the Central Bank building. It was just before 4:00 in the morning when a handful of people ran out of the front entrance of the building. A voice shouted at them to raise their hands and walk toward one of the spotlights. As they approached, another group of people hurried out of the building with hands raised, following the first group.

"You two," a voice shouted, "give us a hand with this lot. We have to pat them down and move them out of the way."

Dillon and Suel followed the officer over to the spotlight. Three men and two women were approaching with their hands raised. One of the women stepped over to Dillon and said, "Please pat me down. I just want to get home. This has been fecking awful." Her face had tear stains in her makeup, and although it wasn't cold, she was shivering slightly.

He lightly patted her down, thinking that's all he needed after spending the better part of sixteen hours out here only to be served with a complaint of indecent action patting her down. He quickly ran a light hand over her back, stomach, and hips and pointed her toward a group assembling further down the street.

More people were coming out of the bank as two Emergency Response Units hurried into the building.

"This is bullshit. Come on, something's got to be happening," Suel said and hurried toward the building.

The bank lobby was just inside on the main floor and off to the right. A handful of people were stepping out of the area, all with their hands raised. Emergency Response officers were in the large lobby. More officers were behind the teller counter and working through the office areas. Dillon and Suel stepped back behind the teller counter and looked around. The cash drawers were still in place. One of the drawers was partially open, exposing a tray still filled with cash. It appeared to have been untouched.

"The vault," Dillon said, and they made their way toward the back of the area and the open Central Bank vault door.

There were three officers inside the large vault as Dillon and Suel stepped in. One of the Emergency Response officers said, "There's no one in here. They must be in the group of folks stepping out front."

Dillon looked around. There were a number of four-wheel carts stacked with empty metal containers. More empty containers were stacked four high against the vault walls. Loose twenty, fifty, and hundred-euro notes were scattered across the floor.

"These containers are all empty. If they took the cash out of these, they wouldn't be sneaking out the front. They'd never get away with it. Look at all these containers. They could never carry it all."

"Then they're still in the building, on the upper floors. Let's go," he said, and the three of them hurried out of the vault.

"Something's not right," Suel said. And began moving a stack of empty metal cases away from the wall. From the floor up six feet, the wall was filled with large safety deposit boxes. All of them still locked.

Dillon moved a stack of empty metal cases and found the same thing. They moved two more stacks with the same result. There were two stacks of empty cases against a far wall. Dillon went to move the first stack, and both stacks moved. They were held together by a metal cable wrapped around all eight boxes.

"I got something here, Paddy," Dillon shouted as he pushed the metal boxes to the side and stared. "Jesus Christ," he shouted and continued to stare at the hole in the side of the vault.

THIRTY-NINE

Dillon said, "Call whoever is in charge and get them back here. I'm going down that hole."

As Suel clicked the microphone on his protective vest, he replied, "Hold on a minute, Dillon. Don't you think you'd better wait until we—"

"We haven't got that kind of time," Dillon said as he pushed the stack of empty metal cases off to the side.

The opening was large, two feet wide by three feet high. Dillon slipped in feet first and worked his way onto a gradual incline. A string of small round lights was attached to the upper right corner of the little tunnel and illuminated it just enough so you weren't completely in the dark. He couldn't quite sit up, but it wasn't completely confining, and a rubber pad led the way along the bottom of the tunnel. As Dillon crawled along the tunnel, he could hear water rushing. A moment later, his feet rested on a large concrete mound, and he realized it was a sewer line. Chunks of the concrete pipe were stacked off to the side. Dillon glanced into the pipe, then cautiously lowered his head into the large opening.

The sewer appeared at least twice as large as the short tunnel he'd just come down and obviously ran beneath the North Wall Quay and into the Liffey River. Just above the opening into the concrete pipe, a four-foot-long steel beam was buried into the ground leaning against the massive concrete sewer. A metal wheel was welded onto the steel beam with a half-inch metal cable draped around the wheel and running into the sewer line. Suddenly, things became very clear to Dillon. He pulled his cell phone from his pocket, took three quick photos, then rolled over on all fours and began to crawl back up the tunnel toward the bank vault.

He was halfway up the incline when he heard Suel's voice. "Dillon. Dillon, can you hear me?"

"On my way up, Paddy. Give me a minute," Dillon said and crawled a little faster. The light from the opening drifted down the shaft, and in no time, his head was rising into the vault, and he placed his arms against the wall to hoist himself back up. Two sets of hands took hold of his arms and lifted him out of the tunnel and onto his feet. He blinked for a moment or two, getting used to the light, and then looked around at the half-dozen men staring at him.

"What did you find down there?" a lieutenant wearing an Emergency Response vest asked.

"I'm pretty sure that's how they got out of here, and I'm willing to bet they spent a number of hours hauling the cash out that way. The tunnel runs down to a major sewer line. The sewer line runs beneath the North Wall

Quay and into the Liffey. Whoever did this hooked a cable up in the sewer, and I'd be willing to bet it runs across to the far side of the river."

"You're talking over four hundred feet."

"Okay, but this could have been done weeks ago. They bundle the cash in plastic and haul it down into the sewer and across the Liffey."

"But they would have been spotted."

"Not if they're doing it underwater. They could have air tanks and bring the euros across to the other side. Two men could make countless trips. Bring it around the corner to the Grand Canal entrance and—" Dillon thought for a moment and said, "Dirty Dick's. It all makes sense. That's where they took the cash. Dirty Dick's."

"Dirty Dick's, that sleaze pit of a pub?"

Dillon nodded. "It's right along the water. They could have someone on shore hauling it into a vehicle. Dirty Dick's. That's why the Meehans were there. That's why Rory Meehan told Calum Gannon he'd give him something to remember him by if Gannon didn't leave."

"Dirty Dick's pub?"

"Do you know it? The place is just across the Liffey. We need to get over there now," Dillon said.

"But what if—"

"Is this your ERU team?"

The lieutenant nodded.

"Look, they're probably ready to leave if they haven't left already. Let's get over there and see. If we catch them, great. If we don't, well, we're no worse. Obviously, they've left this building," Dillon said and nodded at the tunnel. "I can give you directions."

"But you're a bleedin' American."

"With all respect, sir. He knows what the hell he's talking about," Suel said.

"We need to head over there now, sir," a sergeant said.

He seemed to think for a brief moment and then said, "Yeah, let's do it. Dillon, you ride in the front seat and give directions to my driver. Double time to the vehicle, gentlemen," he said, and they followed the lieutenant on the run out to their ERU van parked back toward the Samuel Beckett Bridge. Dillon climbed into the front passenger seat, and the driver started the vehicle. A moment later, he made a U-turn on the North Wall Quay and sped toward the bridge. He skidded around the patrol car blocking the street and picked up speed crossing the bridge.

"Take a left at the end of the bridge and follow that to the end, where you'll take a right. Is there a way to talk to the team in the back?" Dillon asked.

"That receiver over your right shoulder."

Dillon pulled the receiver off the wall and said, "LT, can you hear me?"

"What's up?"

"We'll stop in about sixty seconds. We'll be in front of a building. I'm thinking we break into two teams, go around either side of the building, and we can come onto the rear parking lot from two directions. If they're still there, that's where they'll be."

"Yeah, we're on it."

"Stay safe," Dillon said and hung the receiver back on the wall just as the driver turned off the lights and raced around the corner and up Stevens Walk. "Yeah, that building up on the left, stop in front of it. Once we're out, back up and block the entrance to the parking lot."

As they pulled to a stop, Dillon heard the rear door of the van open. He opened the passenger door and hopped out.

"You stay safe, lad," the driver almost whispered.

FORTY

Dillon slipped out of the passenger seat and joined the team at the rear of the van. They were in two small teams, and the lieutenant directed Dillon and Suel into different teams with a wave of his hand. He gave a nod, and the teams jogged in opposite directions, stopping at opposite corners of the building until both teams were lined up in position. Once they were set, the lieutenant waved his hand, and they headed around the corners of the building, stopping at the far end. The lieutenant slowly peeked around the corner and gave a thumbs-up. He held his hand up and raised a finger as he spoke into his radio, followed by two more fingers a couple of seconds apart. They charged around the corner of the building as the third finger went up.

Dillon was at the back of the line. As he rounded the corner of the building, he saw a small box truck in Dirty Dick's empty parking lot fifty yards ahead. Two men were just stepping out of Dirty Dick's back door. They were each carrying what looked like plastic bags with handles. The bags appeared to be stuffed with currency.

One of the men seemed to stare for a long moment before he shouted something, dropped his bags, turned, and ran back inside Dirty Dick's. A shaved head suddenly popped around from inside the back of the truck.

For a half-second, Dillon thought the man looked familiar. A moment later, the man produced a pistol and fired two rounds. One of the officers ahead of Dillon stopped, aimed his rifle, and fired three automatic bursts. They pinged as they hit the side of the truck, and the man fell out onto the pavement. He bounced as he hit the ground face-first and remained still.

The glass broke from a rear window of the pub as a short burst was fired. The burst was immediately answered by the officers. Three or four bursts shattered the glass. One of the ERU men charged toward the box truck. He pulled a large knife out and slit the front tire on the driver's side of the truck so it couldn't drive off. Two men were on either side of the rear door into Dirty Dick's, and three others disappeared around the corner toward the front of the pub. Suel and another officer were standing at the back of the truck, shouting at someone apparently still inside the cargo box.

Dillon approached, ready to help, as a man walked backward out of truck with his hands raised. Dillon kept his pistol aimed at the man while Suel cuffed his hands behind his back and patted him down. Dillon checked the man with the shaved head on the ground for a pulse but couldn't find one. He rolled the body over and recognized him as the man who had tried to assault him in the men's room the night he was at Dirty Dick's, only now the welt on his forehead had been replaced by a bullet hole.

He caught up with the two officers just as they headed in the back door. They moved cautiously down a hall toward the main barroom, passing two large plastic bags filled with euros. The barroom was empty, and the front door was slowly closing.

Two shots were suddenly fired outside, and everyone ducked, although the shots were apparently aimed in a different direction. They spread out as they entered the empty barroom. One of the officers headed out the front door and immediately fired.

An officer fired three bursts through a front window, shattering the glass, and a moment later, it was quiet. Dillon followed the two officers out the front door. Two men were on their knees with their hands in the air. The sergeant and another team member were in the process of handcuffing the men while a third member kept his weapon aimed at them.

The lieutenant was off to the side and on his knees, apparently giving first aid to a redheaded man, and Dillon wondered if he might be one of the Meehan brothers. Just off to the right, a man was face down on the ground. Based on the wounds and the blood, he wasn't going anywhere. In the distance, a line of flashing lights and sirens was making its way across the Samuel Beckett Bridge. Dillon stepped over to the body on the ground.

The hair on the back of the man's head was gray, speckled with hints of red. He leaned over and looked at the face, bushy gray eyebrows. He stared for a long moment and then hurried back inside and out the back door. Suel and another officer had the handcuffed individual lying face down in the parking lot.

"You okay?" Dillon asked as Suel looked over at him.

"Yeah, what's it like out front? We heard the shooting."

"Everyone's okay. It looks like one dead. I'm guessing it's Liam Meehan, and there's another down. Red hair, so possibly Rory Meehan. The LT was giving him first aid," Dillon said as the noise from the sirens suddenly grew much louder.

In what seemed to be just a minute or two, there were twenty or thirty other officers on the scene. A half-hour after that, two officers were busy photographing the cargo box stuffed with plastic bags of cash. Another one was out front photographing the dead body, while another was photographing the plastic bags in Dirty Dick's hallway.

Most of the officers, Dillon and Suel included, were standing off to the side, discussing what they'd seen. The cash, and there was lots of it, had apparently been brought over by someone or a number of someone's swimming below the surface of the Liffey River. Two wet suits and four air tanks were located in the back room of Dirty Dick's. What was even more surprising was the whiskey and Guinness glasses scattered along the bar. Testimony to the little celebration the group had been having. If they hadn't taken the time to celebrate, there was a pretty good chance they could have loaded the box truck and escaped.

The sun had been up for over an hour. Reporters and cameras were in a taped-off area in front of the building next door. Dillon and Suel were waiting to be interviewed and make their statements. The ERU lieutenant suddenly waved them over and introduced them to some higher-ups in dress uniforms, no doubt here to talk to reporters. Maeve Byrne was not among them. Dillon thought the rank on their uniform epaulets indicated a Chief Superintendent and a Deputy Commissioner. Dillon had met the Deputy Commissioner, Sean Tully, a year or two ago.

"These are the two officers I was telling you about, sirs," the lieutenant said. "DI Paddy Suel and Marshal Jack Dillon, both with Special Branch. If they hadn't found that hole in the vault, we'd still be going through the Central Bank building looking for these knackers. It was Dillon who thought they might have brought the cash here to the pub. God bless, but if they hadn't stopped for a pint, this lot could have gotten away with millions."

The Chief Superintendent's name tag read Mahon. He took a half-step forward and said, "Much appreciated, gentleman. As you know, your name won't be mentioned to the media. No telling who might still be waiting for this lot to arrive with all this cash, but you'll get the good word within the department. You're okay, no damage?" Dillon and Suel nodded. "Good. We'll leave you to your duties, Lieutenant. Thank you," he said, and they both flashed a salute.

The lieutenant, Suel, and Dillon returned the salute. Once they left, Dillon asked, "The redheaded man you were giving first aid to, was he by any chance a Meehan?"

The lieutenant looked surprised and nodded. "Yes, as a matter of fact, he was. Rory Meehan. I think they were taking him to the Mater. With any luck, he'll recover and stand trial. His brother wasn't that lucky."

"Liam Meehan?" Dillon asked.

"Yeah, he took two or three bursts through that window. It's a shame. I would have liked to see him locked up for life. God, but isn't it the damnedest thing? Moving all of that money across the Liffey."

FORTY-ONE

It was just after noon before Dillon made it home. He'd been awake for over thirty hours and had to pinch himself more than once so he didn't fall asleep behind the wheel on his drive home. Lucifer met him at the front door and immediately jumped over the front stoop and assumed the position. Dillon gathered two days' worth of mail at the front door and stumbled into the kitchen, where he was greeted by two of Lucifer's deposits. He couldn't blame Lucifer. The poor little guy hadn't been outside since early yesterday morning. At least he'd been decent enough to use the tile floor in the kitchen. Dillon cleaned up the mess, filled the food and water dishes, and coaxed Lucifer back inside with a biscuit and a long head scratch.

He headed upstairs and debated taking a shower. The next thing he knew, it was almost 7:00 in the evening. He was still dressed, with his shoes on, and waking up on top of his bed.

Lucifer was next to him and licked the side of his face as Dillon rolled over. He remained there for several minutes, then slowly rolled off the bed and undressed. A long hot shower seemed to bring him around. He pulled on sweatpants and a sweatshirt and headed downstairs. Lucifer was waiting next to the front door. Dillon let him out into the garden, then wandered into the kitchen. A plate with the bones of two chicken drumsticks was on the counter, but he had no recollection of eating them earlier. There was a plate with three pancakes in the refrigerator. He microwaved them, covered them with maple syrup, and ate them while standing at the counter. He debated making coffee, decided against it, grabbed the leash instead, and stepped into the front garden. At the sight of the leash, Lucifer ran to his side, and they headed out on a long walk.

Once they were back home, Dillon settled in front of the TV. He phoned Noreen and ended up leaving a message. He watched the news coverage of the Central Bank robbery, including some scenes filmed at Dirty Dick's on the evening news. The two officers in dress uniforms that they had met were interviewed. An Garda Síochána was portrayed as preventing a national embarrassment and saving the country from a potential economic disaster. He checked his phone for a message from Noreen, didn't see anything, and went upstairs to bed.

He felt well rested when the alarm woke him the following morning. Arriving at the office early, he responded to a number of congratulatory emails from workmates and friends. Suel arrived a half-hour later with two pastries, and they settled in the break room and rehashed the events of the past forty-eight hours. They were scheduled for more interviews at 10:00. Just a procedural matter and nothing to worry about.

After the interviews, the eight Special Branch members who had been at the Central Bank met for lunch in Phoenix Park. They sat in the sunshine and, in the case of Dillon and Suel, ate their burritos. They compared stories, all pretty much the same, and then decided that it made sense to meet at the end of the day in the Autobahn pub. Just after 3:00, Dillon received a phone call from Jim Burke in the Tech Department.

"Hi, Jim, what's up?" Dillon answered.

"Just wanted to let you know I received confirmation from Dublin morgue. One of the victims in the Dirty Dick's event has been confirmed as Liam Meehan."

"Good to hear that. I thought that might be the case. I was able to look at him for a moment, and the term bushy gray eyebrows seemed accurate. His brother Rory was wounded. I believe they took him to the Mater, but I don't know that for sure, and I don't have any information on his status at this point. Say, thanks again for all your help on this case. Without you isolating those images of the two brothers and the wheelchair, there's a good chance they'd be resting easy on bags filled with cash."

"You ever get a number on how much they stole?"

"No, never heard anything, but based on what we saw, it was millions, many millions. The thing that still doesn't make any sense is that they actually got away with all that cash, and then they stopped and celebrated with a pint or two, which gave us just enough time to catch up to them in the pub."

"Yeah, Dirty Dick's. I'm guessing they might be looking at being closed down. Still, it's nothing but crazy. All they had to do was load up and drive off," Burke said.

"Thank God they didn't."

"Well, congratulations to you and all the guys who were there."

"And to you, too, Jim. If you hadn't sorted through those millions of hours of tapes, we wouldn't have had any idea."

"Put a win down for both of us," Burke said and disconnected.

Theoretically, Dillon, Suel, and the rest of the officers who participated were on desk duty. Dillon left early to take Lucifer for a walk before he met up at the Autobahn pub with the group.

It was a sunny afternoon. He let Lucifer out into the front garden while he changed into a short-sleeved shirt and grabbed the leash. He placed a call to Noreen, left another message, and figured she was probably having one of those days. The last thing she needed was Dillon suggesting it would be a good idea if he drove out to Skerries and they spent the night together.

The officers met up at the Autobahn and were treated to a free round of Guinness. A patron bought a second round, and a number of people thanked them for their efforts. They ordered dinner, followed by a third round, and suddenly Dillon was home and ready for bed. He settled in with Lucifer to watch the evening news and then made their way up to bed.

The following morning, Dillon pulled into the Headquarters' parking lot just as Suel was stepping out of his car. They walked over to Phoenix Park, and Dillon paid for the tea, coffee, and two raspberry-filled pastries. He left another message with Noreen, this time asking if everything was all right and to please call him. The day was spent closing a series of files connected to the Central Bank robbery. Dillon agreed to meet Suel for a pint at the Autobahn after he took Lucifer for a short walk.

He'd just parked and turned off his car in front of the Autobahn when his cell phone rang. He glanced at the screen. Thankfully, it was Noreen finally returning his calls.

"Noreen, is everything all right? I've been worried about you. Hello? Noreen, are you there?"

"Yes. Yes, I'm here. I've been busy."

"Are you okay? You don't sound—"

"No, I'm not okay. I've been making funeral arrangements for one of my uncles and trying to see my other uncle in the hospital. But I can't get in to see him."

"What the hell happened? Were they in a car accident? A house fire?"

"Stop it. Stop it. Stop it," she screamed.

"Noreen, what happened? Are you all right?"

"Why do you even care? You did this. You and your, your—" She suddenly began sobbing.

"Noreen, what happened? What are you talking about? I've been dealing with the Central Bank robbery. We caught the gang in the act. We recovered the money and—"

"Yes, and you killed Uncle Liam and shot Uncle Rory in the process. Liam's dead, Dillon. I hope you're happy. He's dead," she sobbed. "They won't release his body, and I can't get in to see Rory. They won't let anyone in to see him. What are they doing to him? What?"

"They're just making sure he recovers, Noreen. They're, God—Liam and Rory Meehan are your uncles?"

"Oh, so now I'm suddenly guilty because my uncles are, are—" She started sobbing again, and suddenly the line went dead. Dillon called back, but his call was dumped into voicemail. He called two more times and got the same result.

There was a knock on the driver's window, and Dillon looked up. Suel was laughing and giving him the finger but then stopped and signaled with his hand to open the door.

"Are you okay?" Suel said as Dillon opened the door, shaking his head. "Dillon, what happened? What's going on?"

"Noreen, she was crying and screaming on the phone. She was—"

"Do we need to call the Skerries station?" Suel asked as he pulled his phone out.

"What? No, no, that's not going to help. It's her uncles. Paddy, her fecking uncles are Liam and Rory Meehan."

"Get the hell—are you serious? The Meehans are her uncles?"

"That's what she said. I've been trying to reach her for the last two days. She never answered my calls, never called me back. I thought she was probably just tied up with work. She just called me back now. All upset. Liam's dead, and she can't get in to see Rory. Is he still at the Mater?"

"Yeah, at least as far as I know. Probably still in intensive care. Are you sure? She told you those two were her uncles?"

Dillon nodded. "That's what she said. She's trying to make funeral arrangements for Liam, and she can't get in to see Rory."

"Jesus Christ, I don't believe it."

"Join the club," Dillon said.

FORTY-TWO

Suel had a pint of Guinness while Dillon tried to get his head around Noreen's phone call. He debated driving out to Skerries, and Suel convinced him that might not be the best idea just now. He was home forty-five minutes later and slept fitfully through the night. He was up an hour before his alarm went off and was the first one in his office. For a change, he wore a light-blue button-down shirt, a dark-blue sport coat, and gray trousers. He waited until half-past nine. Suel still wasn't in, and Dillon took the elevator up to the top floor and entered the office of Deputy Commissioner Sean Tully.

There was a front office with a couch, two chairs, and a coffee table. Two framed paintings hung on the walls. One was a view of the Four Courts building from across the Liffey River. The other was a painting of the GPO, the General Post Office building on O'Connell Street.

A female officer was seated at the desk opposite the couch and chairs. Dillon caught a glimpse of Deputy Commissioner Tully in his office as he approached the female officer at the desk.

She looked up, flashed a half-second smile, and said, "May I help you?" Sounding surprised to see him in the office.

"I'm Marshal Jack Dillon. I'm attached to Special Branch, and I met Deputy Commissioner Tully. I was involved in capturing the Central Bank robbers, and I wondered if I might have a word with the Commissioner."

"And this is about what, exactly?"

"I have some information regarding two of the robbers, one of whom was killed and the other wounded."

"Shouldn't you be going through Special Branch?"

"It's a request from a family member of the robbers, and I was hoping Commissioner Tully would be able to help."

She seemed to think about that for a moment and then said, "Let me just check with Deputy Commissioner Tully. Why don't you take a seat." She stood and headed into Tully's office as Dillon headed over to the couch.

A moment later, Tully stepped out of his office and headed over to the couch. "Marshal Dillon, we meet again," he said, extending his hand.

"Sorry to bother you, sir," Dillon said as they shook hands.

"Not a bother, please, come back to my office," Tully said.

"Thank you, sir," Dillon replied and followed Tully into his office. The walls were paneled with three-foot-high dark oak wainscoting. Tully's carved wooden desk was large and stacked with files.

"Take a seat," Tully said, pointing to the two leather chairs in front of his desk. As he settled into his black leather desk chair, he said, "I take it you're on desk duty for the prescribed period."

"Yes, sir, still plenty to do. More interviews yesterday, just making sure all the information is correct."

"And if I recall, it was your idea to head across the Liffey to that pub, correct?"

"Yes, sir, at least initially. My partner and I located the hole in the bank vault that led down to a sewer line. The sewer fed into the Liffey, and the robbers, over the course of a number of hours, moved the stolen funds to the far side of the river and into a pub. It's only luck that they spent time celebrating in the pub instead of making a getaway."

"And you're related to one of the bank robbers?"

"No sir, not at all. I have a friend who is related to them. Two of the robbers were her uncles. I don't know this, but it wouldn't surprise me if they were the masterminds of this event and very nearly pulled it off."

Tully nodded, thought for a long moment, and said, "And she wants to visit them?"

"Not exactly, sir. One of the robbers, Liam Meehan, was killed in an exchange of gunfire. His body is in the Dublin Morgue. She would like to have his body released at some point. Another robber, Rory Meehan, was wounded, and she hoped that she could visit or at least receive an update on his medical condition. She is in no way suggesting that they were wrongfully arrested. I'm sure she is aware that her surviving relative—"

"Her uncle."

"—yes sir, is likely to spend the remainder of his life behind bars."

"What is this woman's name?"

"Noreen Rooney, sir."

"And do you have contact information?"

"I do, sir," Dillon said as he pulled out his cell phone. He read off Noreen's phone number and email address as Tully wrote them down. "She lives out in Skerries, sir. I don't have the address, but I can look it up and get it to you."

Tully shook his head. "We've got the phone number. It won't be a problem."

"I should tell you, sir, that these two men were career criminals." Dillon went on to tell Tully about the fake deaths in Spain, the cremations, and fake graves in Glasnevin cemetery.

"You're kidding! Really?"

"Yes, sir. I only learned about this about a week ago. We largely put it together after attempting to work facial recognition on the security tapes on four earlier robberies. Basically, what they did was rob a bank teller of a small amount of funds, more or less establishing themselves as novices. When we got word that they were in the Central Bank, everyone was convinced they were finally caught in the act, and it was only going to be a matter of time. They released a few hostages every hour or so, negotiating with us. It seemed like a foregone conclusion they'd been caught. But that all changed once we learned they had escaped across the Liffey."

"You know, Dillon, as you're saying this, I'd be interested in talking to this Rory Meehan character."

"I've never met him, sir. In fact, I only learned he and his brother were related to Miss Rooney yesterday."

"How did you learn this?"

Dillon wasn't sure what to say. He thought for a moment and said, "I was beginning a relationship with Noreen Rooney. After the robbery, I phoned her a few times just to let her know I was okay. When she finally returned my call, she was very upset and told me the Meehan brothers were her uncles, and she wanted to have Liam's body released and wanted to check on the surviving brother, Rory."

"What did you tell her?"

"I didn't have a chance to tell her anything. She was upset, and she hung up."

"Have you tried to reach her since?"

Dillon shook his head. "I didn't think that would be the best thing to do."

"Humph, can't say I blame you. I think you made the right decision. Let me check on releasing the body. I don't see a problem there. As far as visiting, that's another story. What we could do would be to get a doctor's report and pass that information on. I don't think it would be wise for the department to contact her, but we could pass on the information to you, and you could contact her."

Dillon nodded and said, "That would be great, sir. I really appreciate it."

"Tell me, Dillon, in your post statements and interviews, did the information regarding the fake deaths in Spain come up?"

"No, sir, it did not."

"Let me ask a favor in return. Would you please write up a report covering this information and send it to me? I find it nothing short of amazing."

"I'd be happy to do that. I'll get on it right away."

Tully stood and held out his hand. "Thank you, Dillon. Someone will be in touch."

"Thank you, sir," Dillon said as they shook hands. He headed out of the office, thanked the female officer at her desk, and took the elevator down to Special Branch.

As he headed for his desk, he walked past Suel, who was on the phone. Suel hung up a minute later and stepped over to Dillon. "How are you doing?"

"I'm okay. I was just up in Commissioner Tully's office talking with him."

"What were you doing up there?"

"I told him about Noreen, hoping to have the body released and wanting to see her uncle Rory."

"What did he say?"

"He's going to check into releasing Liam Meehan's body. He didn't see a problem there. As far as her visiting Rory Meehan, he didn't think that would fly. He's going to have someone call me with an update on his status, and I can pass it on to her.

"That's if she'll take your phone call."

"Yeah, there's always that. Oh, and then I told him about the fake deaths in Spain and the graves in Glasnevin cemetery. He didn't know anything about it, and he wants me to write a report on it for him."

"There you go, Dillon. You're just moving up the ladder."

EPILOGUE

It was another forty-eight hours before Dillon finally got the medical update on Rory Meehan. He'd been moved from intensive care to a private room with an officer posted at the door around the clock. Visitors weren't allowed, but Dillon had updates on the two surgeries he'd gone through, and he was expected to eventually make a full recovery.

The release of Liam Meehan's body was delayed due in large part to Dillon's report on the fake deaths back in 2001. Fingerprints and DNA matched what had been on file, which led to the question of who or what was cremated twenty-two years ago and buried in the back of Glasnevin cemetery.

Noreen finally answered Dillon's phone call. It was the fourth one he'd made since getting the information. He told her that Liam Meehan's body was available to be released and that Rory Meehan had been transferred out of intensive care and moved to a private room in the Mater Hospital. He also mentioned the around-the-clock guard and that visitors were currently not allowed.

There was a long silence, and just as Dillon was going to ask her if there was anything he could do, Noreen said, "Thank you for the information. I think it would be best if we don't contact one another again."

"Wait, Noreen. Noreen?"

But she'd hung up.

Suel had been watching and walked over. "You okay?"

Dillon swallowed the lump in his throat and seemed to consider Suel's question for a moment before he said, "Yeah, I'll be fine. I guess."

"Good, because I'm buying dinner tonight, and you're stuck with me, pal."

THE END

Thanks for taking the time to read the Jack Dillon Dublin Tale <u>Retirement Scheme</u>. If you enjoyed the book please consider leaving a review, it really, really helps. Thank you.

Check out this sample of <u>The Collector</u>, the next book in the Jack Dillon Dublin Tales series.

THE COLLECTOR

PROLOGUE

The gallery was small, just two stories in what was originally an attached house in the section of Dublin known as the Liberties. The sign above the door in gold letters read, 'Local Dublin Art.' Other than a secure entrance door, reinforced windows, and alarm sensors on the windows, not much had changed on the exterior over the last hundred and fifty years. The interior was a different story. The receptionist desk was just inside the front door where, for the cost of only five euros, a visitor could enter and examine the collection of over three hundred paintings by local Dublin artists going as far back as James Brenan (1837-1907). In fact, it was Brenan's painting entitled 'Dublin Girl' that had drawn Connor Byrne to the gallery in the first place.

Connor loved art. He had been visiting museums from the tender age of five and could never seem to get enough of them. His mother never married and broke off her relationship with Connor's father when the boy was just three. She had attempted to give him a wider picture of life, realizing that Connor appeared to be a bit of a loner. She had been correct in her assumption. If she had the funds for an examination, Connor's narcissistic disorder coupled with his antisocial personality would most likely have been identified. But it was a moot point because she didn't then, nor even now thirty years later, did she have the funds to deal with Connor's problems. He was indeed a loner, and his frequent visits to museums and galleries did nothing to change that. The visits did, however, ignite in Connor a fervent desire to obtain a personal collection. Not the easiest undertaking when one is perpetually broke and unemployed.

He smiled at the receptionist as he handed her his five euro note. She smiled back and handed him a 'Local Dublin Art' brochure. He thanked her as he stepped across the narrow hall into what had once been the sitting room. He had caught sight of a camera above the reception counter and adjusted his cap, pulling it just a bit lower.

The room he entered held over eighty works of art, from portraits and landscapes to ivory-carved figures of the holy family, not to mention a silver vase and a pair of crystal wine glasses.

Connor studied the objects intently and searched for another camera before moving to the staircase and the three rooms on the second floor. He climbed the staircase and quickly walked past all three rooms, checking to see who else was there. He didn't find anyone else and crossed his fingers in the hope that he and the receptionist were the only ones in the small gallery at the moment. He walked back to the first room, originally a bedroom.

Once again, he couldn't see a camera anywhere. A painting of Dublin Castle dated 1840 hung above the fireplace and dominated the room. Connor stood and studied the painting for almost ten minutes. As he did so, he felt himself being transported back to the sunny day and the castle courtyard with the two carriages and the elegantly dressed couples seated in the carriages. From there, he moved to a landscape of the flooded Tolka River in 1954. Once again, he felt transported and, after studying the painting for a number of minutes, felt as though his shoes and jeans were wet from the flood waters. A quick check determined that was not the case. A flintlock pistol rested in a plexiglass case on an antique side table with brass feet. More landscapes and portraits caught his attention as he moved to the middle room and, finally, the third and smallest of the three rooms.

As he stepped into the room, he looked around for a camera but didn't see one. He then focused on the painting above the fireplace. The painting was of the GPO, Dublin's General Post Office, during the 1916 Easter Rising. The painting was a study in contrasts, with flames leaping from the windows of the three-story building, screaming death and destruction, framed by a beautiful, magnificently carved gilt frame. Once again, he studied the painting for a number of minutes, and then, almost as if he heard her passionate call, he turned and focused on the James Brenan painting, 'Dublin Girl,' resting in a plexiglass case on the side table with an antique lace table runner and crystal candlestick holders.

The painting was small, just eight by ten inches, sur-rounded by a simple wood frame. The country girl with red hair seemed to call to Connor, and he stepped over. He quickly glanced at the door and the empty hallway. He pulled out his Swiss army knife and gave another quick glance at the doorway. Seeing no one, he opened a blade and slit through the adhesive on the side panel of the plexiglass case. He reached into the case, removed the framed painting, and turned it over. Four small tacks held the frame in place. Using the knife blade, he quickly removed the tacks and returned the empty frame to the plexiglass case. He slid the painting into the front of his trousers, pulled his sweater down over the painting, and headed out of the room. He walked down the hall and took the stairs to the ground floor at a normal pace. He nodded and smiled at the receptionist as he said, "Thank you."

She glanced up from the book she was reading, flashed a quick smile, and returned to her book.

Connor closed the door behind him and headed to-ward the car his mother had bought him, parked just a block away.

ONE

US Marshal Jack Dillon pulled into the security parking lot at the An Garda Síochána Headquarters building alongside Phoenix Park. As he climbed out of his car, he glanced around for Paddy Suel's car but didn't see it. Suel and Dillon were partners and close friends. It wasn't all that surprising that Suel's car wasn't there. It was still early, a good half hour before the standard 9:00 starting time, and Suel was routinely ten minutes late on any day. Not that it mattered since many were the nights they worked into the wee hours of the morning, never taking a break.

Dillon entered the building via the parking lot entrance, inputting the four-digit code number on the keypad, then walking toward the lobby and taking the elevator up to the third floor. A short walk down the hallway brought him to the Special Branch office and another keypad. He input the code, the door buzzed, and he stepped into the office. A few of the desks were occupied, and Dillon headed toward his own desk near the front of the room. He nodded toward two officers on the phone, exchanged "Morning" acknowledgments with two others, and settled in at his desk.

Initially, his desk had been the collection spot for used tea mugs, dirtied plates, and bowls. But that had stopped almost two years ago, not that he missed it. It signaled his acceptance into the hard-core unit, and he was honored.

He unlocked his desk, grabbed his coffee mug from the top drawer, and headed for the break room. Given the chance, he would have gladly strolled out to the tea and coffee truck stationed in Phoenix Park, but he and Suel were submitting paperwork to DCI McCabe later this morning requesting an arrest warrant on an individual named Lorcan Bell, and Dillon wanted to give the file one more look before submitting it.

The coffee pot was only a third full, which strongly suggested it had been on the burner since sometime yesterday. He took a chance, filled his mug, crossed his fingers, and took a sip. The finger crossing didn't work, and he turned off the coffee maker and dumped the contents of his mug into the sink, followed by what remained in the pot. He rinsed out the pot, refilled the coffee maker with water for twelve fresh cups, and turned it back on.

He wandered back to his desk, brought up the file on Lorcan Bell, a suspected Dublin art thief, and began reviewing. Bell had been on the department's radar for over two decades and seemed eternally untouchable. Dillon hoped that would end with their request for a search warrant of Bell's home and the recovery of a seventeenth-century landscape painting by Irish artist Thomas Roberts labeled 'Sunset.' It had been stolen from the Dublin Art Museum four months ago. The painting, once the property of the Vernon family in Clontarf Castle in County Dublin, was valued at upwards of four million euros.

Word of the painting in Bell's possession was made via a woman's anonymous call to An Garda Síochána. The call was then backed up by an email of the landscape painting hanging above a four-poster bed. The image was verified by staff at the Dublin Art Museum as potentially being the painting and it was confirmed that the frame on the painting appeared to be the original frame. Due to the substantial value, Dillon and Suel undertook a background investigation of Bell, where they discovered he'd been charged five different times with art thefts over the course of the past twenty years. Charges in all five cases were eventually dropped due to lack of evidence. Dillon and Suel suspected that the lack of evidence actually meant that Bell had sold the items. He hoped that the issuance of a search warrant would allow them to search Bell's home on the south side of Dublin in an area called Sandymount, one of the wealthier areas of Dublin.

He glanced up from his computer screen when he heard Suel calling out a greeting to someone toward the back of the office. Suel gave Dillon a nod as he set a bag on his desk. He grabbed his tea mug and stepped over to Dillon's desk. "Can I tear you away from your computer long enough to join me for a tea?"

"You can," Dillon said with a nod. "I just put a fresh pot of coffee on."

"You watching a cartoon on your computer?"

"I only wish. No, actually, I was going over our request for the warrant on Lorcan Bell. We have a 10:00 with DCI McCabe, and I'm crossing my fingers we can get the warrant."

Suel shook his head. "Can you imagine hanging a painting like that above your bed? We'll probably never learn who made that phone call, but I'm guessing it was an unhappy woman who spent the night in your man's bedroom and wants to get even for whatever he did or didn't do."

Dillon chuckled at that. "That list could be long. But then I think we probably all have a list like that."

"Probably, only we don't have a painting estimated at four million hanging over the bed. Well, at least I don't."

"That's right. You just have that set of pink handcuffs."

"So? Come on, I need a tea."

"That fresh pot of coffee I made should be about finished."

They sat in the break room for ten minutes discussing what the chances were they'd get the search warrant and settled on a fifty/fifty chance. An anonymous phone call and an amateur photo from someone's cell phone weren't the strongest bits of evidence, but the five previous charges over the past twenty years, even though they'd been dismissed, added some much-needed credibility.

Forty-five minutes later, they were seated in DCI McCabe's office, watching him as he went over their request.

"I'll submit this," McCabe finally said and then shook his head. "Maybe the sixth time is a charm. I was never directly involved with the previous cases, but we all felt disappointed when the charges were dismissed. Each case appeared stronger than the preceding one, but when money is no object, and your man is able to pay whatever price is necessary to avoid serving time, it's an uphill battle. I'll submit this directly, and let's all say a prayer we get the go-ahead. I'll let yous know the moment we get a response. Your man should have been locked up years ago."

"Thank you, sir," Dillon said as he and Suel stood, exchanged nods with McCabe, and stepped out of the office.

"Well, so far, so good," Suel said as they headed back to their desks. Dillon raised both hands with all his fingers crossed.

TWO

Suel was scheduled for a late afternoon appointment, and so they skipped stopping for a pint at the Autobahn. Dillon was home at a reasonable time. He slipped the leash onto his dog Lucifer's collar, and they headed out for a walk. They went up the lane to St. Pappins Road and walked the block to the shops, where they crossed Ballymun Road and headed into St. Albert Park. It was dinner time, and the foot traffic was light. They circled the park, not quite 1.2 miles, and took a second walk around. At the end of their second pass, Dillon led them on a third. Halfway through the third time around, Lucifer slowed and then sat. Dillon tugged on the leash, but Lucifer was having none of it. They settled onto a park bench for fifteen minutes, and once rested, Lucifer agreed to cut across the two playing fields, leave the park, and head home.

Dillon tossed him a biscuit once they stepped into the kitchen, and the dog hurried into the sitting room so he wouldn't have to share. Dillon made himself a grilled cheese sandwich, poured a glass of white wine, and settled in at the kitchen counter. They were upstairs in bed by half-past ten and slept through the night. Dillon was out of bed five minutes before his alarm went off.

He was halfway through his breakfast when Lucifer came downstairs. He let him out into the front garden and then filled the food and water dishes. Ten minutes later, Dillon was backing out onto the lane and heading to the office.

He and Suel worked through the morning and were about to head out to a food truck in Phoenix Park for a quick lunch when DCI McCabe stepped to his office door and called, "Dillon, Suel, a moment of your time, please."

"That was fast. Let's hope they didn't deny the warrant request," Suel said as they headed into McCabe's office.

"Well, we're about to find out," Dillon replied as they stepped across the threshold.

McCabe was seated at his desk behind two stacks of files, each a foot high. "No need to take a seat. Your assistance has been requested in Rathmines. It appears a rather vicious murder," McCabe said and handed a file to Suel. "That's your copy. Contact information is on page one. Garda have been on the scene for a couple of hours."

"We're on it," Dillon said.

"Any response on the Lorcan Bell warrant?" Suel asked.

"Nothing yet," McCabe answered as he pulled a file from the top of the stack closest to him and opened it. "Questions?"

"No sir," they said and headed out of the office.

Suel handed the file to Dillon. "I'll drive, and you can bring us up to date along the way." They headed down to the security parking lot and climbed into Suel's car. Dillon opened the file as Suel started the car.

"Give me the address."

"Number ten, Charleville Close, Rathmines."

Suel punched in the address on his GPS and waited a moment for the map to come up. The GPS displayed a map with a timeline of nineteen minutes. As Suel headed toward the parking lot exit, the GPS said, "At the next corner, turn right."

Dillon began to read the first page of the file. "The victim is a woman named Orla O'Hara. Does that name ring a bell?"

Suel seemed to think for a moment, then shook his head. "No, should it?"

"Just wondered, age 38, apparently found in her home. The unit on Charleville Close." Dillon read on for a moment before suddenly half-shouting, "Jesus Christ. She was decapitated."

"Whoa, that sounds a little on the vicious side. She have a record?"

Dillon scanned through the half-dozen pages in the file and shook his head. "Apparently not, at least no record is listed. She's single and has been employed by a financial firm for the past twelve years. Norman Financial, ever hear of them?"

Suel shook his head. "Doesn't sound familiar. A financial firm, she doesn't have a record, she's single. Maybe a crazy boyfriend or a client who didn't like his bill?"

"Someone had to be pretty pissed off to decapitate."

"Or some completely crazy knacker. I don't know, Dillon, suddenly the stolen painting is starting to look a hell of a lot better than a decapitation. Hopefully, there's a suspect we can focus on and get this off our desks."

They pulled onto Charleville Close twenty minutes later. The houses on both sides of the street were two-story attached structures. Each unit was built on top of a double garage with the entrance just next to the garage door. The front of the structure was gray and buff-colored stone. The second floor featured a modest-sized picture window, with a smaller window next to that, suggesting a sitting room with either a small kitchen or possibly a bathroom. There were three squad cars and two unmarked cars parked on the street. A van labeled Dublin Morgue was backed in front of the garage door. Suel parked three houses away, and they walked toward unit number ten. A uniformed officer stood out in front of the unit. As they headed toward the officer, Dillon pulled out his ID attached to a lanyard and draped it around his neck.

The officer quickly glanced at their IDs and opened the front door for them.

"You been inside?" Dillon asked.

The officer shook his head and said, "No, thankfully. It will be tough enough trying to get to sleep tonight knowing what's upstairs without having to see it."

They both pulled on latex gloves, stepped into the entrance, and headed up a narrow, carpeted staircase. The walls were painted a light cream color. As they climbed the stairs, a sitting room appeared off to the right, just beyond a three-foot wall. The picture window was centered on the front wall and overlooked the street. At the top of the stairs was a short hallway off to the left and an open door to the bathroom. The sitting room had a couch with a coffee table and two upholstered chairs facing a flat-screen TV on a side table against the far wall. Next to the TV was a framed copy of the Mona Lisa painting, only this Mona Lisa had a streak of white hair across the top of her head. Two men in white hazmat suits were placing items in plastic evidence bags and loading them onto a cart and a large open case on the floor. Plastic bags containing wine glasses and a wine bottle rested on a small dining room table. The hazmat suits identified them as Tech Lab officers. A man in blue trousers and a light blue button-down shirt was seated on one of the upholstered chairs. He looked up from a file on his lap as Dillon reached the top of the stairs.

"DI McCall?" Dillon asked. The man nodded. "Marshal Jack Dillon and DI Paddy Suel from Special Branch. We just got word and headed over."

"You've got the file?" McCall asked and nodded at the file in Dillon's hand.

"Yeah, we went through it on the way over. More than a little shocking."

"To say the least," McCall responded. "I've two teams knocking on doors at the moment. The Morgue team is in the bedroom photographing and doing their usual. Approximate time of death is listed as a few minutes after midnight. At this stage, no sign of drugs."

"Suspects?" Suel asked.

McCall shook his head. "Not at this point."

"If there was a decapitation, is the head still at the scene?"

"It is," McCall said and exhaled.

A man in a white hazmat suit opened a door on the far wall and stepped out. He carried three evidence bags and looked familiar, but Dillon couldn't recall a name.

"Rowan Derry, how you holding?" Suel said.

"Oh, Paddy, God bless. Wonderful to see you again. Been a long time. Sorry it's under these circumstances."

"Goes both ways," Suel replied.

"How can we help?" Dillon asked.

McCall nodded at the evidence bags Rowan Derry held. "Rowan, I've the forms for paperwork in the boot of my car if you need them."

"Thanks but we're good, Logan. We're wrapping up our initial work, but I'd like to get all these items back to the Tech Lab as soon as possible. How long do you think it will take you two?" he said to the other two men in the protective suits.

"We should be good to go in the next half-hour, maybe an hour tops."

"Lads, let's step outside so we'll be out of the way," McCall said to Dillon and Suel. They both nodded and followed McCall down the staircase. Once they were outside, McCall took a deep breath and said, "Oh, thanks, lads. I just had to get my ass out of there. One of the more vicious attacks I've had to investigate."

"Anything on suspects?" Dillon asked.

McCall shook his head. "Nothing at this stage, but it's still early. It looked like there was a dinner guest. Two place settings, wine glasses, and the lot. Unfortunately, the dishwasher had been run. We've finger-printed everything and—" The front door suddenly opened, and two men walked out carrying a gurney with a body bag strapped to the top. They stopped as soon as they were out the door and extended the legs on the gur-ney. As they extended the legs, the gurney shifted slightly from left to right, and Dillon noticed what had to be the decapitated head rolled inside the body bag.

"Hey, Noel, how's it going?" Dillon called to Noel Leonard, one of the two men at the gurney. As Leonard glanced up, the look on his face made Dillon immedi-ately regret his question.

"To tell you the truth, Dillon, I've had better days."

"No doubt. I was stupid to phrase it the way I did," Dillon replied.

"No surprise," Suel said, which brought a smile to everyone's face. "Other than the decapitation, anything else stand out?"

Leonard shook his head and said, "Nothing really at this stage. Whoever did this was behind the victim with a serrated knife. She does not appear to have been assaulted prior to the incident. No bruising. She still had her jeans on, although the belt and the fly were undone. Her blouse was draped over the back of the desk chair in the bedroom, and her bra had not been removed. Initial examination suggests no sexual assault. For what it's worth, my thought is whoever did this was a known individual. Most likely male, given the strength required, and someone who she would be comfortable undressing in front of. We'll have more information over the course of the next twenty-four hours." He gave a nod to his partner, who had opened the rear doors of the morgue van. They pushed the gurney onto the rack, and as the legs folded beneath, they pushed the gurney into the van.

Leonard shook his head and said, "Sorry, lads, but if it's okay, I'd like to head back and get started on our examination. Hopefully, get whoever is responsible off the streets before they do something like this again."

"I'll touch base with you at the end of the day," Dillon said.

"Thank yous," McCall said to Leonard and his assistant as they climbed into the van, gave a nod, and headed back up Charleville Close on the way to the Dublin Morgue

THREE

They were back upstairs in the bedroom of the unit. The far corner of the otherwise light beige carpet was soaked in a pool of blood. Now, after ten hours or more, the color was closer to black than red. A trail of blood ran across the carpet off to the left of the pool, indicating the direction the head had rolled. Everything else in the room appeared to be in order. The queen-size bed was neatly made. There was a makeup table with a chair that had a white silk blouse draped over it. A small notebook lay open on the makeup table.

Dillon stepped over to glance at the notebook. Three words were written, 'milk, eggs, tea.' A digital clock and a lamp were next to the bed on a small nightstand with three drawers. The alarm wasn't set on the clock.

"Has anyone touched the clock?" Dillon asked.

McCall shook his head. "Not to my knowledge. Strict instructions were not to touch anything until the Tech team was out of here."

"Interesting that the alarm on the clock hasn't been set."

"Yeah, although that may be one of the last things she would do before climbing into bed. Given the dinner plates and wine glasses, it's possible she was entertaining, and the couple entered the bedroom with the idea of enjoyment. Unfortunately, whoever was with her had another idea."

"Do you have anyone looking into the firm where she was employed, Norman Financial?"

McCall shook his head. "No, that's one of a number of reasons we requested help from Special Branch. We just don't have the manpower."

"Can you post her image?" Suel asked.

Dillon looked around and lifted a framed photo from the makeup table. Three attractive women were in the photo, two blondes and a dark-haired woman. They were all dressed in formal attire. McCall pointed at the dark-haired woman and said, "That's Orla O'Hara."

"You mind if I take this? We'll head over to Norman Financial. Speak to her boss and, hopefully, some people she may have been close to. We can start to establish a list of contacts and maybe even some possible suspects."

"By all means, be my guest. Let me just get an evidence form so we don't lose track of that photo. I've got a form in my file out in the sitting room," McCall said. He took the framed photo from Dillon and stepped out of the bedroom.

Dillon and Suel looked around the room for a long moment. "No offense to the victim here, but if she was in here getting undressed, wouldn't you think your man would have waited until they'd finished the intended event?"

"One of many questions without an answer at this point. My first thought would be he didn't want to leave any potential DNA. Of course, maybe he thought he couldn't get undressed without revealing the knife. A serrated edge. Like Noel Leonard said, we should probably check the kitchen and see if there's a knife like that."

"Good idea," Suel said and stepped out of the bedroom.

Dillon looked around for a long moment. Eventually, he shook his head and headed out of the bedroom. DI McCall was seated in one of the upholstered chairs, filling out the evidence transfer form. The framed photo rested on the end of the coffee table. Dillon was about to say something when Suel called his name.

"Dillon, in the kitchen. We've something here, possibly."

Dillon stepped over to the kitchen, a small U-shaped area open on one end with wooden cabinets on top and bottom on the three walls. A white refrigerator, about half the size of Dillon's, stood in the right corner. A stove with a built-in microwave above it was centered on the back wall. A dishwasher and the kitchen sink were opposite the refrigerator. Suel was standing back by the stove. Dillon took three steps and stood alongside Suel. McCall stepped just behind Dillon.

"Check this out," Suel said. "Your man Leonard said a serrated blade was used. This knife rack is missing a knife. Based on the empty slot, it's a large knife. There are seventeen slots, and only sixteen knives. The O'Hara girl heads into the bedroom to get undressed. Your man says he'll be there in just a minute. He steps in here, looks at the knives, chooses the serrated edge, and heads into the bedroom. She's just about to slip off her jeans. Her back is to him. He grabs her chin, slits her throat, and maybe saws back and forth a few times."

"That could be what happened," Dillon said.

"You didn't touch the knife rack, did you?" McCall asked.

"I've more sense than to do that," Suel huffed.

McCall shook his head and said, "My, how things have changed."

One of the men in a hazmat suit came up the stairs. "Anything else you want us to look at, McCall? We've samples and photographs. Our team will grab the bed linens, the blouse, and a few other items."

McCall pointed at the knife rack and said, "There's a knife missing from the rack here. A large knife based on the empty slot. You'd best wrap this up and run it for fingerprints and DNA."

"Mmm, how in the hell did we miss that?"

"You were busy dealing with your woman's head," McCall said.

"God, it will be at least a week of not sleeping very well."

"We'll all be lucky if it's just a week," Dillon replied.

The man nodded and said, "I've got a box out in the van I'm gonna get." He hurried down the steps and out the door.

"I just need your signature on that evidence transfer, and you'll be good to go," McCall told Dillon as he headed back into the sitting room and the upholstered chair. He set the form on the coffee table and handed a pen to Dillon so he could sign his name. McCall picked up the form, tore off the yellow copy from the back of the form, and handed it to Dillon along with the framed photo. "Keep me posted on Norman Financial."

"I'll call you when we're finished there," Dillon promised.

They said their goodbyes and headed for the staircase. They waited as the officer in the hazmat suit hurried up the stairs with a box. He gave a friendly nod, thanked them, and hurried into the kitchen.

Dillon and Suel headed down the stairs and outside. They got a friendly nod from the uniformed officer near the entrance and hurried to Suel's car.

FOUR

It was a twenty-minute drive out to the coast and a bit south to the area known as Dún Laoghaire. While Suel drove, Dillon was on the phone and got the name of the CEO at Norman Financial, Aidan Norman. The company was located in a five-story brick building on Clarence Avenue. The office was on the third floor of the Casement Building. It overlooked the West Pier and the Traders Wharf in Dún Laoghaire Harbor and, beyond that, the Irish Sea. The building was named after Roger Casement. He was hung by the English in London in 1916 for his participation in the Easter Rising, the only participant executed outside of Ireland.

Suel pulled into the parking lot and amazingly found a parking place. They climbed out of the car and headed into the building. There were two elevators located at the far end of the lobby. Between the elevators was a framed list of all the businesses in the building and their office number. Norman Financial was located in unit 312. They rode the elevator up to the third floor. As the elevator rose, they draped their IDs around their neck.

Unit 312 was halfway down the hall. They stepped into an attractive lobby with four couches. Two of the couches were arranged in an 'L' shape on either side of the entrance. Two coffee tables covered with financial magazines were centered on the couches. An attractive red-haired receptionist sat behind the counter and watched as they approached. Hanging on the wall behind her was a three-by-five-foot painting of a man who appeared to be maybe fifty. The painting and frame looked to be from the 1940s. The man stood in front of a large fireplace holding four rolled documents with red wax seals.

"Good morning. How may I help you?" the receptionist flashed them a smile.

"Hello. We're with An Garda Síochána, and we need to speak with Aidan Norman," Suel said as he held out the ID draped around his neck.

"Do you have an appointment?" she asked, not sounding all that convinced her question to two Garda officers was even appropriate.

"No, this is regarding an incident that occurred a few hours ago, and we need to speak with him now. It's an urgent matter," Suel said.

Her brown eyes seemed to grow wide as she nodded and picked up the phone. She punched in three numbers and, a few seconds later, said, "Yes, Thomas. I'm sorry to bother you, but I have two gentlemen here from An Garda Síochána, and they said it's urgent that they speak with Mr. Norman." She listened and then responded, "Just that it was an incident that occurred a few hours ago. Yes, please. Thank you," she said and hung up. "Mr.

Keane will be out in just a moment. If you'd like to take a seat."

"Is Mr. Norman unavailable?" Suel asked.

"He's here, but all things regarding Mr. Norman have to go through Mr. Keane."

"But Norman is in the office, correct?"

"Yes, he is, and—" The door suddenly opened, and a dark-haired man with bright blue eyes stepped into the lobby. Dillon pegged him for maybe forty years old and in very good shape. "Oh, Mr. Keane, these are the two officers."

Keane smiled and held out his hand. "Thomas Keane, how may I help you?"

Suel shook hands as he introduced himself. "DI Suel, An Garda Síochána Special Branch." He took a half-step back as Dillon approached.

Dillon shook Keane's hand, "Marshal Dillon with An Garda Síochána."

"You're an American?" Keane asked.

"Yes, I've been assigned to Special Branch for a couple of years now. We need to speak with Mr. Norman. Is he in?"

"He's very busy. Perhaps I could help you."

"There's been a serious incident concerning one of your employees, and it would be best if we spoke with Mr. Norman, and then we would like to talk to some of your employees. If you wouldn't mind taking us to Mr. Norman, that would be most helpful."

Keane seemed to think about that for a moment and then said, "Does this involve investments or a financial situation?"

Suel shook his head and said, "No, it does not. But, it's imperative that we speak with Mr. Norman."

Another pause from Keane before he nodded, "All right, follow me, please." He led them out of the lobby and through a large area with maybe twenty desks, all occupied. They headed down a hallway toward a set of double doors. A brass plate on the wall read 'Aidan Norman' and below that, 'CEO.' Keane knocked on the door three times, followed by two more, apparently giving a signal.

"Yes, Thomas, enter," a voice called from inside the office.

Keane opened one of the doors, stepped inside, and held the door for Dillon and Suel.

The office was large, with a leather couch and three matching wingback chairs off to the right. Just ahead was a large, carved, antique desk. The desk was devoid of anything like a file or papers. A large computer monitor and keyboard were off to the side. A credenza with four crystal glasses and a matching decanter filled with what appeared to be whiskey was just behind the desk. To the left of the desk was a bookcase with four shelves apparently holding law books and maybe two dozen ring binders arranged on the top two shelves. A large flat-screen TV hung from the wall just above the bookcase. At the moment, a yoga video was playing, displaying a man on his back holding a large, round, gray ball with his right leg and his left arm. The man's left leg and right arm were extended.

On the floor in front of the bookcase, lying on a blue mat, was Aidan Norman. He was in the exact same position, only he was holding a large, bright blue ball. He was attired in a blue gym outfit with a sweatshirt labeled 'Gentleman's Club.'

"Sir, I have the two men from An Garda Síochána."

"Bear with me, Thomas. Ninety seconds remaining," Norman said and continued to maintain his pose. Suel and Dillon shot a quick look at one another and then waited.

The man on the video called out both the remaining one minute and the remaining thirty-second times. Then, with ten seconds left, he counted down to zero, "Ten, nine, eight… Well done, now for our next—" Norman dropped the large ball onto the floor. It rolled up against the bookcase. He picked up the remote, turned off the TV, and stood. "Gentlemen, thank you for your patience. I understand you have a concern. Perhaps a question on investments? How may I help?"

"Unfortunately, I'm afraid this concerns one of your employees," Suel said.

"One of our employees? But who? Thomas, are you aware of anything?" Norman asked, quickly looking over at Keane.

Keane shook his head. "No sir, this is the first I've heard of anything. Who, exactly, does this concern?"

"A woman by the name of Orla O'Hara," Suel said.

"Orla O'Hara. Good lord. What has she done this time?" Norman asked.

"We're sorry to report that she has been murdered. We would like to speak—"

"Murdered? Oh, for God's sake. You know, in a way, it's not surprising. I'm sorry to say she has a knack for pushing all the wrong buttons on people. Her father is one of our largest investors and has served as her guarantee for employment. You said murder? There…there…isn't some tie to our organization, is there?"

"We're not aware of anything like that at the moment, and that's why we would like to speak to you and your employees. See if anyone might have an idea of some problem, maybe a relationship break up, financial difficulty, or perhaps a family situation. Any information you may have would aid in our investigation."

Norman shook his head. "Good lord, I can't believe this. Thomas, would you have HR pull the O'Hara file, please? Miss O'Hara led our service department. In all honesty, it was the position where she would do the least amount of damage. That said, there's been an exodus of a number of potentially good employees over the years. Oh, please don't let this be tied to the company. Oh my God, I just can't believe this. Has her father been informed?"

"We're just getting the investigation underway. I would think he will be informed in the next two or three hours. As a matter of fact, let me just send a text to the officer in charge, and he'll let you know when that has occurred," Dillon said. He pulled out his cell phone and began typing a text message to DI McCall. "May I have your cell phone number, sir?"

Norman gave him the number and then said, "Thomas, better have HR send me that file as soon as possible. We'll want to have everything covered when I speak with Niall."

"We would like to meet individually with people who knew her and worked with her. See if anyone is aware of a problem, maybe a family matter, something that may have led to this situation," Dillon said.

Norman nodded. "Yes, yes, of course. We have a conference room you can use. Thomas, after you speak with HR, arrange the conference room. While you gentlemen are reviewing that file, we'll schedule her department. I must warn you. Miss O'Hara was not well-liked by the people she managed and, well, actually not well-liked by many in the organization. Thomas, if you would see to it that the department is organized and everyone participates in an interview. Thomas will set this up for you, gentlemen. Is there anything else?"

Dillon and Suel looked at one another, and then Suel said, "We appreciate your assistance. The sooner we meet with people, the better."

"This can work in our favor, eliminating a problem and suggesting a promotion. We'll hopefully be able to get the department back on track. Yes, let's get started," Norman said.

TO BE CONTINUED . . .

Thank you for checking out the sample of <u>The Collector</u>, the next book in the Jack Dillon Dublin Tales series. Things are about to get complicated, better grab a copy and check it out . . .

BOOKS BY MIKE FARICY
CRIME FICTION FIRSTS

A boxset of the first four books in four crime fiction series:

Russian Roulette; Dev Haskell series
Welcome; Jack Dillon Dublin Tales series
Corridor Man; Corridor Man series
Reduced Ransom! Hot Shot series

The following titles comprise the Dev Haskell series:

Russian Roulette: Case 1
Mr. Swirlee: Case 2
Bite Me: Case 3
Bombshell: Case 4
Tutti Frutti: Case 5
Last Shot: Case 6
Ting-A-Ling: Case 7
Crickett: Case 8
Bulldog: Case 9
Double Trouble: Case 10
Yellow Ribbon: Case 11
Dog Gone: Case 12
Scam Man: Case 13
Foiled: Case 14
What Happens in Vegas… Case 15
Art Hound: Case 16

The Office: Case 17
Star Struck: Case 18
International Incident: Case 19
Guest From Hell: Case 20
Art Attack: Case 21
Mystery Man: Case 22
Bow-Wow Rescue: Case 23
Cold Case: Case 24
Cash Up Front: Case 25
Dream House: Case 26
Alley Katz: Case 27
The Big Gamble: Case 28
Bad to the Bone: Case 29
Silencio!: Case 30
Surprise, Surprise: Case 31
Hit & Run: Case 32
Suspect Santa: Case 33
P.I. Apprentice: Case 34
Rebel Without a Clue: Case 35
Puppy Love: Case 36

The following titles are Dev Haskell novellas:
Dollhouse
The Dance
Pixie
Fore!
Twinkle Toes
(*a Dev Haskell short story*)

The following are Dev Haskell Boxsets:
Dev Haskell Boxset 1-3
Dev Haskell Boxset 4-6
Dev Haskell Boxset 7-9
Dev Haskell Boxset 10-12
Dev Haskell Boxset 13-15
Dev Haskell Boxset 16-18
Dev Haskell Boxset 19-21
Dev Haskell Boxset 22-24
Dev Haskell Boxset 25-27
Dev Haskell Boxset 28-30
Dev Haskell Boxset 1-7
Dev Haskell Boxset 8-14
Dev Haskell Boxset 15-19
Dev Haskell Boxset 20-24
Dev Haskell Boxset 25-29

The following titles comprise the Jack Dillon Dublin Tales series:
Welcome
Jack Dillon Dublin Tale 1
Sweet Dreams
Jack Dillon Dublin Tale 2
Mirror Mirror
Jack Dillon Dublin Tale 3
Silver Bullet
Jack Dillon Dublin Tale 4
Fair City Blues
Jack Dillon Dublin Tale 5

Spade Work
Jack Dillon Dublin Tale 6
Madeline Missing
Jack Dillon Dublin Tale 7
Mistaken Identity
Jack Dillon Dublin Tale 8
Picture Perfect
Jack Dillon Dublin Tale 9
Dublin Moon
Jack Dillon Dublin Tale 10
Mystery Woman
Jack Dillon Dublin Tale 11
Second Chance
Jack Dillon Dublin Tale 12
Payback Brother
Jack Dillon Dublin Tale 13
The Heist
Jack Dillon Dublin Tale 14
Jewels To Kill For
Jack Dillon Dublin Tale 15
Retirement Scheme
Jack Dillon Dublin Tale 16
The Collector
Jack Dillon Dublin Tale 17

Jack Dillon Dublin Tales Boxsets:
Jack Dillon Dublin Tales 1-3
Jack Dillon Dublin Tales 4-6
Jack Dillon Dublin Tales 1-5

Jack Dillon Dublin Tales 1-7
Jack Dillon Dublin Tales 6-10

The following titles comprise the Hotshot series;
Reduced Ransom! Second Edition
Finders Keepers! Second Edition
Bankers Hours Second Edition
Chow Down Second Edition
Moonlight Dance Academy Second Edition
Irish Dukes (Fight Card Series)
written under the pseudonym Jack Tunney

The following titles comprise the Corridor Man series:
Corridor Man
Corridor Man 2: Opportunity knocks
Corridor Man 3: The Dungeon
Corridor Man 4: Dead End
Corridor Man 5: Finger
Corridor Man 6: Exit Strategy
Corridor Man 7: Trunk Music
Corridor Man 8: Birthday Boy
Corridor Man 9: Boss Man
Corridor Man 10: Bye Bye Bobby

Corridor Man novellas:
Corridor Man: Valentine
Corridor Man: Auditor
Corridor Man: Howling

Corridor Man: Spa Day

The following are Corridor Man Boxsets:
Corridor Man Boxset 1-3
Corridor Man Boxset 1-5
Corridor Man Boxset 6-9

THANK YOU!

Contact the author:
- Email: mikefaricyauthor@gmail.com
- Twitter: @Mikefaricybooks
- Facebook: Mike Faricy Author
- Website: http://www.mikefaricybooks.com

Published by

MJF Publishing

www.ingramcontent.com/pod-product-compliance
Lightning Source LLC
Chambersburg PA
CBHW070340010826

48976CB00017B/468